THE BITTER AND THE SWEET

ANESSA SEWELL KENT

Sydney -
I hope you love Vernadine &
Johanna as much as 🌹 I do! ♡

Black Rose Writing | Texas

Anessa Sewell Kent

The author grants the final approval for this literary material.

First printing

This is a work of fiction. Names, characters, businesses, places, events, and incidents are either the products of the author's imagination or used in a fictitious manner. Any resemblance to actual persons, living or dead, or actual events is purely coincidental.

ISBN: 978-1-68513-187-6
PUBLISHED BY BLACK ROSE WRITING
www.blackrosewriting.com

Printed in the United States of America
Suggested Retail Price (SRP) $20.95

The Bitter and the Sweet is printed in Garamond

*As a planet-friendly publisher, Black Rose Writing does its best to eliminate unnecessary waste to reduce paper usage and energy costs, while never compromising the reading experience. As a result, the final word count vs. page count may not meet common expectations.

"I dedicate this book to my parents and eternal cheerleaders, Wade and Pat Sewell. There are not enough words to express my deep love and thankfulness for you both. I love y'all dearly."

Acknowledgements

The journey of writing *The Bitter and the Sweet* was not a road traveled alone. Without the constant encouragement of family and friends, this process would have been a long and hard hill to climb. Thank you to my inner circle. Words cannot adequately express my sincere appreciation for your love and patience you all so freely gave to this weary and worn traveler. I would especially like to thank Wade and Pat Sewell for listening to every word of my story for over a year and for your never ending cheers of support that kept me propped up and moving along. To Keith Kent, your encouragement and expertise in keeping me on track with technology was a lifesaver! To Jordan Kent, Celeste Sewell Stonicher, Shannon Gilbert Rizzo, Ladeana Cook Richardson, and many more of my dear and treasured friends, you listened, you loved, you cried and laughed, and bolstered me on the course. I love all of you dearly. To my high school English teacher, Karen Jeane, you read every word, offered suggestions, kept me true to my voice, and wrote many side notes of correction in the margins of the manuscript with your green pen. Thank you for taking this journey with me! I am thrilled you are still my teacher!

I would also like to thank Reagan and the Team at Black Rose Writing for offering me the opportunity to realize a longtime dream of mine of finally becoming a published author! Thank you, thank you, thank you!

With love, from the bottom of my heart,
Anessa

THE
BITTER
AND
THE
SWEET

"She was beautiful, but not like those girls in magazines. She was beautiful, for the way she thought. She was beautiful, for the sparkle in her eyes when she talked about something she loved. She was beautiful, for her ability to make other people smile, even if she was sad. No, she wasn't beautiful for something as temporary as her looks. She was beautiful, deep down to her soul. She is beautiful."
—F Scott Fitzgerald

Louanna Parsons

Spit's Creek, Alabama
September 1960 to April 1961

By everyone's opinion Louanna Parsons was a beauty, and by far the prettiest girl in Buford County. She was popular among the boys at Buford County High School and not so popular with the girls. Slender and tall, she could wear the latest fashions like a magazine model. Though not from a wealthy family, she carried herself with the confidence and grace of a girl that had been offered the training and exposure to the finer things of life. Her long blonde hair was wavy with natural highlights, her eyes were hazel green complimented by long dark eyelashes, and her mouth was a perfect full pout which she accentuated with a frosted pink lipstick. Even without makeup she was stunning. She was outgoing and friendly to everyone, and because of that, it made it even more difficult for the girls to hate her, but they tried really hard. She was captain of the cheerleading team and sang soprano in the school choir and the First Methodist church choir. She was an honor student and most interested in English Literature, music, art, and fashion. She was unsure what she wanted to study after high school, but going to college was definitely her plan. She would be the first from her family to attend college and they had already accepted her for the upcoming fall semester at Plains University. Maybe she would double major in Literature and Art, then figure out which career path she could pursue?

Either way, she was going to travel the world, visit exotic cultures, learn to speak foreign languages, and reinvent herself from a small town South Alabama girl to a worldly sophisticated woman of style and distinction; and forever shake the dust off from her family farm, the dirt roads of Buford County, and Spit's Creek, Alabama forever. She spent hours fantasizing about her grand life full of possibilities, and she voraciously read every National Geographic from the city and high school libraries. Her plan was to be prepared for the world. She subscribed to Vogue, Teen, and Petticoat magazines, and spent hours studying fashion, hairstyles, and modern make-up techniques. Afterwards she would spend even more hours in front of the mirror trying to perfect her new and chic look. She knew she was beautiful and unstoppable.

Louanna was the leader and role model of fashion and beauty at BCHS, and the whole county. No one would admit it, but Louanna's phone rang off the hook most nights with girls, and even some of the mothers, calling her for beauty tips and advice. She even moonlighted for extra money by making house calls when she was asked, which was frequent. Her nest egg was growing by the day. She saved each dollar in cigar boxes she kept hidden in the back of her closet for her debut into the world after high school and college. The moonlighting money also allowed her frequent shopping trips to Montgomery and Birmingham, where clothing choices were more modern and unique.

In the fall of 1961, Louanna's senior year, she began dating Tommy Smith, the quarterback of the BCHS football team. They were the perfect couple. Tommy was dark haired with an olive complexion and brown eyes. Standing together, they were like sunlight and night. Without dispute, they were the sweetheart couple in town. When Louanna was voted Homecoming Queen, Tommy was the proud escort during her walk on the field at half time. She was a sight to behold in her dress and crown, and many of the women left the ballgame angry at their husbands, who made no secret about their thoughts and desires regarding Louanna Parsons.

Louanna liked Tommy because he was good looking, funny and popular, but she found him intellectually boring and unchallenging. He was awkward in the ways of romance and passion. He was jittery and nervous, and she found that bothersome and unattractive. They spent plenty of nights parked by the river, necking and heavy breathing, but once things got to a fevered pitch, Tommy would not know what to do next. Louanna was left breathless and frustrated. So, by the end of the fall quarter, Louanna lost interest in Tommy and in her mind he was immature and not sophisticated enough for her. She kept Tommy dangling on the line, however, because she would still need dates to dances and parties for another few months until graduation.

Louanna had taken notice of Sheriff Frank 'Bull' Smith, Tommy's father, months earlier. Bull was the man-version of Tommy; dark and tall and very handsome. Louanna spent time around Bull when visiting Tommy at his home, and she noticed him looking at her inappropriately. He would look at her from head to toe, and wipe the sweat from his brow. In the beginning, the gazes from Bull made her uncomfortable, but her feelings of uneasiness took a turn for intense curiosity. She was primed for sexual exploration and she was ready for it.

On a fall afternoon, Louanna stopped at Mrs. Ruth's café for a milkshake and a piece of chocolate cake. As she was sitting there reading her National Geographic, Bull Smith walked in for his coffee break. When Louanna saw him in his uniform she began sweating, her heart began racing, and she felt flustered. After ordering his coffee, Bull walked over to say hello. In a matter of a few minutes and a short conversation, a rendezvous was planned for that evening.

"I will meet you down by the river, on the last road to the left, just passed the double oak trees, at eight o'clock," said Bull with a wink and a smile.

Louanna was speechless and bursting inside. Without saying a word, she looked at him and nodded her head in agreement. She choked down her cake and gulped her milkshake. She had to hurry! She rushed home, took a long bubble bath, painted her fingernails, fixed her hair and makeup and pulled out a clean halter top and a pair of cutoff shorts.

With her money she had saved, she bought a lacy bra and underwear and kept it hidden in the bottom of her shirt drawer. She had been saving them for a special occasion, and tonight was the night.

After dressing and primping, Louanna left her house at 7:45 PM and began her drive to the river, feeling nervous and excited at the same time. She knew what was going to happen at the river and she also knew she was living her last few moments of purity on that car ride. She could have stopped the car, turned back toward home, ran inside and locked the doors, protecting herself from herself, but she didn't. Even through nerves and uncertainty, nothing was going to stop her from this night. It was eight o'clock on the dot when she pulled down the dark dirt road that ends at the river. She could see Bull was there waiting for her, and the reflectors from his patrol car shined like beacons in her headlights; directing her towards exploration and unbridled passion.

After Louanna parked her car, Bull said, "I will be right back." He walked down the lane and pulled a large, broken oak tree limb across the entrance. He had it all figured out. Maybe the limb would dissuade anyone from driving down the lane, and because it was dark, an intruder's headlights could give them enough warning to set an innocent scene. When he made it back to Louanna's car, he could see small beads of sweat on her upper lip and chest reflecting in the overhead car light. "Hello," said Bull, "I brought some whiskey, would you like a sip?"

"Sure," said Louanna.

"Just a little something to help you relax," said Bull.

Louanna stepped out of her car, took the whiskey bottle, turned it up and took a long drink. Bull placed the bottle on the hood of Louanna's car then pulled her in tightly for a hard, impassioned kiss. The kissing stopped long enough to walk to a blanket Bull had laid out on the soft river side. They were wild with each other. The magic of passion was there and Louanna finally knew she was being kissed and touched and ravished by an experienced, hot blooded man. She had dreamed and thought about this exact moment for a long time with a faceless stranger, but this time, she could see a face. The sensations she felt almost paralyzed her and knew she would want to feel this way often and regularly, and with Bull Smith. The fact he was married and that he was the father of her on again-off again boyfriend didn't bother them. They were lost in each other and nothing else mattered. They decided, as they were lying there, breathless and sweaty, they would meet every Thursday night. Louanna knew she would have to purchase more lacy bras and panties because she would need them and that excited her. They both knew this would not be love, just plain lust, but Louanna knew she would be more prepared when she struck out on her own, to her wide open future, full of possibilities and excitement, and Bull would return to his wife and family, and the law and order of Buford County.

Louanna and Bull had continued their weekly meetings at the river for months and somehow they had both been able to keep their secret from everyone. Had anyone known any better, it would have made sense why Bull had been so light hearted, not too hard on his deputies, and he even looked different. He looked younger and full of himself, but not in a bad way. He was twenty pounds slimmer with a new wardrobe. A few sneak away trips to Birmingham and Montgomery for shopping and short stays at motels with Louanna had transformed him into a hip and even more attractive forty-year-old man, and the salt and pepper hair around his temples added an air of maturity and sophistication. The music played louder than usual in his car, and people even noticed him at red lights singing and dancing along with the beat. What had happened to Bull? Everyone wondered.

At home, his wife certainly noticed the changes, but didn't inquire too much. She noticed he was sweeter and more attentive to her. She figured it was a mid-life crisis and as long as she was reaping positive changes in her husband and marriage, she would happily go along. In fact, she got on the band wagon too and made a plan to lose weight, change her hairstyle, and buy new clothes. Maybe even a new slinky nightgown? A shopping trip was definitely in her immediate future. Even the romantic spark in their marriage had accelerated, and she felt young, alive, beautiful and willing for the first time in years. Bull loved his wife and not wanting to jeopardize his marriage, he knew his actions towards his wife during this time had to be irreproachable, loving, and attentive, to keep the wolves at bay and suspicion low.

Louanna's classmates and parents were also noticing changes in her at school and home. The outgoing friendly girl had now become snobby and overconfident. She even walked, talked and dressed with an air of majesty and her parents found her too big for her britches. Arguments at home settled into their daily routine and the stress level ran high. Her classmates assumed she had been reading too many beauty magazines, National Geographics and travel books. Louanna appeared as if she had mentally moved ahead of her classmates, life in Spit's Creek; and she could barely tolerate their presence. The feeling was mutual, and for once, the guys and girls agreed on the feelings of dislike for Louanna Parsons.

In March 1961, Birdy, Sheridan, and Celia invited Louanna for a spring break trip to Panama City Beach. Because of her recent coolness, the three figured she would tell them no, but to their surprise, she agreed. All four of the girls pooled their money for a room at the Beachcomber Resort Motel. With its beachside pool and screened porches, it was definitely a step above most of the motels at the beach.

On a Saturday morning, the girls piled into Birdy's VW convertible bug, with all of their luggage and towels and let the top down. The weather was beautiful and warm for March, and they were all excited for their week of adventure and freedom. The music boomed from the speakers, and the girls honked and waved at everyone they passed. Shortly after the girls checked into the motel they changed into their swimsuits and headed for the salty, foaming water. Birdy and Celia's mom, Patricia, had packed bologna sandwiches, chips, dill pickles, and the new craze in sweets, the Little Debbie crème pies, for a picnic lunch on the sand. Life was grand.

In between trips to the pool and the beach, Birdy mentioned to Sheridan that Louanna was looking plump in her bikini. Everyone couldn't help but stare at Louanna fully clothed, but in a bikini, she was a sight to behold. The girls also noticed on the ride to the beach they had to make many stops because Louanna was sick. She told the girls not to worry, it was just a stomach bug and it would pass soon. Probably something she ate… it all seemed odd, and no one dwelt on it long. She devoured two bologna sandwiches in no time, and had two oatmeal crème pies for lunch. Oh well, they were on vacation, so indulgence was okay.

The week flew by with parties in motel rooms, games at the pool and in the surf, lots of yummy seafood and lazy pajama mornings. Louanna was often absent from the morning discussions, because of her stomach bug, and she remained sick the whole week.

Packing the car at the end of the week was bittersweet, and the girls could not remember when they had so much fun. A trip next spring break was a definite, and during making plans for next year's trip, it was noticeable to all of them Louanna seemed sad and depressed and deflated. Birdy wanted to ask her if she was okay, but she stopped herself. She figured she was tired from being sick all week in the sun.

When April rolled around, what Louanna had feared the most was confirmed. She was pregnant with Bull Smith's baby. Scared to death and in deep despair, her grand plans of becoming a woman of the world began disappearing at a rapid pace. She began arriving at school without makeup and her hair in a ponytail. Under her eyes were puffy purple bags and she walked with drooping shoulders. The school was buzzing with chatter and whispered comments as she walked by. 'What is wrong with Louanna?' No one would say the word 'pregnant' out loud, because it was too scandalous. Everyone assumed Tommy was the father, but no one dared ask.

Louanna knew she had to tell Bull. He had to know and he had to help her. He could give her some money, and she would be gone as soon as she could. She was very surprised her parents had not kicked her out of the house or banished her from the family when she told them her news, while also concealing the identity of the father. They assumed like everyone else that it was Tommy and she did not confirm or deny their suspicions. Graduation was only a little more than a month away and Louanna knew she could conceal the pregnancy long enough to receive her diploma; but after that, she was not sure what she was going to do or where she was going to go. She figured her only chance for a new start was to move to Atlanta or Birmingham, attend beauty school, and use her talents of hair styling, fashion, and makeup. She would carve out a life for her and her baby, away from the prying eyes and gossip of Buford County. All of her grand plans for world travel, riches, and society life vanished with each minute and she wept constantly, as she counted down the days of her departure.

The following Thursday night she met Bull at the river. On this night, Louanna didn't take her long bath, wear her halter top and cut-off jean shorts. She was too upset to care. All she knew was she had to tell Bull and get back home. At 8 PM, his headlights shined down the lane, and when he got out of the car, Louanna was leaning against her car looking very pale and bloated and different. She blurted it out, through tears, when he walked up, "I am pregnant, Bull, and the baby is yours. I am leaving town to have the baby as soon as I graduate, all I need from you now is some money to help me get started in a career and pay for an apartment deposit. This will be a clean break. I will say nothing to anyone about you and me. My parents know I am pregnant, but I didn't tell them about you, they assume Tommy is the father and I plan on leaving it that way. I figure five hundred dollars from you, along with the money I have already saved, will be enough to help me get settled. I am not sure exactly where I am going, but it will be far from here. You can count on that. Please have the money to me by Saturday morning. I can meet you at Mrs. Ruth's at 10 AM. Stop by my table and drop if off, then head on your way."

"How in the heck do you expect me to get five hundred dollars by Saturday?" Bull yelled.

"I don't know," said Louanna. "But, I figure you would rather come up with five hundred dollars instead of having to live with the public shame of fathering another woman's baby. You are up for re-election in a few months and you wouldn't want to lose would you? Just get the money and I am out of your life and out of this one horse town for good."

Bull continued, "And how in the heck do I know that baby is mine? Everyone has seen you and Tommy running around together for months and for all I know you have been fooling around with him too! You can't prove it's me, Louanna," said Bull.

"Bull, I have not been fooling around with your immature, inexperienced, over-inflated-ego son. He is way below me. I have only used him for dates and that is it. We have talked about my relationship with Tommy before, so don't throw that back in my face. All I know is I am seventeen. I had plans to leave for college at the end of the summer. I have plans for my future and they don't involve you, Tommy, or a baby. So, I figure you would rather pay me off than jeopardize your career and public persona. The public expects you to uphold law and order, not to fool around with a girl that's half your age, and who is the girlfriend of your teenage son; then get her pregnant and abandon your responsibilities. Just get the money and we will be out of each other's lives shortly.

As Louanna was talking, even in the darkness, she could see Bull's face turning red and distorted. He had a look in his eyes she had never seen before, and she was getting more frightened and desperate by the minute.

"I will not get you any money! I will not help you! You are on your own and no one will believe a girl like you over the Sheriff! No way. No money. Now, get the heck outta here, you and your illegitimate child", Bull growled. Bull laughed out loud with a scornful expression on his face that sent Louanna into dark places in her heart and mind. In anger, she lunged at Bull's face and clawed his cheeks and neck. He reached for her neck with both hands and squeezed. Louanna was a fighter, she kicked and tried with all her might to break the hold Bull had on her. She could feel herself losing vision and breath as her strength left. After a few minutes of struggle, Louanna was gone. Bull released Louanna's neck and her body crumbled to the ground. He panicked, checked for breathing and a heartbeat. Nothing. Louanna was dead. Beautiful Louanna. What was he going to do? Frantic and breathless he dragged her lifeless body under the brush and tried to think. Two things he knew for certain, he was in big trouble and he would go to prison. Bull walked to the rear of the patrol car and opened the trunk, hoping to find a shovel to dig a grave. The only items in his trunk were a rope, a fishing boat anchor, Tommy's lettermen jacket, and a pair of Tommy's tennis shoes. Taking the jacket and shoes out of the trunk, he placed them on the ground. Retrieving the anchor and rope, he wrapped the rope around Louanna's torso and attached the anchor. He picked up Louanna's lifeless body, dragging the anchor and rope, and put her in the brisk current of the river and watched her body float away in the moonlight. Acting quickly, he covered up the anchor drag marks in the sand with a broken limb he found lying on the ground. Running back to his car, he jumped in and sped away, leaving Tommy's jacket and shoes on the riverbank as he disappeared into the cover of darkness.

Spit's Creek, Alabama

1926-1927

The Town of Spit's Creek, Alabama, in Buford County, is the county seat and the largest town for miles around. The centerpiece of the downtown square is the courthouse, and businesses and community services span the six city blocks. Like a watchful eye, the court house towers over every building downtown. The red brick, two story structure, designed by an architect from Atlanta in the neoclassical style, is an imposing reminder of law, order and justice to all who gaze upon it. The ornate clock tower crowns the majestic structure, and a large bell rings every hour, of every day, and can be heard for miles around. The clock, shipped from a Charleston clock maker, is the official timekeeper for the town's residents.

The Dixie Pharmacy on Main Street, owned by Mr. Potts, is always a bustle of activity. Selling everything from Carter's liver pills, which ease a variety of ailments from headaches to digestive disorders and aids bile flow in the liver; to the popular cure-all Asafetida that aids in the treatment of asthma, epilepsy, flatulence, weak digestion, and influenza. But, the top seller, month after month, and the one that Mr. Potts could not keep in stock, is Hadacol. Marketed as a 'vitamin' supplement, Hadacol has a preservative of twelve percent alcohol volume and is a must-have for every lady, young and old, sinner and saint in Buford County. Hadacol is never stored in the bathroom medicine cabinet; each bottle has its own special hiding place in most homes. The purchasing of

Hadacol is not a common topic of conversation among the women, but each has her own understanding and appreciation for the power of the 'vitamins' in those brown bottles with the red, white and blue label; and they swear to the effectiveness of the warm, soothing elixir.

Along with Mr. Potts' thriving medicine sales, the Dixie Pharmacy is also the main social gathering place for the town's teens. The soda counter is always three to four people deep, especially after school, and the ice cream, root beer floats are magical. Suffice it to say, Mr. Potts is one of Spit's Creek's wealthier citizens, but his quiet demeanor and non-assuming personality keep him very approachable and loved by the community.

Next door to the Dixie Pharmacy is the 'Clip and Curl' beauty shop, owned by twin sisters Zilly and Dilly. Their innovative and modern hairstyling is known for miles around and their 'special' hairspray, 'Glamour Glue', is shipped on the railroad each week from a beauty warehouse in Mobile. One appointment a week, topped off with Zilly and Dilly's 'Glamour Glue', will hold a hairstyle for a solid week, sometimes two weeks, if left untouched; but eventually the head itching from a week of no hair washing keeps appointments at a regular weekly shuffle.

The general mercantile, one block over, sells everything from canned and dried foods to dressmaking patterns and materials to hardware and farming supplies. Besides the mercantile, Woolworth's sells affordable and fashionable clothing along with various housewares. At each checkout line, the display of twirl pops, lollipops, and old fashioned sticks, all the way from The American Candy Company in Selma, beckons each child who waits impatiently in line for their treat.

Mrs. Ruth's café, owned by Ruth Spruel, sits on the adjacent corner from the First Baptist Church, and her Sunday 'meat and three' gathers a faithful and hungry crowd each week. Her specialty though is her fried catfish dinners, served on Friday evenings from 5 to 9 PM. Folks from all over the county come each week, and wait in long lines, for the fresh, cornmeal battered crunchy catfish. Her coleslaw is renowned and served before the meal, with a bowl of pickles, raw onion and a basket of fluffy hushpuppies. Mrs. Ruth's is one, if not the main social and information hub in the county, and the townspeople all know if they need any 'news', it can be quickly found there. Mrs. Ruth bought the building with insurance money shortly after her husband, Thurl, suffered a death at the hands of his tractor. It was not a secret that Thurl enjoyed his moonshine, and one afternoon, while plowing his field, he fell off of his tractor and was run over by the back tire. Dr. Smith said he never felt a thing and Ruth was thankful for that. Before Ruth was informed of Thurl's death, she was fired from the school cafeteria as a sandwich maker because she had just discovered she was pregnant with her eighth child. Her boss told her they could no longer allow her to continue in her job if she would not stop having babies. So, with another baby on the way, Ruth was without a job, her husband was dead, and she had to support herself and her eight children. The insurance money from Thurl's death was her lifesaver, and she worked hard to build her restaurant into a thriving and lucrative business.

The rest of the small businesses downtown serves the community well, and for the town's modest size, everyone can purchase what they need without making the one-hour journey to Montgomery, the State Capital city. The Carnegie Library is the largest library south of Birmingham and commands half of a city block. The Classical Revival architecture style is a point of pride for everyone, and by far the most ornate building downtown. The First National Bank on Railroad Avenue runs a close second in beauty and size, and both buildings, along with the court house, add an air of refinement to Spit's Creek and Buford County.

The First Baptist, First Presbyterian and First Methodist churches sit on their own corners, and the sound of church bells resound every day throughout the town. On any day, "Amazing Grace", "In the Sweet By-and-By", and "Jesus Paid it All" can be heard in a muddled harmony for miles. Having the distinction as the 'bell ringer' is quite a compliment and a privilege to the recipients, and they take their job seriously. In fact, an unspoken war rages in the heart of each bell ringer, as they work their hardest to out-ring their competition at 8 AM, noon and 6 PM.

Two railroad tracks run through downtown, adding another layer of activity and excitement to town. The steam trains arrive and depart daily carrying passengers, freight and mail from Chicago, Atlanta, Memphis and Birmingham, heading further south to the white sandy beaches of the gulf coast. The train depot, with tall ceilings and multi colored stained glass, is a popular place to people watch. Guessing where people are coming from and going to is a pastime for the older residents of Spit's Creek and the young boys, who are in awe of the massive, steaming machines.

The Spit's Creek Elementary School is on the edge of downtown and instructs grades one through eight, and the school auditorium is used for plays, pageants, political rallies, and the annual fall Southeast Alabama revival, featuring notable evangelists from as far as North Carolina. Due to the growth of the county, the brand new Buford County High School, south of town, sits on a large parcel of land donated by a local and wealthy landowner. The school boasts a large gymnasium, a football stadium with home and visitor stands, and state-of-the-art science labs. The former high school, next door to the elementary school, was purchased by the State as a school for the deaf and blind, and is considered another accolade to the county.

North of downtown, large oak trees line the streets and drape majestically over homes of varied size and architecture styles. Each lawn is expertly manicured, and the area is highly sought after as a status symbol of success and wealth. Each Christmas season, folks come from miles to stroll the streets and admire the twinkling lights and luminaries that adorn each house. On every corner, Christmas carols are sung by church choirs and the Girl and Boy Scout Troops. Hot chocolate and spiced cider is sold by the Daughters of the American Revolution as their annual fund raiser, and the Ladies Auxiliary club sells their cakes, pies and cookies. For those who arrive late, they miss the opportunity to buy the popular Alabama 'Lane' cake; a white batter cake, iced with chopped nuts, coconut, raisins, whiskey, eggs and sugar cooked together in a yummy and sticky goodness. The delectable 'Ambrosia' cake runs a close second.

West of town, the Alabama Mill, is the largest employer of the county and specializes in fine fabrics, blue jeans and other household textiles. A small village of homes surrounds the mill and basic household needs can be purchased at the small mercantile in the center of the village. Fresh milk is delivered every morning from the Meadow Gold Dairy, along with fresh eggs from a chicken farmer south of town.

South and East of town, rich, gently rolling, red dirt farm land nurtures cotton and soybean fields. Bright green pastures feed large herds of prized Angus and Hereford cattle, and running throughout the rolling land are miles and miles of winding dirt roads. Scattered around the fields are small sharecropper farms growing vegetables, cotton, peanuts and sugar cane. Farming and agriculture is the second largest occupation in Buford County and the farming families take great pride in their efforts and products. By far, everyone agrees that Spit's Creek is a self-sufficient community and a beautiful place to live. New families arrive daily and there is an ever changing excitement to the town.

Fletcher and Irene Turnipseed arrived in Spit's Creek as newlyweds in the fall of 1926. Moving from the nearby community of Inner Banks, Fletcher purchased a small farm on the south side of town and planned to grow cotton, raise a modest herd of cattle and grow chickens. After their arrival in Spit's Creek, Irene realized she was pregnant, and the following summer, they welcomed their new baby girl. Vernadine Dawn Turnipseed was the first child born to Fletcher and Irene Turnipseed. Of German descent, she was the largest baby that Dr. Smith had ever delivered in his 3o years of country practice in Buford County. Weighing in at thirteen pounds, just the sight of her was overwhelming. From the moment of her arrival, she was commanding; commanding in extraordinary size and demanding in her deafening cry. Her appetite was shocking, and her head was covered in deep brown hair. Irene knew they would be overjoyed once the shock of seeing their large baby girl subsided.

Irene had never understood the compulsion for marital relations, or the desire for that matter. She didn't think to inform Fletcher of her opinions on marital relations until after they were married. On her wedding day, her mother reminded her it was her Christian duty as a wife to submit to her husband in such private matters. The courtship of Fletcher to Irene continued after their honeymoon, and in the third month of marriage, Fletcher caught Irene at a weak moment. The next morning, she was so embarrassed over what she had done that she didn't speak to Fletcher for one week. A shaken Irene went to church, even when services weren't scheduled, just so she could feel close to God and pray for forgiveness. She thought about visiting her mother to cry on her shoulder, but she knew that her mother would offer no sympathy, and more likely, Irene would receive a tongue lashing about not being a submissive wife, so she quickly abandoned that idea. One year to the day of their first anniversary, Vernadine Dawn Turnipseed was born, and that's also the day that Irene almost died. The physical trauma and near death experience from the birth confirmed Irene's original thoughts on marital relations, and she vowed to herself, that day, that there would be no more babies born into her small family of three. Because she felt so strongly on the matter, she now had no reservations about telling her mother, or anyone for that matter, that marital relations could cause possible death, and she would not consider taking part any longer in such activities, no matter what her momma or The Bible said. No, Vernadine Dawn Turnipseed would be the only child of Fletcher and Irene. Period. In the future, she would be happy for the other women in her community when their new babies arrived, and when she returned home to her pink, frilly bedroom, she would pat herself on the back at how smart she was to make the life-saving decision to have no more babies. Call it mother's intuition, but she knew in her heart that raising Vernadine could equate to raising multiple children, and she was ready for the challenge when she felt better and could get back on her feet.

Vernadine

Since their arrival in Spit's Creek in 1926, Fletcher, Irene and Vernadine had thrived. Fletcher's farm proved prosperous and provided them a comfortable, yet modest, lifestyle. Irene showed herself to be an efficient homemaker and a loving mother to Vernadine. She attended a ladies bible group every week and took part on the social committee at church, organizing pot luck dinners.

Their church, First Believers Victory Church, was the center of their social life and Vernadine, now sixteen, enjoyed the activities offered to the youth. Vernadine was now a junior at Buford County High School. She was a mediocre student, a member of the glee club, FHA, and the 4H club.

Each fall, Fletcher and Vernadine would show one of their prized calves at the county fair, generally winning first place. Vernadine proudly wore her first place ribbon, pinned to her blouse, for one solid week after the competition, and snickered in the faces of the boys at school and church. Vernadine brushed against the grain and she liked that about herself.

They spent Wednesday nights at church. A pot luck supper began at 5 PM, and the chance for fellowship was always a welcomed mid-week refresher. After supper, the adults would adjourn to the sanctuary for a roaring mid-week message from Brother Lester Scarborough. His wife Shirley played the piano and sang a lot of solos, and was always a little too sharp. 'The Old Rugged Cross' never sounded quite right, but everyone sang anyway… Loudly.

The ladies kept their handkerchiefs and fans handy for the occasional tear or sweat bead. They were always prepared. One never knew when the power of the Holy Spirit would overtake them.

As the adults made their way to the sanctuary, the youth would move into the fellowship hall. There was always a short bible study led by Coach Bud Caruthers, the health teacher and basketball coach at BCHS, followed by rowdy games of bible scripture quizzes. And, always, always there was a pick-up game of basketball outside in the field, beside the church, after the closing prayer.

On this particular Wednesday night, one of the 'regulars' was out sick. The team needed another player, and Vernadine piped up, barreled through the group, grabbed the ball and said,

"I'm in!"

The boys complained to Coach Caruthers and said, "Come on coach, girls don't play basketball!" But, Coach said, "It's ok, Vernadine, go for it! Boys, put a lid on it!"

So, there she was, in her blue jean skirt, long brown hair, dominating physical presence, aggressive and bulldogged demeanor, barreling and dribbling down the dirt court. She possessed a look of determination and a serious gleam in her eyes that Coach Caruthers had not witnessed out of the boys that had tried-out for the center position for the upcoming basketball season.

Coach Caruthers could not believe what he was seeing, and he was even more shocked at the thoughts forming in his mind. Could it be possible that a girl could play basketball on an all-boys high school team and be taken seriously? Would they laugh him out of town and lose his future as a coach if he even mentioned his idea to anyone? No, he would have to abandon this idea completely. It would never work. As soon as he resigned his mind to forget the idea, Vernadine maneuvered her way through the crowd of teenage boys, ran straight for the hoop, and slam dunked the ball! At that moment, Coach Caruthers abandoned his doubt, ran to Vernadine, grabbed her arm, held it up and exclaimed, "Boys, meet your new center for the BCHS basketball team, but only if Vernadine agrees!"

The loud gasps from the boys sucked all of the air out of the atmosphere as they waited to hear what Vernadine would say. Prayers were mumbled, and they directed threatening glances at her, while she figured quickly on her response. For what seemed like a moment, frozen in time, Vernadine finally answered. "Coach, are you sure? I am a girl!"

"Yes, I know you are a girl! I will take this risky chance on you if you agree to join the team. Your raw talent, physical presence, and determination on the court are worth the gamble, and I will survive the mountain of mean comments and threats that I will receive from this decision. What do you say, Vernadine?" Coach Caruthers asked.

Vernadine inhaled the last bit of oxygen in the air and exclaimed, "Coach, I will do it! I will be your new center! Thank you for taking this risk on me. I won't let you or the team down!"

The boys just stood there, mouths gaping and shoulders slumped. Some felt like crying, but quickly dabbed their eyes. They just knew that their basketball team would be the laughing stock of Alabama and maybe even the entire country.

They were so angry that their coach had betrayed them, and every one of them thought he had absolutely lost his mind. Most, if not all of them, would have quit right there on the spot, but when they thought about how Vernadine barreled through the team, the way she did, to score like that, they bit their tongues and silently prayed everything would work itself out. There was no denying Vernadine's talent, and they knew it. And because of that, they had to accept they were an all-boys high school basketball team in South Alabama with a girl center. The only one in the country.

"It's settled then," Coach exclaimed. "Practice starts tomorrow after school. We have a lot of work to do to prepare for the upcoming season. I can see on your faces the mixture of anger and disappointment on my decision to invite Vernadine to the team; but I have a feeling about this, a strong and indescribable intuition, that we are going to have the best basketball team that BCHS has ever seen."

The guys shuffled their feet and kicked the dirt. Not one of them could bear to look Coach in the eyes and show him their fear and anger. The shock and disbelief were almost unbearable, and if they could run off, they would have, but that would admit defeat and they weren't ready for that just yet.

"You guys and gal are just going to have to trust me on this," As Coach continued. "This decision and feeling is something that I cannot adequately explain, but if you will believe in me, I will believe in you. I have a feeling deep in my soul that is telling me we can do this! We can make history. Be prepared for many people to laugh at us, call us sissies, berate our talent, point and stare at school and around town. You will probably hear more than you want to about how ridiculous and scandalous our team is. Believe me, I will hear just as much ridicule as you, much more I am sure. I will be the laughing stock of coaches like no one has ever seen; but we are going to prove them wrong. I just feel it in my bones. This decision seems ridiculous, and I mean no harm against you, Vernadine, but on the face of it, this is the craziest thing I have ever heard of in my life. What I will need to know by the start of practice tomorrow is if I have a commitment from each of you to continue on the basketball team for the entire season. We cannot have half-hearted effort. We cannot have indecisiveness. We cannot have dissension of any kind. You will have to defend Vernadine with all that you have in you, and you will not contribute to gossip and slander. Even if you try to remain on the team, and I get any reports of mean and unsportsmanlike comments and behavior, you will have no other option than to be dismissed from the team. We cannot afford to spend our time practicing, learning our strategies, working hard to improve, and lose a valuable teammate before the season starts. That will devastate the entire team, and if that happens, it will be your fault if we fail. No boys and gal, this is do or die. I mean it. So, if any of you already feel the need to quit, then go ahead right now. I won't hold it against you tonight or tomorrow afternoon at the start of practice, but if you quit mid-stream, I will hold it against you and so will the rest of the team. You can count on that. Go ahead and alert the remaining team members tonight, or in the morning, so they have time to make their decision; the time for indecisiveness is over when I blow the whistle."

Coach Caruthers paused, removed his ball cap, and scratched his head. In an exhausted moment, he drew in a deep breath and said,

"Now Vernadine, I need to be very direct and frank with you here. You are going to be seen by every man, boy, woman, child, sinner and saint as an imposter and a threat to this sport and all boys' sports, for that matter; and you will be seen as a disgrace to the women folk. You are going to suffer the biggest blows and insults that will be thrown, and honestly, I understand why that will be. I am going to be on the hot seat with you. Heck, I might even lose my job tomorrow and be driven out of town on a rail, but you have to know, that you know, that you know you are strong enough emotionally to handle this massive storm that is approaching. The burden that will be on your shoulders will be tremendous and possibly much more than you can even imagine. So, knowing this ahead of time, we all need to hear from you that you can see this through. The same goes for you as with the guys, you can't quit when the heat is too hot, you can't quit when your feelings are being run over by a train, you can't quit when you think you have reached your wits end. Your promise and dedication to the team is just as important as the guys. Can you look at me and your team mates that are standing here tonight and say, without hesitation, that you are in this for the long haul? I understand if you can't. I know I am calling you to the rug, but this is no joking matter and nothing to be taken lightly. Unfortunately, you will not have the same opportunity to give me your answer tomorrow at the start of practice, because everyone, and I mean everyone, in town will know by 9 PM tonight that I have asked you to join the basketball team. So, time is not on your side. What will it be?"

No one standing in the circle had moved for the ten minutes while the Coach spoke. Breathing was shallow and the sweat beads on everyone's faces glistened in the moonlight. The air was thick and oppressive and stomachs turned all waiting on Vernadine to give her answer. The truth was that even the boys didn't know their answers either and the pressure was building in all of them. After what seemed like an eternity and with all eyes on Vernadine, she drew in hot air, studied each face, staring at her and said, "Coach, after listening to you these past few minutes, I admit I am scared and unsure. I want to think that I am strong enough to withstand the storm and fury that is going to descend on me and my family, and you and the team. I want each of you to know that I understand how this is a punch in the stomach, and one that you didn't ask for. If anyone would have told me I would be in this situation, I would have laughed them off the face of the earth. I have been told by my parents, my entire life, that I was created for something very special and unique, and I have always believed that. I have been loved and encouraged to be myself and my momma has always told me she did not want to have to share all of her love with more than one child, so that's why I don't have any brothers or sisters. Both of my parents have encouraged me to use my imagination and dream big dreams. I know I sound flowery and like a girl, but I am a girl. I am a girl with ambition and conviction and loyalty to what I believe in. I believe in myself. I believe I can stand the heat and the pressure. I know I will be made fun of. I know that I am an outsider, here in this circle, and at school. I know I am not traditional in the sense of most southern girls. I mean, all you have to do is look at me. I am not the wilting gardenia that needs a protector. I am rough around the edges, and not polished or feminine; but what I am is capable, strong, determined, and unyielding. For once, these qualities will work to my advantage."

Vernadine took another long breath and knew she had to give an answer now, and she also knew everyone was waiting in high anticipation for her to finish her thoughts. She looked at the ground and swayed back and forth, digging deep within herself for her final answer. After a few moments, she looked up, straightened her back and said,

"I know that a girl on an all-boys high school basketball team is the last thing that should ever happen. I know you guys want me to say 'no', but I also know that I have the talent, skill and drive to pull this off. Coach, I will commit to my answer of 'yes'. Boys, it's going to be a struggle, but like Coach said, if you will believe in me, if you will believe in our team, if we will trust our Coach and work very hard, we can do this. No, it's not going to be easy. We are going to have conflict on the court, but let's try to shift any conflict and prejudice that we have against each other into drive and determination and energy. If we can do that, we could be unstoppable, and I truly believe that. This is too strange and too odd of an opportunity for all of us to pass up and miss out on. So, Coach, I am agreeing to play the Center position on the team and see it through, come hell or high water."

Everyone exhaled in unison. The question was answered. Vernadine said 'yes' and now they were on their own to decide for themselves what their answer would be. At least they had time to think until tomorrow, and they were thankful for that.

Coach Caruthers looked at Vernadine and the boys and said, "Well, let's call it a night. Everyone needs to get home, get some rest, soak in everything that has happened tonight, and make some decisions."

So with the decree from the Coach and the answer from Vernadine, everyone turned around and walked away without saying one word. Coach stood there, took a deep breath, and prayed that he was making the right decision for his career, for the school's reputation, and for the game of basketball. The boldness and passion which he felt while talking to his team, and the conviction with which he delivered his strong words, felt less-than and depleted now. Now, all he felt was deflated and scared. Would Vernadine hold true to her words? And how in the world were they going to really pull this off?

Without uttering a word to any of the departing church members, as they made their way out of the sanctuary, bound for home, Bud walked into the sanctuary and headed straight towards the altar. He knelt, clasped his hands and closed his eyes, and pleaded with the Lord for guidance, strength and perseverance. He asked for the Lord to light his path in this uncertain and challenging journey he was embarking on. Coach knew in his heart that it would take a miracle to pull this off, but he believed in miracles, and at the end of his prayer, his heart and mind were filled with peace and a strength that he knew was from God. He just knew that his miracle would come.

Brother Lester entered the sanctuary to turn out the lights for the evening and saw the Coach praying at the altar. News had already shaken the congregation about Vernadine and the team, so he understood why the Coach was kneeling and praying. The pastor also knew that there were many men huddled around the Coach's car, waiting on him outside. The murmurs of the crowd were getting louder and Brother Lester knew that the Coach's storm and troubles had already arrived.

Even though he did not know why Coach Caruthers would ever ask a girl to be on his basketball team was beyond him, but he knew Bud to be a man of faith, true conviction and very skilled as a coach. He knew he would hear all he wanted to know from the townspeople, but he also knew he would have to partner with Bud during this uncertain and treacherous time as his pastor and his friend. Bud rose from the altar and turned around to see Brother Lester in the back of the sanctuary, waiting on him. Bud also heard the noise outside from the men talking and his fear of facing his decision and risk was in front of him.

"Well, Pastor, I guess it's time to face the crowd outside. I have created quite a storm. I apologize for keeping you late, but thank you. I had to spend some time right here, praying. Well, mainly begging, if you want to know the truth," Coach Caruthers forced a smile, but Brother Lester could see the emotions all over Coach's face.

"It's ok, Bud; I will unlock these doors anytime, day or night, for you and any of the congregation when there is a pressing need to beseech God," Brother Lester said. Then he continued, "In fact, if you remember, the church used to be kept unlocked for that very reason, because this is God's house and not mine, but after that unfortunate scene with Deacon Dwight and Sister Maylene skinny dipping and drinking whiskey in the baptismal at midnight a couple of years ago, I took all of the spare keys away from every one of the Deacons. If you recall, it was the Janitor, Mr. Green, that caught them and he quit right on the spot. He ran out of here like a shot and never looked back. He sped over to my house and woke me and Shirley up to give us the news. I flew out of the house and raced over to the church. When I pulled up to the front door, I was welcomed with a broken whiskey bottle and two sets of wet footprints on the front steps. Chills ran all over me and I was stricken with fear of what I would find inside. The floors were wet and the water in the baptismal pool was still swirling. I have heard that this incident caused Mr. Green's backslidin', but I don't know that for sure. I know he was pretty shaken up, seeing them laughing and splashing around as naked as the day they were born. I should pay him a visit soon," Brother Lester wiped his brow; the thought of the episode still caused him stress. But he continued.

"It has taken us over two years, as a congregation, to get past the scandal of knowing that two naked church members, of the opposite sex, were having fun in the baptismal. I have never figured out what in the world they were thinking or how they thought that they could get away with this crazy act in this small town, with no one finding out. They didn't last a week in town after that. A couple of days after the incident, Shirley went to her weekly ladies Bible study and, for some strange reason, she returned home much later than usual. I remember asking her if everything was ok. She just smiled at me and said, 'Oh yes, dear, we spent quite a bit of time in prayer over Deacon Dwight and Sister Maylene. We were laid out prostrate on the floor asking God to help them see the error of their ways and we lost track of time.'

"And that's all she said. I didn't think another thing about it," Lester said. "But, the next day, when I heard that 'SINNERS' had been spray painted in red paint on the doors of his car, and 'YOU WILL PAY' on the hood, I began to suspect something, but quickly removed it from my mind. I wanted to believe that the ladies bible study group, led by my sweet wife, would be so far removed from this tragedy, that again, I erased the thoughts. When word got 'round about Dwight's car, some of the townspeople told me that they saw Dwight spray painting white over the red paint to cover up the vandalism, and I just could not get rid of the growing, sinking feeling in my stomach that someone very close to me had gone off the deep end. Then, I heard later that day his car was spotted speeding like the devil through town with cars following behind them. Can you believe that folks lined the streets like they were watching the annual Christmas parade, as this white car with pink 'SINNERS' raced by them? I was told that when his car hit the railroad tracks at eighty miles an hour, the tires exploded, the muffler fell off, and the hood flew open. I understand from the impact of hitting the tracks that he lost control of the car and abandoned it on the street. The last anyone saw of Dwight and Maylene, they were sprinting down the road and heading into the woods like their lives depended on it. When I came home from church, after preparing for Sunday's sermon, I noticed Shirley's front two tires were flat and the rims were unrecognizable. I thought to myself, 'what in the blazes has happened here?' Then I opened the driver's door and tried to move the seat back to get in and look for any inside damage, but the seat wouldn't budge. By this point, my nerves are shot and my panic mode is kicking in. I got out of the car, looked under the seat, and low and behold, and to my horror, there sat an empty can of red spray paint! I buckled in the knees, hyperventilated, and a moan from the bottom of my lungs sprung forth. I just knew that my whole world and my years of ministry were all but over. 'I am finished as a pastor and I am married to a complete and utter stranger!' I thought to myself as I raced into the house and called for Shirley. She had locked herself up in the bedroom and wouldn't answer me. I beat on the door and said 'WOMAN OF GOD, GET OUT HERE NOW!', but all I could hear was mumbling and groaning and something about hitting a dog and wrecking the car. I said, 'Shirley Pearl Scarborough, now I KNOW that you didn't hit a dang dog! There ain't a dog that's ever been born that would have done that kind of damage to the vehicle! No ma'am, you were on that high-speed chase escorting Dwight and Maylene out of town, weren't you!? I found the empty can of red spray paint under the driver's seat! You cannot get out of this!' Do you know that Shirley stayed locked up in the bedroom for three days after the incident? When she finally came out, dehydrated and starving, she said, 'God worked wonders in three days, look at Jesus, and that she felt much better.' That is all she would say. I knew my wife and the ladies' bible study group vandalized Dwight's car, and most likely, Shirley was driving the lead car right behind Dwight on the way out of town, though no one would confirm this. The damage to her car was too extensive and the story about hitting a dog was ludicrous. I was so exhausted and embarrassed my wife, a preacher's wife, had led the rebellion and furious mob that day against Dwight and Maylene. I didn't have the energy to fight with her, so we carried the burden around like a heavy weight on our backs and conscience. When I did not see any remorse or regret in Shirley's behavior, I was reminded of my earlier thought. 'I am married to a complete and utter stranger!'"

"The next day, after Dwight and Maylene ran into the woods, Mr. Green's father-in-law brought his wrecker to pick up their car and he hauled it back to his junk yard. Instead of putting the car in the smash pile, he left it parked on the outside of his fence, on the highway, with the pink paint 'SINNERS' and 'YOU WILL PAY' visible and lighted each night with spot lights. He hand painted a sign and stuck it in the ground beside the car that says 'Be sure your sins will find you out!' This is so strange; I couldn't make this stuff up!" Brother Lester said.

"I clearly remember this entire story like it was yesterday. It's still a very popular subject of conversation around town. I remember hearing rumors about Shirley and the Ladies bible study group being the cause for the dramatic ending to Dwight and Maylene's residency in Spit's Creek, but since it was not confirmed, I just moved on from speculating. But, wow, Pastor that is some story. I can only imagine your dismay and horror at the whole thing, from the skinny dipping and drinking whiskey in church, to your wife leading the mob and chasing Dwight and Maylene out of town. I understand why you felt defeated and embarrassed, but I will say you are one strong man to continue, after such horrific events, to stand in the pulpit each Sunday and deliver the powerful sermons you do," Bud exhaled.

"I told Shirley I am going to commit the next month of Sundays to sermons strictly on how we are not supposed to 'judge our neighbors' and 'vengeance is mine sayeth the Lord', and you know what she and the ladies bible study group did? For four solid weeks, they were all 'sick' every Sunday. You remember how we had to sing our hymns a cappella? That's because Shirley refused to come to church and play the piano. Now, how does that make me look as a minister, when I can't even get my own wife to act right and not separate her actions from worldly behaviors?! Pitiful, that's what!" Lester took a seat in the pew and wiped his defeated brow again. "Rumor has it Dwight and Maylene high tailed it across the state to Marion. I heard Dwight is an auto mechanic and Maylene went to beauty school and is working in a beauty parlor." They both reflected for a moment on the biggest scandal that has ever happened in their church, or Spit's Creek, for that matter.

"But, I think what is happening with you now, Coach, might make that old memory of Deacon Dwight and Sister Maylene seem like child's play. I say all of this to comfort you. All you have to do is ask, and I will meet you here and unlock the doors. If kneeling at the altar is where you need to be, it would be wrong of me to keep you locked out," Brother Lester said as he collected hymnals and the coach rested on the end of a pew.

"But, getting back to the present, I know you hear the group of men that have gathered outside and are impatiently waiting on you," Brother Lester said.

"Yes, I hear them and I have to face them. I won't keep you any longer tonight. Thank you again," Coach Caruthers began the walk to the front doors of the sanctuary.

"Hey Coach, this is none of my business, but you might want to wait until tomorrow to face the people? I have heard just enough about what is going on, and you're right, this is a doozie. I have an idea.... what about slipping out the back door with me and let me drive you to the Golden Cherry Motel where you can spend the night in peace and quiet? I have heard some of the men say that a crowd has also gathered at your house. If we can get you into your back door without being seen, you can grab your clothes and a toothbrush without anyone knowing a thing. I can pick you up early in the morning and bring you back to the church to pick up your car. The way I see it, you will need the rest tonight so you can face your giants in the morning. What do you say?" The Pastor asked and waited.

"Ok, by the sounds of it out there, I am going to need help tonight and for a long time. Thank you for your kindness. Kindness is something I am going to miss from others for a while. Please pray for me and the team. Vernadine is going to need an extra anointing, I suspect," Coach said through labored breaths.

And with that, the two of them turned out the lights and made a run for it out of the back door and jumped into the preacher's pick-up truck. Coach was still closing his door as Brother Lester punched the gas, heading into the safety of darkness for his friend Coach Bud Caruthers.

Vernadine is a Southern Sensation

Buford County High School, 1943
Spit's Creek, AL

When Vernadine jumped in the car with her parents after church service, she jumped into a hornet's nest. Irene was weeping, and Fletcher was stoic. The combination of her parents' emotions let her know they were not happy with the sudden news about her joining the boy's high school basketball team. It never occurred to her that either of them would consider this bad news. In fact, she thought quite the opposite. She was sure that both of them would be proud of her new venture of breaking stereotypes, asserting herself, taking advantage of an opportunity, even though it was an unconventional opportunity. They had always encouraged her to take risks, to be true to herself and to believe in herself. And now that she had just taken the biggest step of her life; she was met with disappointing resistance from the two people that had encouraged her for the last sixteen years of life. This will not be good, she mused inwardly.

A confused and dumbfounded Vernadine broke the silence and said, "So, I guess you have heard the news about me joining the basketball team? Either that or Brother Lester delivered a powerful sermon tonight that have you both stirred up? But I guess this reaction is not about the sermon?" There was no response.

Vernadine sat as far back into her seat as possible, thankful for the darkness, and wished she could disappear. It appeared her bold decision to be 'herself' was not turning out to be a good idea after all. Like a wave of salty water knocking her off of her feet and stinging her eyes, she now regretted her decision and commitment she had just given to Coach Caruthers and the team. What in the world was she thinking? Of course girls are not supposed to be on a boys sports team, that's why girls have their own teams. Why didn't she just play on the girls team instead of upsetting what appeared to be the whole town? She felt stupid, embarrassed, reckless, alone and afraid all at the same time.

She felt sure that what she was thinking was the same thing her parents were thinking. She also felt fairly confident that they also wanted to know why she had not asked them first, bounced the idea off of them, sought their counsel and guidance instead of dropping a bomb on them with no warning at all. They would have kindly told her she was crazy. They would have lovingly re-directed her thoughts and energies in a completely different direction. Showing her prized calf and winning first prize against the other boys in the 4H club was one thing, but playing on a boys' basketball team was something completely different. Conventions have their place in society. Men and women are different. Not everything is meant to be equal. She was right. Irene and Fletcher were blindsided with the news and that was all there was to it, and they also did not know how in the world they were going to clean this mess up.

By 9 PM, the news was all over town. Coach Caruthers and the Turnipseed's were the laughingstock of Buford County and they could all thank Vernadine for that. The car ride home continued in complete and awkward silence. When they returned home, they all got out of the car and walked into their bedrooms, closed the doors and turned out the lights for the night. Each of them praying that this was all a bad dream, that come morning, all would be forgotten. Each praying that their peaceful and normal family life would greet them with the morning sun and each breath that they took would fill their lungs with joy and comfort. Sleep did not come easy for any of them tonight.

When the sun rose, Spit's Creek was abuzz. Coach Caruthers dressed, then ducked into the small café at the motel for coffee and toast. Thankfully he only had to wait a few minutes for the Pastor to give him a ride to the church to get his car. Once Bud rounded the last curve in the road to the school, it appeared every car in Buford County had descended upon it. The road and property surrounding Buford County High School looked like an oversized parking lot. Bud considered sinking lower in his seat and just passing the school on by, but he knew if he ran away today, he would never be able to face the consequences and response to his decision about Vernadine. At the same time Bud was putting his mental armor on and praying without ceasing, the school secretary, a bible study friend of Irene's, called Irene and advised Vernadine to stay home from school. Vernadine agreed to stay home from school, but she insisted she would show up for the first basketball practice that afternoon in the gymnasium.

"Oh my Lord," thought Bud, "What in all that's good and pure has happened to everyone? It's not the end of the world. A girl playing on a boys' team is unusual, for sure, but to warrant an uprising this size seems like too much?" He could smell the trouble around him as panic and fear gripped him to his core.

Coach parked his car in his usual parking space, surprised that no one had blocked him. He struggled amid the crowd and endured rude remarks as he made his way to his office. Men yelling, "You're done here, Coach", "You are a disgrace to our school" and "You have lost your mind" lingered in the air like poisonous gas. Once inside his office, he was greeted by the Superintendent, Principal, Athletic director, Brother Lester and the attorney for the school district. He swallowed hard, then choked on his breath. With no greetings or niceties at all, the conversation began.

"Coach Caruthers, I have been running faster that a one-legged man in a butt kicking competition, trying to put out this firestorm that you have created. What in the devil are you thinking by asking a girl to play on the boys basketball team? That is the dumbest idea that I have ever heard, and this genius move of yours is probably going to be the extinction of your coaching career. Mark my words, son. Why, do you know you have completely upset this entire community? You have brought shame and embarrassment to this school and school board. We have always regarded you as an outstanding coach, a great role model for the youth, and an excellent teacher, but this takes the cake for a major lack of judgment. We have all gathered here among the fierce mob outside to ask you directly, 'what in the devil, boy?!!' We were threatened as we made our way through the crowd. We were told that 'our heads would roll' along with yours. Coach, you and I have always had a great relationship with mutual respect, and my boys always looked up to you as their coach, but we are in a pickle here and none of us know what to do about this situation that has come straight from the bottom of burning hell." The Superintendent said as he took another puff from his cigar.

"Yea, the dumbest idea I have ever heard of and the threats outside were real. Those faces are full of rage and insult and there was one moment when I felt my death was certain," said the Principal. "I didn't get one wink of sleep last night. Angry father's repeatedly beat on my front door from 9 PM last night until 2 AM. How in the heck are we supposed to handle this scandal?"

Brother Lester silently prayed for his friend, Bud, and the school board attorney stared into his coffee cup, trying to figure out the legal grounds the school board may have to fire Coach Caruthers right there on the spot. So far, he was not having any luck in his recall. Yes, this was a scorcher of a situation. This was unchartered territory for every single one of them.

After Irene hung the phone up from the brief conversation with the school secretary, she plopped herself in a chair at the breakfast table and laid her head down. Fletcher sat at the other end of the table, blowing on his hot coffee and blankly staring at the wall. Vernadine was frozen in an upright position, not knowing what to do. Nothing had yet to be said by either of her parents and the silence was killing her. She walked across the kitchen and poured herself a glass of fresh milk, and sat down at the table with her parents. She knew she had some explaining to do.

"Momma and daddy, I know you are both upset. Even though neither of you have said a word to me. I know you are shocked, disappointed, and probably angry at me for this mess I have created. You know I never want to hurt either of you, and I am going to do my best to explain how this happened. Believe me when I tell you that this is just as much of a shock to me as it is to you. We were outside playing basketball, and the next thing I knew, Coach Caruthers asked me to join the team. Everything happened so fast. Everyone was shocked, including Coach, but what happened out there was something unpredictable and spontaneous. I would never seek out playing sports on an all-boys team. Coach saw something in my ability that only a coach can see. He is risking his career and reputation by going forward with this plan. I am risking the three of us being laughed and scorned out of town, but I know that I can do this. Please forgive me for bringing this upset into our family. I have made a commitment to Coach and the team that I will not back out, no matter how hard things become. We are in for hard times in the immediate future, but the payoff is going to be worth it. I know I am asking a lot from you. I know that if you told me I cannot pursue this hair-brained idea, that I would have to listen to you and back out, but please don't ask me to quit before we even get started. I am asking you to trust me. I know that I could be very wrong, and that this could be a huge disaster, but I really don't think it will be." Vernadine said as she swirled the milk in her glass without looking up.

After what seemed like an eternity, Fletcher spoke for the first time in hours. "I don't know what to say, other than this has the potential to run us out of town, away from our home, farm, church, family and friends. What you have decided to do could have serious consequences. Me and your mother have heard what you have said. I know you have committed to being on the team and you are supposed to be at practice this afternoon, but your mother and I need time to think and to pray. We will give you our answer before the end of the school hours." And with that, Fletcher left the kitchen table, put his coffee cup in the sink, walked out the back door and disappeared into the barn to begin his daily work. Irene made her way to the sink to wash the breakfast dishes and Vernadine retreated to her bedroom to wait it out.

The rest of the day at school was a total whirlwind. The men left Coach alone after the morning bell rang, still not sure what to do. The one thing they did let him know was they would all be back to watch the practice and the circus in the gym after school. Bud was left to maneuver his day amidst the comments and dirty looks, and Vernadine sat alone in her bedroom thinking the worst.

This had been the longest day that Vernadine could remember. The waiting on her parents' decision was brutal. Fletcher and Irene spoke briefly and prayed, mostly. At 2:15 PM Fletcher knocked on Vernadine's door. "Come in," she said.

"Vernadine, your mother and I have talked. We are not in total agreement in this matter, and you know that we always try to agree on big decisions. We always have. Nevertheless, your mother feels that you should quit the team. It breaks her heart to know that her only child would face harshness, crude remarks, and isolation from your peers. Do you honestly know that you can withstand all of what you are about to face? You are sixteen years old. You gave your word, and we agree that this is important to keep, but I think in this situation, if you backed out, it would be okay. You can always blame it on me and your mother."

"I know Daddy, but I don't want to back out. I want to do this," Vernadine said.

"Well, if at any time you feel that the burden is too much. Anytime you feel that the criticism is too harsh and if you feel along the way that you cannot compete with the boys, let me know and I will talk to the Coach. I want you to succeed. I want this to be a great learning experience for you. So, go ahead to practice. I will drive you and stay with you the whole time."

Vernadine jumped off the bed, put on her sneakers, and ran out of the front door to the truck. Irene stood behind the screened door and wept as she watched them drive away. She just knew that her daughter was the lamb headed for slaughter.

Just as Coach thought, his day had been a complete storm. The final bell rang for the day. He grabbed his whistle, play book, a cup of fresh coffee for a caffeine jolt, and made the walk from his office to the gym to begin practice. The noise coming from the gym was loud, like a game was being played. He paused outside of the heavy door and took a deep breath, uttered a silent prayer, and hoped the next two hours would not be the end of his long coaching career. He chided himself a bit and questioned his judgment for this situation he had created. Maybe he was committing career suicide? A death wish for a future in coaching. He felt inadequate to handle the pressure. He was a calm, easy going man, not a fighter. But, things were as they were now, and he had no choice but to face the maddened crowd. He opened the door and walked in with his chin cocked high. Faking confidence might just get him through this.

Just as promised, the Superintendent, Principal, and the entire school board, complete with the attorney who still had not discovered legal grounds for firing the coach, was standing in a huddle waiting on the first row of bleachers. Brother Lester had placed himself on the top row like a beacon of hope on high. Vernadine and her father were sitting down looking as scared as someone on death row making their last walk, as people mingled around them with angry expressions and audible grunts. The boys gathered in another huddle, also looking scared and unsure about everything that was happening. Coach walked over to the team bench and placed his playbook and coffee down. He blew the whistle, and everyone went quiet.

"Team, huddle up!" The team gathered around him. When the team was in place and ready for instruction Coach billowed out, "Folks, thank you for being here, but this is our first practice as you all know. And, while normally we don't have spectators for practice, let me remind you that if you insist on being here, this is not a game. This is practice. I am in control here. If I feel that the noise is too much or proves a distraction for my coaching and the team, then you will have to leave. We have work to do for the upcoming season and that's what we are going to focus on. So, please respect the rules I have set forth. We all know why you are here, but this is not the time to speak up or say anything. You will really be upset when our team hits the court in the upcoming season and are not ready to compete. So, please be respectful to these team members... All of them."

With that, the crowd ceased their noise and Coach turned his attention to the team. He called the role and found that everyone on the team was accounted for.

"Boys, Vernadine has given her answer of 'yes' to be a team member. I asked you boys to give me your definitive answer at the beginning of practice on your commitment to the team. So, if anyone has something to say, now is the time. No going back after you give your yay or nay."

Coach waited. He scanned the faces of the boys trying to get a read on their answers. No one spoke. Another few moments passed in silence, Coach asked, "If you are committing to the team, for the entire season, raise your hand." Little by little, hands rose. The boys looked at each other waiting for responses. More hands went up. By the end of the silent vote, every one of the hands were raised. No one had quit. The curiosity was too high. The consensus was they would not miss being a part of the unfolding story of being the oddest boys basketball team in the nation, no matter how mistreated they might be by everyone. Coach was stunned. It amazed him at the character displayed in his young men and gal. Seeing the strength and determination in the faces of the team laid the foundation for him of mental fortitude. If these young teenagers can stand upright, he thought to himself, then so could he. He didn't know whether to laugh or cry from relief. So, instead of doing either, he said, "Vernadine, take the center, Slim, take the point guard, Jimmy, take the small forward, Johnny, take the power forward and Lester, take the shooting guard. The rest of you guys, take the defense."

The team filled the court. Coach threw the ball to Johnny and blew the whistle. The dance on the court began as Johnny dribbled and looked for a space to run. He tossed the ball to Lester and, through flying arms, he took a shot from the shooting guard position. The ball hit the ring, bounced off, and Slim grabbed the ball from under the net and tossed it to Vernadine. In a moment of panic, Vernadine dribbled the ball, looked for the shot and was knocked down flat on the floor.

Was that how it was going to be? Panic, fear and knock downs? Girls cannot handle the strength of her male counterparts. This will not work. Everyone silently agreed. The noise level rose for the first time since Coach's speech to the onlookers. Coach put the whistle to his lips and blew in loud spurts. He blew harder and longer until the crowd quieted more. "See, Coach, this is a horrible decision on your part. A girl cannot play on a boys' team!" One father yelled. "Yeah, get her off the court!" and "This is embarrassing!" echoed through the hissing and yells.

Coach walked over to Vernadine, grabbed her hand and pulled her up. He checked on her, then patted her on the back before walking to the middle of the court. Without saying another word, he blew the whistle and signaled with his hands for play to resume.

Another play stopped Johnny from running. He tossed the ball to Jimmy, Jimmy tossed to Vernadine, Vernadine tossed to Lester. Everyone was blocked. At least they knew their defense was strong. Lester tried for the shot. He missed. Vernadine ran towards the net, grabbed the ball, knocked over a teammate, firmly placed her feet and threw with all of her strength. Two Points!

Vernadine's score shut the onlookers and haters up in a second. With no delay, the ball was in motion. Plays were called by Lester, the shooting guard. And even though Vernadine did not know the calls yet, she hung in there out of sheer determination and athletic ability. The offense scored again. After fifteen minutes of play time, Coach blew the whistle to stop play. Offense ten, defense zero.

And so it went every afternoon after school. Practice for three hours Monday through Friday. The hazing subsided over the next couple of weeks as the idea of Vernadine on the team took on a different light. She was an asset. She was talented. She could block and she could score. She was a team player. The iciness from her teammates were thawing as they all became adjusted to the reality that Coach Caruthers was indeed right in his pick of Vernadine. They believed that they might have a decent chance of being a real competitor for the upcoming season and possibly win over their rival, Lee County High School.

Talk around town, in the barbershop, at the company coffee pots, and waiting in line at the Woolworth's diner for lunch changed from disgust and fury to 'can you believe it?'

The school board made a 'temporary' decision to not fire Coach Caruthers, but allow him to finish out the basketball season with the hopes of a miracle and success for his career and for the school.

Coach Caruthers was finally able to take full breaths now and the line of cars waiting for him after school from angry parents had almost come to a complete stop. He could now go home after school and stop hiding out. For all of this, he was very thankful and very proud of how he had trusted his instincts about Vernadine. She was quickly becoming exactly what he needed for the center position.

Vernadine settled into the rhythm of her new normal. Hazing and rude remarks were still hurled at her from the boys and girls from school and church, but the sting had worn off and her resilience was at an all-time high. She was thankful the boys on the team had trusted her skills and had even begun including her in their conversations of play call strategy and small talk.

Life in Spit's Creek and Buford County was well on its way to resuming the normal hum and tempo of the small town and county that it is. The dark clouds were clearing and even the chirping melodies of the birds seemed happier. Out of the mouths of everyone was the name 'Vernadine Turnipseed, the girl basketball player'.

Word spread quickly to the newspapers and radio stations in the State and every day there were at least two or three newspaper journalists at practice trying their best to get the latest 'scoop' on the team's progress and their girl player. Coach Caruthers did not want to, but felt he had no choice other than to let the spectators and the press continue to sit in for practices. There was just too much interest in what was going on inside the school gymnasium. His rules were supreme, though. No talking, no cheering, no yelling, and no rude remarks. Anyone that broke the rules was banned from practice from now on.

No discussion or arguments allowed. Period. No one could speak to any of the players. If one player was caught with a comment in any of the news articles, they were benched for the first two games of the season. Just the sting of that kept their mouths closed.

Practices were going well. Everyone involved seemed pleased and the reality of the season kick off was only days away. The tension was running high; the pressure was on, but everyone felt confident in their positions and the playbook. Slim Perkins had proved himself to be just the leader the team needed and his kindness to Vernadine was noted not only to the team, but also to Vernadine, who was particularly keen on his kindness.

Soon after the 1943 season began, the basketball team of Buford County High School was in every newspaper from Montgomery to Birmingham and Atlanta to Nashville and beyond. The whole of the Southeast was in shock and disbelief that a girl was playing on a boy's high school basketball team and they were even more shocked that the team was winning every game.

People drove in from towns near and far, to watch this fascinating saga play out, as Vernadine charged her way around the court, game after game. The ticket sales and concession stand proceeds were going through the roof, and the school board was ecstatic. The crowd was so overwhelming, and nothing like this had ever happened before in Buford County, Alabama.

It was so crowded in the gymnasium that the cheerleaders and band were asked to cheer and play outside of the gym in the hallways, so there would be more space on the floor and in the bleachers for spectators and sports writers. Loudspeakers were wired on the outside of the gym for the overflow crowd in the parking lot, so they could still hear the play-by-play action of the game.

The local AM radio station, WJHO, broadcast the games. Fortunately, the game could be heard on the radio all over the South to the Midwest, and on a clear night, all the way to California. Their basketball team was in the spotlight and on the lips of thousands of people around the country, but the name that rose above every name on the team was Vernadine Turnipseed, and she was their star.

Vernadine was in disbelief, and she was not prepared to handle all of the attention she was receiving. So when the radio announcer caught up with her after a game, wanting to interview her, she froze. She looked at Coach Caruthers as she remembered his rule of no interviews with his players. She excused herself and walked over to ask him what she should do. Her name and her team were all over the airwaves and newspapers, and she knew eventually someone would have to say something.

"Coach, what should I do? I keep getting asked every game to answer their questions. I know you said not to, but the way I see it, folks want to hear something from us, from you and me and the guys. What we are doing here is catching the attention of people everywhere, near and far. Why don't you do an interview with the radio announcer? You speak for all of us because sooner or later, you are going to have to say something. What do you say, Coach?" Vernadine stepped back and waited for Coach's response.

Coach Caruthers knew Vernadine was right. He had worked very hard to shield his team and himself from any more hassle, insult, and mockery. But, because of the undefeated season, insults and mockery had turned into jubilation and cheers of support. Yes, he should take advantage of the moments to capitalize on their success, because it may not last. The crowd's fury was always on the horizon, ever threatening. It amazed him at how well his team had performed, way beyond his expectations. There was a small flame of hope and a dream burning in his heart, that just maybe, this team could make it all the way to the state championships. He was also very cautious, because what was unfolding in front of everyone was nothing anyone had seen before. The falling from grace would be a very long fall, and they all knew it.

"You are right Vernadine. Everything you said is right. Folks are eager to hear from us, that's for sure. What I will do is let the broadcasters and sports writers know that at the start of practice tomorrow afternoon, we will offer them ten minutes for questions and comments."

Coach liked the idea. That would give him time to think and collect his thoughts before he 'went on the record'. So, the Coach walked over to the sportswriters and radio announcers and told them they will have ten minutes at the beginning of tomorrow's practice for questions. No more. Then, the Coach turned around to his team and told them they needed to think long and hard about tomorrow's interview. That in no shape or form, if asked negative or probing questions about Vernadine, should they answer except positively. He reminded them they are a team, not individual players. They are succeeding as a team and they will fail as a team. One for all and all for one.

Each player went home and thought about their true feelings for their team. They each knew that the risk was too great for them personally, and as a team, if ill-will or dissention came out in their comments tomorrow. No one could deny that they were winning every game, and that Vernadine was a key asset to their success. She wasn't so bad. She was hanging in there, just like a guy. She wasn't whining or asking for special treatment. She was playing her hardest and they could all see she was faithful to the commitment she made to be a team player. She wasn't asking for fame or accolades; she wasn't asking for leniency; she was all in, just like the guys, and a miracle was playing out in front of everyone, and they were all thankful for that.

The school day was long. The tension was high as the clock ticked towards the last bell of the day. At 3 PM, the team members rushed to the locker rooms to change into their uniforms, and by 3:10 PM, all of them were accounted for and seated in a row on the bottom bleacher. Coach Caruthers was standing beside his team as the writers and announcers filed into the gymnasium. Tension was high.

"Good afternoon, men. Thank you for coming today. I know you have some questions for us. We have ten minutes set aside for your interview, that's it," Coach said firmly. "You may go ahead."

Coach remained standing, but rested his hand on Slim's shoulder for support. He was shaking and so was Slim.

"So, Vernadine, I understand that you have never really played basketball and you being on the team happened by accident? Is this correct?"

"No, sir, I haven't played all that much and I guess you could say that, about being an accident and all," she meekly said.

"So, you didn't realize that you had undiscovered athletic talent?" asked the broadcaster.

"No, sir, not really," said Vernadine.

"So, what brought you to this moment, the star of Buford County high school basketball, and the only girl player on a boys' team?" the reporter prodded.

"Well, I don't know, other than my church youth group needed another player for our Wednesday night pick-up game, because one boy was out sick, so I figured I might as well try to play. So, I did, and here I am. Coach Caruthers is my youth pastor, and I guess he saw something in me he needed for his team. I still can't believe it," Vernadine smiled slightly.

"Vernadine, do you know that people all over the South, and beyond, are keeping up with your team's season?" asked the reporter.

"Well, everyone in town is talking about it, but all we want to do is play basketball and maybe go to the state championship finals, if we make it that far. Other than that, we try not to pay attention to what is being said about us. It could be a distraction and we don't want that. Coach Caruthers keeps us focused on the game and winning," said Vernadine.

"Just one last thing. Have you heard that you are being called a 'southern sensation'?" asked the reporter.

"Yes, I have heard that, but I really don't know why? I am just trying my best and so is the whole team. It takes all of us to win a game. I don't think I should be the only one mentioned in the news articles just because I am the only girl on the team. We have a lot of talented players on our team that are much better than I am. All of us try very hard and our efforts are paying off, so far. Coach Caruthers is a great coach, and his coaching has brought the best out in all of us. Thank you for asking me these questions, but you should ask someone else a question now," Vernadine smiled and took a deep breath. 'That wasn't so hard,' she thought to herself. She did not like the 'Southern Sensation' title, though. That much she knew.

The reporters turned to Coach Caruthers. There were only two minutes left for the interview. Coach had been keeping the time. It did not surprise him that Vernadine was the principal topic.

"Coach Caruthers, you took a major career risk by asking a girl to play on an all-boys high school basketball team. Many people believe that what you did was wrong, that you were insulting the sport, and ignoring the definition of an all-boys team. Vernadine should play on the girls' basketball team, don't you agree?" asked one reporter.

"Men, life is a mystery. I am well aware that I have upset many people with my decision regarding Vernadine. Some things cannot be adequately explained, but what I do know is this, I am not trying to ignore or upset the tradition of boys basketball. I did not set out to cause a war. What you see happening here is something none of us would have ever dreamed of. This team represents our school and our community. My job, as the basketball coach, is to win games. My job, as the coach, is to teach my team how to play the game of basketball successfully. My job as a coach is to find the best group of young people in my high school that can excel in this sport, and that is exactly what I have done. Yes, this is very unconventional. There is no denying that, but we are in the middle of an undefeated season. We are all in awe of that. Every one of us. But I am doing my job, and this group of guys and our gal are succeeding, and they are working together for a common goal. They have learned to set aside their own prejudices and negative thoughts to make a cohesive team. They have risen above the hurtful words and the shunning from their peers and their fellow townspeople; and against all odds, the strength and maturity of this outstanding group of young people makes me prouder than I have ever been. We have already won. We are a united front. We are dedicated and challenged to be the best basketball team that Buford County high school has ever seen. We will continue on our path. We will continue to work hard together. Thank you for your time today. Our ten minutes is up." With a renewed strength, Coach Caruthers blew the whistle. It was time to play basketball.

The practice went well and no one held any grudges against Vernadine, since she and the coach were the only ones asked questions during the interview. They all knew that the only reason why their team had any attention and notoriety was because of her. They were relieved that they were not asked questions, and they were not upset that their names went unmentioned. They were undefeated. That's all they cared about. Undefeated and known all over the country.

Totally unaffected by her notoriety, Vernadine was tired and hungry after practice ended and she wanted to get home, but out of the corner of her eye, she saw her teammate and point guard, Slim Perkins, walking towards the door. She ran to catch up with him and he walked her to her car, where her parents Fletcher and Irene were waiting. Slim shook Mr. Turnipseed's hand and said goodbye to Vernadine and Mrs. Turnipseed. And even though it was dark outside, her father could tell that Vernadine was blushing and smitten.

"Oh, Lord," thought Fletcher, "that boy is too skinny for her. She will kill him."

They pulled out of the parking lot as Vernadine stared out of the back window, with a gentle smile on her face, watching Slim walk away. Fletcher chuckled to himself, shook his head, and thought, 'Oh goodness, here we go. Vernadine's first crush.'

The State Basketball Championships

Foster Auditorium
Tuscaloosa, AL 1943

The basketball season of 1943 was an undefeated success, and Buford County High School was on the lips of every basketball fan, and even those who weren't, far and wide. The 'Southern Sensation', Vernadine, was now known as 'The Queen of Basketball' throughout the nation. A title that she didn't like, and found embarrassing, but she also knew there was nothing she could do about it.

The time had come for the end of season finals and BCHS had rolled over every team to reach the Championship games in Tuscaloosa. They fought hard against the top eight teams in the State and were now down to the last game and the winning trophy. Their worthy opponent was Opelika High School. This was the first time for either of the two teams to make it this far in their seasons, and the spectators for both teams turned out in droves. The parking lot was full of every church and club from Spit's Creek and Opelika, selling fresh baked goods, boiled peanuts, and crocheted blankets and doilies for fundraisers. The school marching bands competed from opposite ends of the parking lot, and the cheerleaders screamed through their bullhorns, "victory is ours" in unison. It was loud, it was raw, and it was a territorial fight.

The game began and went strong, fast-paced, and fierce for one hour. With the score neck and neck, BCHS took possession of the ball and Vernadine threw a hail Mary pass from center court and rang the basket as the clock counted to zero. Their girl player had scored the winning points and they were now the 1943 Alabama State basketball champions! The gymnasium went wild with screams, chants, tears, and hugs. The team picked up Vernadine and bounced her all over the court, with arms and legs flying everywhere, with the fans following behind waving the school banner above their heads. Slim Perkins helped carry Vernadine around the court and placed himself right under her rear end as they suspended her in the air. There was just something about her that drew him in. He didn't know exactly what it was. Maybe it was her sense of command and take charge attitude? Whatever it was, it drew him to her like a bee is to honey. Even in all of the excitement of being suspended in the air and the roar of the crowd, Vernadine knew the extra squeezing and rubbing on her rear end was from Slim, and she liked it. At that moment, her world stood still. She wasn't thinking about being the 'Queen of Basketball', or winning the State championship. She was thinking about Slim and his touch and how she wanted him to squeeze her some more.

This was history and they knew it. The war raging against Hitler was far away from Alabama, and all everyone wanted was to have a moment of happiness; to forget the tragic war outside of the gymnasium, on the other side of the world, where their sons and daughters were dying to protect their freedom. The trophy was handed to Coach Caruthers, as he relished his proudest moment surrounded by his team. His team, from a little town, with a girl center, had given him the best victory in his entire coaching career. He knew he had earned his place in Alabama sports history, conversations at the barbershop, picnics and town gatherings for years to come. He had made history and chartered unfamiliar territory with the help of Vernadine Turnipseed, 'The Queen of Basketball'. This would be a moment that none of them would ever forget.

The Queen of Basketball is a Senior

Spit's Creek, 1944

The excitement in Buford County after the 1943 Championship was palpable. If the excitement could have been called a disease, it would have been. An epidemic of jubilance and happiness was everywhere. The excitement from the state championship continued into 1944 and into another highly anticipated basketball season. Coach Caruthers and his team knew they had a job to do. They had to repeat their 1943 season, so they forged ahead.

Vernadine was still in the newspapers and on the lips of everyone, near and far, but the team maintained their focus because they knew it would take each and every one of them to have another winning season.

As expected, the season went undefeated. Crowds of people descended on Spit's Creek every game. Mrs. Ruth's cafe was reaching record sales from the last two seasons, and her Catfish Friday's were becoming well known as far as Birmingham and beyond. The churches had exceeded their fundraising efforts from all of the homemade cakes, pies and cookies sold in the high school parking lot at each game, and it was rumored that the First Baptist church and First Presbyterian church could finally begin additions and build larger and updated kitchens with modern fellowship halls. The School Board was also pleased to announce that because of the ticket and concession sales from the games, a new roof could replace the leaky roof at the high school, and the auditorium improvements that were sorely needed.

When the time arrived for the end of season games, Tuscaloosa hosted the finals at Foster Auditorium with eight teams from across the State. Each team traveled in their school buses while the families, friends, fans, bands, and cheerleaders followed in their cars and trucks. Banners and painted car windows proudly displayed the support of 'their boys' and, in Buford County's case, 'their girl and boys'. The nation's sport fanatics were also keeping up with the advancement of Vernadine and her team, and barbershops across the nation were packed out listening to the game on the radio. After the first day of finals, four teams remained. The cities represented were Spit's Creek, Opelika, Daphne and Muscle Shoals. In between games three and four, with BCHS still undefeated, Coach Caruthers told the team to take a rest. So, players from the final two schools all took a spot of their own on the bleachers and reclined in a moment of recuperation. The spirits were running high, so the rest did not come easy. Coach Caruthers thought he saw Vernadine and Slim slip out of the back door of the gymnasium during the break, but he was exhausted and didn't have the energy to investigate their departure.

Vernadine and Slim had been looking for this exact moment. They had anticipated time alone, away from the team, the fans and their parents. In a mad rush, they sprinted to the Buford County school bus, jumped in, and locked the door. It was dusk, so they laid low in the back seat until darkness arrived. They were both smiling ear to ear, unsure of what to say and a little nervous. But Vernadine did what she does best; she took over. She grabbed Slim's narrow boney body and pulled him in with force and laid a kiss on him that made his head swim. After the initial shock, Slim's apprehension subsided and he returned her kiss with reckless abandon. After months and months of playing this scene over in their heads, they couldn't hold back from doing everything they had been taught and scorned not to do in mixed, unchaperoned company. They were in love and the world was theirs for the taking, and so they took from each other all that was intended. A shuffling noise outside of the bus startled them, and they had no idea how long they had been away from the gymnasium. In sheer panic, they regained their composer, exchanged a small kiss, and sprinted back to the door they had escaped from, and of course, Vernadine out ran Slim. In all of the excitement and darkness, neither one of them realized Vernadine had put her jersey on inside out, so when Coach Caruthers spotted them, he knew immediately what had happened to Slim and Vernadine. Since warm-ups were going on for the last battle, he didn't have time to scold them or inquire. He already knew it was too late for a talk. His concern was winning the next game, and he figured he couldn't fight the battle between the game and human nature on the same night. He was there for another championship, not a health class lecture.

The championship game against Daphne High School began at 7 PM sharp. The noise in the gymnasium was deafening. The nerves and excitement were high. The tip off gave Buford County the advantage from the start. Johnny dribbled and threw the ball, and two points scored right off the bat. The game was neck and neck for all four quarters. With two minutes remaining, Slim wrangled the ball from his opponent and ran for a slam dunk from the outside. Now BCHS led by two with possession. Daphne retrieved the ball and scored two points to tie the game. This was a full speed fight to the finish. With seventeen seconds on the board and Daphne with possession, a long shot was thrown from the outside. No one breathed. The ball looked like a sure shot. The Buford County team and Coach Caruthers saw their fame and championship disappear in those frozen seconds. Out of the corner of her eye, Vernadine saw Slim sprint towards the goal and jump with all of his strength. He tipped the ball and it missed the net. The entire team knew Vernadine was a sure shot. Slim tossed the ball to her with two seconds on the clock. She moved quickly, got the ball off towards the net and waited. Two Points! BCHS was again the State Basketball Champions for 1944 and their girl player had scored the winning point! Bands played, cheerleaders screamed and jumped, parents and friends hugged and cried and cameras flashed bright lights. The small town school from Spit's Creek with the girl center had done it again. Coach

Caruthers found his feet wouldn't move. He was stunned and shocked and dazed. Two championships back to back definitely secured his place in Spit's Creek sports history for many, many years to come, and Vernadine would never be forgotten.

***

After the excitement began to temper over the championship, Vernadine, her teammates and Coach Caruthers could start resuming normal life again. After the few minutes in the school bus in Tuscaloosa, Vernadine and Slim publicly declared their love for each other, and the knowledge of that sent another shock wave through the school and town, and left everyone scratching their heads wondering what in the world Slim saw in Vernadine? They both ignored the comments and insinuations.

Spring was warmer than usual in South Alabama, and graduation was approaching. The girls busied themselves, buying dresses for their ceremony and parties afterwards. Irene loaded Vernadine in the car to go downtown to the new department store Haegdorn's, but Vernadine was not looking forward to the shopping trip. She was not a small, petite flower of a girl and she already knew anything she could wear would be in the women's department and not fashionable for a seventeen-year-old girl. And besides that, she wasn't feeling herself these days. After the excitement from the championship in March, by mid-April, she was sick every day. Her get up and go, had got up and went. Her appetite was off and her mother had commented about her not wanting to eat and when she did, it was very little. She also spent her mornings before school in the bathroom overcome with nausea. The thought crossed her mind more than once "maybe I am pregnant?" but since the one time on the school bus with Slim, they both saw the error of their ways and promised to each other they would be pure. So, they worked really hard at not placing themselves in situations where their fleshly desires could take over. Vernadine had not paid attention to Coach Caruthers' health class when sex education was being taught. The discussion of the details was horrifying, gross, too personal, and extremely embarrassing. She was dismayed and panicked, thinking to herself, "It was just one time. IT can't happen after just one time." But, as time went by, she knew she was pregnant and she knew she needed help. She also knew that she had to tell someone. The next Saturday morning, Fletcher was in the field tending to his crops, and Irene was cleaning up the breakfast dishes.

"Mother, I need to talk to you, and it's very important. Can you please sit down?"

Irene looked startled. "Ok, sure, are you okay?" said Irene.

"No, ma'am, I don't think so. I am very troubled over something and what I am about to tell you is the hardest thing I have ever said to you. You and Father have raised me right. You have raised me in the church and encouraged me to follow Jesus, and I am so thankful for that. You have allowed me to play a man's sport without embarrassment and have encouraged me. You have been proud of me as your daughter and told me that I am pretty and special, and knowing that I am not pretty, you told me anyway. You have provided a safe, loving and structured home to live in and I love you both dearly."

She paused in deep thought, realizing that she had said all she could think of to stall the actual news, and she also knew that what she was about to tell her mother would be the worst news her mother could ever hear from her.

"Mother, you know that Slim and I have been interested in each other since the end of the last basketball season? He is such a nice guy, and he is the first guy to ever pay attention to me romantically. I still don't understand it because, well, you know, look at me. I am awkward and large, not feminine and petite, and have no physical beauty to speak of. But he likes me anyway. He says he loves my 'take charge' attitude and he doesn't seem to mind that I insist on being right all of the time. He thinks I have a good heart. I don't understand half of what he says about me, because I have never noticed or really thought that I had any good qualities in me at all."

"Oh Vernadine, you have always been a great daughter. You have always listened to me and your father and have always tried to do the right thing. You are a free spirit, and I am thankful for that. You have leadership skills that I could never possess," Irene said.

"Mother, thank you, but let me finish. At the last championship game in Tuscaloosa, Slim and I slipped off during one of our breaks. We ran outside in the dusk to the school bus. One thing led to another and, well, what I am trying to tell you is... I am pregnant, Mother."

Just hearing those words come out of her mouth for the first time sent a floodgate of tears forth. She couldn't even look at her mother, who she noticed had not moved or said anything at all. She rested her head on the table and continued to cry and heave. All she could do was cry. Cry from the realization that she was pregnant, cry from knowing she had devastated her parents, cry from knowing that everyone in town would cast her out. No more "Queen of Basketball", but now just a loose floosy with an illegitimate child. She was pure disappointment all the way around. She could never show her face in Spit's Creek and Buford County again. Ever. She was a disgrace and she felt like a fraud.

At first, she didn't feel the gentle, warm, loving hand of her mother touch her arm. But when her tears subsided, she noticed, touched her mother's hand and looked into Irene's weathered face. Her mother was quietly weeping and wiping her tears with the dainty flowered handkerchief she always kept in her apron pocket. No words would come from either of them. They sat at the table for what seemed like an eternity, both in their sorrow over the situation and both over the sorrow of knowing that life would never be the same. Plans for college seemed like an unreachable goal now. All Vernadine could see was a life on the run from her mistakes. Having to move to another town, maybe get a job as a waitress or assistant basketball coach in some other small town where no one knew who she was. She would have to walk away from everything she knew and all of the dreams she had planned.

"Vernadine, look at me," Irene said.

It took all of her strength to lift her head and look into the face of her quiet-spirited mother, and not feel crushed knowing she had just deeply wounded the one person who loves her more than anyone else in the world. But she mustered her strength and resolve and waited for her mother to speak.

"This is a troublesome situation and one I never dreamed we would encounter, but I have a plan. I think, my dear, this is going to be the one and only time your size is going to help you. Help you hide this pregnancy. The fashions today are changing, and with some thought, we can disguise your pregnant belly with little effort. Graduation is in a month and you will look no different by then," Irene said at a quickening pace.

Vernadine and Irene sat at the kitchen table for what seemed hours, talking through their plan. As breakfast turned to lunch, Fletcher walked in from the field and he immediately knew that something was not right because of the handkerchiefs and red swollen eyes, but being the quiet, reserved man that he is, he just figured it was girl stuff. And he was right. Irene had comforted Vernadine earlier in the morning, assuring her, "Don't worry about your father. I will deal with him."

It amazed Vernadine that the woman she saw today was strong, capable, cunning and calm. Irene was driven and resolute. Vernadine already knew that about her mother, but seeing her today, she was a force to be reckoned with and in complete control of this 'plan' hatching in front of her eyes. Vernadine felt comforted to her core for the first time in weeks. After a much needed conversation break, and a warm lunch of tomato soup and grilled cheese sandwiches, Fletcher retired for his daily thirty-minute nap. Irene and Vernadine walked outside to hang the laundry and continue to talk away from fatherly ears.

"This is what we will do," Irene broke the silence. "You will continue on with the remainder of the school year and graduate with your class. If anyone asks you what your plans are after graduation, just tell them you are still deciding between going to college at Plains University or maybe staying here to help Coach Caruthers with the new basketball team. No one will find either of those answers odd. Then, when you are in your seventh or eighth month of pregnancy and it's too hard to hide anymore, you will go to your Aunt Marie's in Mobile. We can tell everyone that Aunt Marie is not doing well and needs full time help. No one will be the wiser. I will write to her, explain the situation, and I feel very certain that she will help us. She has always been your Father's favorite sister and he her favorite brother. Then you will have the baby and place the baby up for adoption. After that, you can return home and start college the very next quarter. You will be free to move on with your life, like nothing has happened."

Vernadine pondered for a minute or two, and she liked the idea. The idea of no one knowing, the idea of keeping her reputation untarnished, the idea of a future and college seemed great to her. But, at the bottom of her heart, she felt a tug and a growing sadness. "But, Mother, what about Slim? Shouldn't I tell him?"

"No, let's keep it to ourselves," Irene said. "He's a boy and will notice nothing different in your shape. He will not think it odd for you to go to Mobile to help your sick aunt. The fewer people that know the truth, the better."

"Do I ever tell him? Don't you think it's unfair for him not to know?" Vernadine said as she wiped a tear from her cheek.

"You don't worry about that. Time will settle a lot of the details. Now, go inside and rest. You have had an exhausting day. Let's just stick to the immediate plan. Now, go on, I have my chores to finish and I have to figure out how I am going to tell your father." Irene grabbed a sheet and popped it in the wind.

Vernadine walked away with slumped shoulders, made her way inside, went to her bedroom, closed the door, and fell onto her bed. Before drifting off to sleep, she thanked the Lord for her strong, capable, and loving mother, and she knew she would not have to walk through this situation alone.

Vernadine Sticks to the Plan

Spit's Creek, Alabama
May 1944

Graduation at Buford County High School is always a grand affair. The students, faculty, school board and various volunteers turn out in mass to help decorate the gymnasium. The stage is lined with red, white and black bunting. Ferns are donated from the school horticultural club greenhouse; the podium is loaned from the Second Baptist church, along with the chairs on the platform. Streamers hang from the metal ceiling rafters and a red carpet is placed between the two sections of chairs where the graduates sit, the girls on the right side, and the boys on the left. The high school band plays from the bleachers, where the proud parents and relatives sit to watch their sons or daughters receive the high school diploma that most of them never received. The school choir opens the ceremony with the Star Spangled Banner and leads the crowd in the pledge of Allegiance. The local pastors rotate every year for the opening prayer. A reception is held under the oak trees on the grounds after the ceremony, and the local Ladies Auxiliary Club and the Daughters of the Confederacy prepare the punch, sweets and finger sandwiches. It takes a full week of preparation, but the result is always a showstopper and a very proud moment.

This year, however, in 1944, with the war still reeling in Europe, many of the graduating boys are leaving for active duty on the bus immediately after graduation. For this reason, this ceremony is bittersweet for many families and for the entire community, the promising young men of Spit's Creek and Inner Banks leaving to fight for freedom, knowing that many will not return home. Despite the sadness, everyone gives a genuine effort to keep the mood jubilant and happy. This year, everyone could not help but notice that on the outside of the gymnasium, the gymnasium name was covered with a red drape, along with the scoreboard inside. They wondered what that meant?

Irene had sewn a dress for Vernadine of white cotton covered in eyelets, especially for graduation. Her collar was long and angular, like the latest fashion, with a red bow at the nape of her neck. She wore smart black heels with no hose since hosiery was still hard to find. Vernadine looked herself, only better, in her new dress, and she was thankful that her secret was still hidden.

The moment came. All of the graduates filled their seats while the band played the school alma mater. After everyone was seated, the pastor from The First Presbyterian church led the convocation. As each student rose to walk across the stage, the crowd cheered and yelled for their children. Vernadine and Slim both received their diplomas and smiled at each other across the aisle. Their relationship was still going on, to the surprise of everyone, including Vernadine. She still held her secret to her chest tightly, but was often tempted to tell Slim. She was hoping she and Slim could get married soon. He had told her weeks earlier that he loved her, and weren't couples supposed to get married if they crossed the lines? Isn't that what it meant, true love?

At the end of the ceremony, as people were preparing to stand for the closing prayer, the school board President, Mr. Mills, came to the podium and asked if everyone would take their seats for a brief presentation. "Ladies, gentlemen, students, and distinguished guests, today is a proud moment in the history of Buford County High School. As you well know, our communities have been extremely proud of our basketball championships these last two years. We have been extremely proud of Coach Caruthers and his entire team of talented athletes. You folks have blessed our high school with many years of pride and bragging rights. You have put us on the map for Alabama High School Athletics. Now everyone knows that country boys... and girls... are tough, strong, capable and athletic. But the reason for this special ceremony is to unveil and dedicate our high school gymnasium to one special person. This person is the most unlikely athlete we have seen; an athlete that no one gave any credit to, an athlete folks scoffed and jeered at, and questioned the sanity of Coach Caruthers. An athlete that quickly received the attention of our community, state and nation. A proud moment for all of us was watching our BCHS basketball team give their all, beat the competition game after game, and not only brought home the trophy in 1943, but also continued the momentum into 1944. I know you are all shaking your heads because you know I am referring to our BCHS center, Miss Vernadine Turnipseed," Mr. Mills yelled.

The crowd screamed and cheered. Everyone stood on their feet. The band struck out with the fight song. It was loud and Vernadine had not moved. She didn't stand up and all she could do was look at her lap and count the eyelets on her white cotton dress. Her face was as red as the ribbon bow on her dress. She even felt sick. What a moment. A moment of utter surprise and disbelief. A moment of humility that her community loved her the way they did, especially after such an auspicious and hurtful beginning.

"Everyone, may I have your attention again?" Mr. Mills spoke loudly into the microphone. "I know you all have noticed the draping over the name of the gymnasium and on the scoreboard above your heads. By the authority and honor vested in me as your School Board President, I proudly declare by unanimous vote, the name of the Buford County High School gymnasium is now the 'Vernadine D. Turnipseed' gymnasium!"

A roar consumed the gymnasium, unlike any other. Vernadine fainted. Half on and half off of her chair, her classmates jolted her, grabbed her face, shook her back awake. She was awe struck, speechless, limp.

"Miss Turnipseed, please make your way to the scoreboard and meet me there?" said Mr. Mills.

It took all the strength she could muster, but she got out of her chair and walked to the end of the gym to stand underneath the scoreboard. A string was hanging from the draping. Mr. Mills asks Vernadine, "Miss Turnipseed, will you please pull the string?"

Vernadine gave a firm pull on the string and the draping fell to reveal a shiny new scoreboard. On the very top of the scoreboard, it read "The Vernadine D. Turnipseed Gymnasium, Buford County High School." On the bottom of the scoreboard, it read "State Basketball Champions 1943 and 1944." Underneath the score board was a large photograph of the entire team and Coach Caruthers standing proudly holding their trophies.

By this point, Irene, Fletcher, Coach Caruthers, Slim and the rest of the basketball team had joined her underneath the sign. Everyone was crying and hugging. Mr. Mills had made his way back to the podium. "One last thing, folks. Miss Turnipseed, if you, your family, Coach Caruthers and your teammates please walk outside to the entrance of the gym. Wait for the closing prayer and adjournment of the ceremony and we will all meet you outside in a moment."

As Vernadine and the group made their way outside, they made the closing remarks for the graduates and their families. The pastor prayed a closing prayer and everyone filed outside. Excitement and jubilance and laughter filled the air. Once outside, Mr. Mills had to scream over the crowd, but asked Vernadine to pull the string to the draping. Revealed underneath was a new bright and shiny aluminum sign that read "The Vernadine D. Turnipseed Gymnasium".

Vernadine was completely numb. She didn't know what to say. She didn't know what to feel. She knew she was happy and honored, but she was also sad. Sad because she carried a secret. Had anyone else but her mother known her burden, this would have never happened to her. Her community, that stands so proud of her and her team, would be disgusted and horrified if they knew the truth about her situation. Still, this has happened, all of it, and for the moment, she reveled in her happiness and felt the honor given to her from the communities of Spit's Creek and Inner Banks. They immortalized Vernadine in the history of Buford County High School and The State of Alabama, and that realization was quite overwhelming. She knew this would forever be one of the proudest moments in her life.

There's a New Girl in Town

Spit's Creek, Alabama
May 1944

Pastor Eldridge had been the minister of First United Methodist Church in Spit's Creek for five years. In the true tradition of John Wesley, the eighteenth century minister who founded the Methodist Church, he believed a minister loses his effectiveness if he stays too long at the same church, in the same community; so, with a new assignment in hand, the pastor and his family moved to Opelika, Alabama in April. It excited pastor Eldridge and his family about their new church family and community, and the congregation welcomed them with open arms.

That same month, the new minister for Spit's Creek arrived from Dothan, Alabama. Along with the new minister, Pastor Jacob Wright, were his wife Elaine and their seventeen-year-old daughter Marigold.

Spit's Creek and Inner Banks welcomed Pastor Wright and his family exactly the way they expected. The ladies' ministry organized a dinner on the grounds. There was so much fried chicken on enormous platters that it was truly a sight to behold. Mrs. Ruth offered to fry the chicken in her industrial fryers and donated all of the chicken from her café as her welcome gift to the new family. Alongside the fried chicken, spread on long banquet tables with white tablecloths, were collard greens, potato salad, tomato aspic in bundt molds surrounded by celery leaves, corn on the cob, creamed corn, white acre peas, boiled and fried okra, bread and butter pickles, cornbread, rolls, every dessert known to a southern kitchen and lots and lots of sweet tea.

It was a perfect spring day with a gentle, cooling breeze. Chairs and blankets were set around on the grass, and families piled up together to eat. The children, just out of an hour long church service, were running wild everywhere. It was a great and happy occasion. Even people from the community that weren't members of the church showed up for the lunch to get a glimpse of the new minister and his family. Word had spread among the teenage boys that Marigold was a sight to behold. They couldn't wait to see what all of the fuss was about, and the girls all held their breath and braced for devastating confirmation that Marigold was indeed beautiful. The girls had already decided that they didn't like Marigold, even before they met her.

The basketball team invited Slim to go with them to the church service and picnic. He figured God isn't only at the First Believers Victory Church and Vernadine would understand if he missed one Sunday with her, so he agreed to go, anxious to see firsthand just who this Marigold Wright is, even though he was pledged to Vernadine.

After the boys found their seats in the back row, elbows began punching. "Look, Slim, that has to be her," said Johnny.

Slim, annoyed by the punching, punched Johnny in the arm, then looked towards the front of the church. On the very front row, there she was… Marigold Lily Wright. Slim was speechless. His mouth hung wide open, yet he struggled for air. He had never seen a girl so beautiful in his life. She was the essence of pure beauty. Trying not to be too obviously stricken, and to hide his embarrassment, he forced a cough, looked down, then smoothed his hair back into place, and straightened his back again. "Yeah, she's ok," said Slim, trying to hold back a real cough this time.

"Man, you must be blind or stupid or both. She is beautiful," said Johnny.

"Shut up, Johnny, you are the stupid one. Don't you know you are not supposed to talk in church? Now shut up. You are embarrassing me," Slim growled underneath his breath.

"You shut up, Slim, and for the record, you are the stupid one! You are the one dating Vernadine Turnipseed," Johnny protested quietly.

"Man, I will take you outside right now, in front of God and everyone, if you say another word about Vernadine! She is a great gal and she is very loyal. Just because she isn't a beauty on the outside does not mean that she isn't beautiful on the inside. You wouldn't understand because you are an immature jerk!" The worshipers began turning around to see what the ruckus was, so they both nipped it, embarrassed and red faced.

After Slim's blood pressure returned to normal, he began thinking about Johnny's comments and Vernadine. Not that he agreed with him, quite the opposite, but he had to admit to himself that his feelings for Vernadine had waned, and he hated himself for that. He had told Vernadine that he loved her before graduation, and he really believed he did. But, over the last few weeks, he was becoming unsure about his true feelings for Vernadine and he was in knots about his future. He knew Vernadine was counting on the unspoken commitment of matrimony, and she was expecting a proposal any day now. At the time his feelings were cooling off for Vernadine, in walks this southern beauty, named after beautiful delicate flowers, a beauty like none he had ever seen. An ethereal and timeless beauty. A girl with long blonde hair in soft waves, skin the color of alabaster, and eyes as green as the ocean. A waist the size Scarlett O'Hara fought for and the sweet innocence of purity. She was everything that Slim had dreamed about as his true love. Now, he was truly in a dilemma. He hated to break Vernadine's heart, but he could not pass up the opportunity to meet Marigold Lily and pledge his heart to her if she would have him. Everything was happening so fast. He would not have believed that he was a fickle guy. He had given his love and heart to Vernadine, and now, without even speaking to Marigold, he knew that his course was changing. The winds of uncertainty were blowing.

Set on pursuing this delicate beauty of a young woman, he spent the rest of the sermon daydreaming about Marigold. He could see her in a beautiful white wedding gown, meeting him at the altar of the First

United Methodist Church with her father, the pastor, officiating. He also knew the perfect motor court motel in Panama City Beach for their honeymoon. Once his thoughts turned to the honeymoon, he remembered he was in God's house and thinking about marital relations in church had to be a major sin. Slim jerked himself back to reality when the sermon ended and the last hymn was sung. Feeling ridiculous, he knew he was too confident about his new plan with Marigold. The dreaming and scheming over a girl who doesn't even know he exists could be a set-up for failure. Slim also knew that he would have to see Vernadine that very afternoon to break up with her, and this would break her heart. He prayed for strength and for the right words to say to her. Vernadine would be devastated. He knew he was assuming a lot, because Marigold may not even like him, after all. But he was going to take the chance. Either way, Vernadine would lose because he knew he couldn't continue his relationship with her when his head and heart could turn so quickly, and for that he felt terrible and ashamed.

After an inspiring message of hope, everyone was deeply moved and certain their new pastor was a pleasant addition to their church family. Pastor Wright asked his wife and daughter to join him beside the pulpit for introductions. You could hear a pin drop. Everyone was so eager to see his family, especially Marigold.

"Congregants, I am proud to introduce my wife, Elaine. She has been my faithful companion for twenty years. She has supported me in my ministry in more ways than I can count. I know the Lord made her especially for me. She is a wonderful cook and hostess. She loves working with the ladies' ministry and visiting the elderly in our church and community. She enjoys bible studies and organizing bazaars. She is always ready for a tea social at a moment's notice. She is very outgoing and has a genuine servant's heart. I just know you will welcome her into the fold, as you have done for me." The church offered a genuine welcome with hand claps and smiles. Elaine felt warm inside and excited about their new home in Spit's Creek. Change was always good, and she was excited to get to work in her new church and community.

After the clapping quieted, Pastor Wright signaled for Marigold to join her parents at the pulpit. She was nervous and never felt comfortable being the object of attention, even though attention seemed to follow her everywhere she went. Marigold stood up and smoothed the front of her linen dress with her gloved hands. She made her way to the pulpit, took a place beside her mother and grabbed her hand. She looked out over the congregation and offered a kind and innocent smile. "Friends, this is our daughter, Marigold Lilly Wright. She is a senior at Dothan High School and will not be officially joining us until after her graduation at the beginning of June. She is still undecided about her plans for college, so in the meantime, she will help here in the church office and also with the children's department, organizing and assisting with the activities." A murmur flowed through the congregation, murmurs about her beauty and murmurs about how sweet it is for her to help her father in the church. Slim was excited to know that she would be staying in town for a while. That would give him an opportunity to pursue her and possibly win her heart before she left for college. "Please welcome Marigold to her new church and community," Pastor Wright beamed. They extended another genuine welcome with hand claps and smiles, except the girls. A stirring closing prayer was offered while the Pastor and his family walked to the back of the church to greet the congregation as they departed the sanctuary.

A special table was set for the Wrights to enjoy their lunch, while everyone made their rounds and welcomed their new leaders to the church. The afternoon was filled with laughs and warm exchanges, and the Wrights felt at home.

Slim and his buddies enjoyed the feast of southern delectables and dared each other to speak to Marigold. Every one of them chickened out, except Slim. Slim walked over and stood in the line that had formed in front of Marigold. Many times he considered backing out from sheer nerves and panic, but what kept him there was the daydream he had during the church service. Another reason he considered backing out was because of Vernadine. But Slim reckoned simply meeting and welcoming a newcomer to town was reasonable and kind, but he knew his intentions crossed the line with his relationship with Vernadine. He knew his intentions were not to only say 'hello' to Marigold, he wanted to love Marigold and he wanted her to love him back.

After what seemed like an eternity, he finally found himself face to face with the most beautiful girl he had ever seen. His breathing quickened, his palms were sweaty, but he pressed on with his opportunity. "Hello Marigold, my name is Buddy Perkins, but everyone calls me 'Slim'. I want to welcome you to Spit's Creek."

"Thank you, Buddy, I mean, Slim," Marigold smiled.

"I hope you will like it here. This is a friendly community and there are lots of people here our age. I just graduated this year myself, from Buford County High School. I am not sure what my future plans are, just like you." They both chuckled.

"Well, that's nice. Yes, deciding on the future is difficult. But, I think I will like it here and I will have time to decide what I want to do. So far, everyone I have met has been friendly. I am looking forward to making new friends," Marigold said.

Slim knew that a window of opportunity had just miraculously opened for him. So, he took her last words of looking forward to making friends, to invite her on a ride around the county to show her around. "Would you like to take a ride with me later this afternoon or tomorrow? I will be happy to show you around and introduce you to some folks," Slim said.

Marigold was surprised at the invitation. She did not know this Buddy 'Slim' Perkins and to take a ride in the country with a stranger was not what she would normally consider, but there was something about his demeanor, and the light and sparkle in his eyes, and his warmth that jolted her interest. She pondered for a moment, but she knew that she would need to ask her parents first before committing to an answer. "Slim, thank you for asking me to join you. It sounds fun to me. But, I will have to ask my parents first. I think it's best if we walk over to them. Let me introduce you and you ask my father if it's ok with him if you escort me around town."

Slim froze, but not too much. He rebounded quickly and said, "Ok, that is fine with me. You lead the way."

It didn't occur to Slim that he was at a community gathering, walking around with the prettiest new girl in town, and that maybe the news might get back to Vernadine. He was lost in the storm of his emotions, with no other thought in his mind but winning the heart of Marigold Lilly Wright. He could already hear the wedding bells, but he knew he would have to speak to Vernadine. Slim excused himself after meeting Marigold's parents, then found a payphone on the corner and called Vernadine. They agreed to meet at 3 PM.

Slim and Vernadine Have a Talk

Spit's Creek
June 1944

Vernadine spent all afternoon excited and nervous about seeing Slim, since they had spent little time together after graduation. Slim had been busy telling her he needed to focus on his plans for the future. This excited her greatly, because she knew that his future plans were her future plans, too. Maybe he was proposing to her today; she prayed he would. Maybe they could hurry and get married, and she could share the excitement that the baby in her young womb was a honeymoon baby? She had given him time and space to let him think and plan. Her future was secure. She didn't need to know all of the details. Just knowing she could marry the man she loved and keep her baby was all she needed and wanted to know.

Slim was due at her house at 3 PM. He had called in the middle of lunch asking to see her. Vernadine spent all afternoon curling her hair and dressing in her white eyelet dress Irene had made for her graduation. She even tried a little rouge and lipstick for the occasion. Today was special, and probably the most important day of her seventeen years. She just knew that today would be a day that she would never forget.

At exactly 3 PM, Slim pulled down the driveway and parked his truck. Before he could make it to the door, Vernadine rushed out to meet him. A few thoughts entered her mind as she saw Slim and wondered why they bothered her, but she quickly erased them as Slim lightly kissed her on the cheek. "Hello Vernadine, it's nice to see you. You look pretty today. Have you done something different with your hair? And are you wearing lipstick?"

Vernadine blushed and giggled and said, "Yes, thank you Slim." "Let's take a walk if you are up to it. You may be too dressed up for that, but the weather is beautiful today and it's too nice to be inside."

"That's fine with me," she said.

As they began their walk down the dirt driveway, Vernadine noticed Slim did not take her hand as he usually did, so she grabbed his instead and smiled. "Tell me how you have been, Slim? I am eager to hear what you have been thinking about since we saw each other last. Have you decided on anything? About the future, I mean."

Slim gently pulled his hand away from hers and looked deep in thought and very serious. "I have been doing a lot of thinking about a lot of things lately. I can't decide if I want to join the Navy and help win this war, or if I should stay here and help my father? He expects me to take the business over when he retires. And then, there is the basketball scholarship to Plains University. They are pressing me for an answer. I just don't know. I guess I should be thankful I have so many choices, but I just wish I had a clear picture in my mind about it all."

They continued further down the road. With each step, Vernadine thought she would bust. She wanted to tell Slim about the baby, but she had promised her mother she would say nothing. She was also nervous because Slim acted distant and distracted. In everything he had just said to her about his future possibilities, not once did he mention her or them. Again, she dismissed her doubts and growing anxiety and asked, "Well, what are you feeling the strongest about?"

"Well, I can see all of those as great options. Vernadine, listen, there is something that I have to tell you. Here, let's sit down on this log and rest for a minute. We have had a great time together and shared many new moments, and we have made some really great memories. There is a reason I cannot decide about my future, which seemed so clear to me yesterday, but today it isn't." Slim rubbed his hands together and looked at the ground.

"It's okay, Slim. It's normal to be confused. After all, we are only seventeen. We can't be expected to have all of the answers."

"Yes, that's true," Slim said. "But it's not so much that I am confused over the choices for career or college that have me stumped. Vernadine, I know you and I have talked about a future together and we have made a lot of plans. But, I think we are rushing into things too fast. How do you know you love me enough to marry me? How do you know you aren't making a mistake? If I left for the war or college, it would separate us for a long time. Who wants to marry and immediately be separated from their new spouse? My scholarship states that I cannot be married and, well, the war is in Europe. I would not want to tie you down in marriage or in a promise of marriage with everything so uncertain. Do you understand what I mean?" Slim hung his head. He could not bring himself to look at Vernadine, but he noticed the tear stains on Vernadine's dirt covered shoes, and at that moment he felt like the worst person in the world. He knew his words had devastated her and caught her by complete surprise. Slim waited for Vernadine to say something, anything, to him, but Vernadine did not speak.

At that moment, all of her hopes and dreams of marrying Slim were stripped away. She also knew that she would be left alone to carry their child in secret with an uncertain future for herself. She knew that even though Slim was asking her these doubtful questions, what he really meant was that he was the one questioning his own desires. He was the one who had doubts, not her. Her mind raced. She wanted to convince Slim that whatever career path or decision he made about his future would be fine with her as long as his plans included her; that their love and commitment would carry them through anything life threw at them. But because of Slim's continued silence, she knew there was no need to convince him of anything. His mind was made up. There were no words that would change his mind. She now realized the last few weeks of silence had been the warning bell of the end of their relationship and their future together. Heartbroken and devastated, Vernadine calmly stood up and smoothed her dress. She straightened her shoulders and back and stiffened her chin. She took a deep breath, turned on her heel, and began a brisk walk back to her house alone.

Slim just sat there, humped over as he watched Vernadine walk away. He didn't stop her because he knew there was nothing left to say except how sorry he was. He knew Vernadine was a sweet, loyal, and great girl who did not deserve to be left without knowing the truth. But the truth did not come easy for Slim today. He knew that Vernadine was already hurt and disappointed at what he had told her, and he just couldn't bring himself to tell her that he didn't love her enough to marry her. He couldn't bring himself to tell her about meeting Marigold earlier that day, and that his intention of pursuing her was the one thing in his life that he was certain about.

At the same time Slim was convinced of his fresh course, Vernadine was convinced of hers. Before she was jilted and rejected by Slim, she would short circuit the pain and embarrassment. She would be leaving town and walking away from Slim and her future with him. She knew she had to talk to her mother immediately. Her mother would comfort her and remind her of their plan, but she decided on that dusty road back home she would leave for Mobile as soon as possible and would be gone for a very long time. Maybe forever. She had no idea what tomorrow would hold, but she knew what she had to do today. She was right. This would be a day she would never forget.

Vernadine Leaves Town

Spit's Creek and Mobile
June 1944

June 6, 1944, was the pivotal beginning of the end for Hitler and his tyranny. While the world waited for their sons and daughters to come home, the allied troops invaded Normandy in 'Operation Overlord'. The long debated invasion was originally scheduled for May, but on this fateful day, 156,000 men from The United States, Britain and Canada landed on the beaches of Normandy to a barrage of German resistance under the command of General Dwight D. Eisenhower. Many young men lost their lives that day and this day will forever be remembered as 'D-Day'.

Meanwhile, on the other side of the world, Vernadine was reeling from her own personal D-Day. This day had become a blind attack of what she had planned for herself and Slim and their unborn child. Her future was planned, or she thought, but now she would have to set out on a new course altogether. Early the next morning, Vernadine settled into her bus seat with a suitcase; a book, and a paper bag filled with two ham sandwiches, a dill pickle, and a red apple. Irene also gave her a thermos of hot coffee with cream and sugar for the trip. The exhaust fumes from the bus were nauseating, so she used her mother's floral print handkerchief to cover her nose and mouth. She sat quietly and prayed she could make the four-hour trip without getting sick. The morning sickness had subsided, fortunately, but the sickness she felt this morning was heartbreak and the pain was indescribable.

She could still picture Irene and Fletcher waving her goodbye from the bus station, and this broke her heart. She knew she had to leave Spit's Creek and give herself time and space to think about her future and the future of her baby. Irene called Aunt Marie as soon as Vernadine returned heartbroken and inconsolable from her walk with Slim, explaining the plans had changed and Vernadine needed to get away immediately. So, in her gracious and loving way, Aunt Marie welcomed Vernadine to Mobile and to her home, and told her she would be at the bus station waiting for her arrival. Irene and Fletcher helped Vernadine pack and gave her fifty dollars for expenses and incidentals. They reminded her to let them know when she needed more money. They couldn't and didn't expect Aunt Marie, living on a widow's pension, to be financially burdened.

Seated on the bus, headed to Mobile, she closed her eyes, and wiped away silent tears for the first two hours of the journey. She would have to come up with a plan. Her own plan. She had struggled with the idea of giving her baby up for adoption, but never mentioned her feelings to her mother. She understood the reason for 'the plan' was to protect the future of Vernadine's prospects for matrimony and reputation; and as much as she appreciated her mother's wisdom and input, she instinctively knew she could not part with her own child. She would figure something out. The more miles that separated Vernadine from her parents and Spit's Creek, the more determined and resolute she became in her decision to keep her baby and raise the child alone. She knew she would have to get a job, but who was going to hire a single, young pregnant woman? She knew she had a little time before the pregnancy showed, so she plotted and planned and schemed for the last two hours of the bus ride.

When she stepped off the bus to the warm greetings and tears of Aunt Marie, she stepped off a different girl than she was four hours before. With her tear stains dusted off with face powder and red lipstick re-applied, she held her head high, her back straight, and she seemed to float on a cloud of self-assurance as they made their way to the car for the ride home. Aunt Marie was full of questions about her parents, graduation, and her plans for the future. Vernadine was relieved the questions were not too probing.

Aunt Marie lived in a three bedroom cottage in the Oakleigh garden district, an area with tree-lined streets, parks, fountains and varied architecture style. Vernadine had never seen any place as beautiful as this. All at once, and to her dismay, she felt ill-equipped, untrained and inadequate for such finery in more ways than one. She immediately took notice of her dress and shoes and knew she looked like a country girl, out of place and out of style. She knew she would have to spend some of her fifty dollars on new and stylish clothes, a new hairstyle, and new shoes. She remembered seeing a beauty parlor just a few blocks from Aunt Marie's house on the drive home and made a mental note to take a walk later and set an appointment. Maybe the stylish women of Mobile could help transform her? She was certainly praying they could and she was counting on it.

After unloading the car and walking into Aunt Marie's beautiful home, she realized she was extremely thirsty and exhausted. She excused herself after drinking her sweet tea and took a long nap on the feather bed in one bedroom that had been set up especially for her. She was in heaven, she just knew it. Yes, she thought to herself, this was definitely heaven and Mobile was going to be her new hometown. The dust and dirt roads and small communities of Buford County seemed, all at once, backwards and slow and behind the times in many ways. After only one hour in Mobile, it changed her. Her horizon was endless, her opportunities abounded, and she no longer wanted to be Vernadine Turnipseed, 'The Basketball Queen', the not-so-pretty girl, the girlfriend of Slim Perkins, and the mother-to-be of an illegitimate child. No, she would recreate herself. A new, updated and modern version. A war widow that is pregnant and free to start life over again. She couldn't wait to get started. She would go to the beauty shop after her nap.

After a long and rejuvenating nap, she combed her hair, changed clothes into her white eyelet dress, and collected her purse, hat, and gloves. Before saying goodbye to Aunt Marie, she noticed a sewing machine in the butler's pantry and made a mental note to herself that she may have to learn to sew. She knew her money would have to last her a while, so making her own dresses would be more economical. As she walked down the sidewalk towards the beauty shop, she remembered seeing a general store, a ladies dress shop, and the Oakleigh Realty Company and made a mental note to visit both stores and inquire about the 'receptionist wanted' position at the real estate office. With each step she took, she reassured herself today would be the beginning of her new life and her new identity. She would introduce Aunt Marie to her 'new identity' when she returned home later for supper. She would explain her plan in detail so Aunt Marie would know how to answer questions about her niece when passing folks in the street or seeing her friends at church and around town. Aunt Marie and her parents would be very uncomfortable agreeing with her new 'story', but they would come around. She would convince all of them she was the one that needed to make the final decision about her life and that keeping her baby was her choice, and the right thing to do. She knew she was young and not wise to the ways of the world at seventeen, but in this instance, she would not be swayed.

Vernadine arrived at Sally's Hair Boutique at 2:30 PM. The receptionist was very polite and accommodated Vernadine, asking her if she would not mind waiting in the reception room for Sally to finish styling her current client. Fortunately, an appointment had just been cancelled at the last minute and she could take her right in. She took a seat, rested her feet and took notice of her surroundings. In the center of the reception room was a white-clothed table with a pitcher of iced lemonade with floating lemon slices, cheese wafers, and dainty finger sandwiches filled with cucumber and cream cheese, ham salad and egg salad. The sandwiches were neatly arranged on glass cake platters covered by glass domes. She realized she was hungry and had not eaten for hours, so she meekly walked to the table and helped herself to the unusual food. She had read about 'tea parties' and looked at pictures in the Ladies Home Journal of beautifully prepared food and tables, but she had not seen it in real life. She knew she had a lot to learn about becoming a proper southern lady, and she knew her Aunt Marie could teach her, but she made a mental note on everything beautiful in front of her. She would learn to make her life refined and beautiful and respectable.

Tastefully placed around the salon were palm plants and hanging ferns. The walls were painted a soft and soothing pale yellow. Gold chandeliers hung from the ceiling, and each styling station had a crisp white chair and large framed mirrors. In the background, Glenn Miller's 'Moonlight Serenade' softly played from the wooden framed radio. The floors were hardwood and shined so bright from the sunlight beaming through the windows. There was a smell in the air of hairspray and gardenias. Sally brought bouquets of clippings from her yard and placed the beautiful, fragrant white flowers on every station and on the center of the reception table. This salon was the fanciest place Vernadine had ever seen. She reminded herself to sit up straight, cross her ankles, place her linen napkin on her lap, and to pat her lips after every bite. Her training to becoming a proper young lady was well underway. She was so excited she thought she would bust. It crossed her mind, though, that she needed to be very cautious about what she tells people about herself, especially in a beauty parlor. Until she talks to Aunt Marie and fills her in on her plan and new identity, she will just be Marie's niece from Spit's Creek that wants an updated hair-do.

"Miss Turnipseed, I am Sally. It's so nice to meet you dahlin'. If you will follow me, I will wash your hair and we can talk about what you would like today."

"Thank you, Mrs. Sally. I appreciate you taking me in at the last minute," Vernadine said as she followed Sally to the hair washing station.

"Oh, heavens, I am just glad you walked in. I can't stand it when people cancel at the last minute. Don't they realize that I have rent and bills to pay? And I spend over an hour every morning before work preparing the sandwiches, crackers and lemonade."

Sally sprayed the warm water on Vernadine's hair and began a vigorous scrubbing on her scalp. She didn't miss a beat… "And honey, driving that food around town without it spilling in the floorboard of the car… oh my, it's nerve wracking!" She rinsed Vernadine's hair and wrapped her head in a warm towel. "But I do it because it's a trademark of mine and my clients expect it, so I shouldn't get too worked up over things. Aside from rants, I am always happy to help ladies update their looks."

She stopped and turned around. "Oh, please don't take that the wrong way. I try really hard to not always speak what is on my mind, but when you have dealt with the public as long as I have, you become quick to take notice of fashion and style and bad manners, and it looks like you could use a new lease on your hair and fashion. Here we are, have a seat and get comfortable. You are Marie's niece, aren't you?"

"Yes, ma'am, I am. She and my father are brother and sister," Vernadine said, as she realized she was giving away more information than the question warranted. She would have to practice really hard to only answer the questions that were being asked and not elaborate.

Sally brushed through her hair and dabbed extra water off of the ends with the towel. She lifted the chair, wrapped the cape around her neck, ran her fingers through her hair, and studied for a minute. "You have nice hair, Vernadine. It's very thick and healthy," Sally mused. "Tell me what you are thinking about for your new style?"

"I love the look of the 'Victory roll' and the 'pin curl'. Do you think I have hair long enough for either of those styles?" Vernadine asked.

"Not the 'Victory Roll', but definitely the 'pin curl'; Let me trim a little off of the ends and let's get to pinning. You will need to sit underneath the dryer for a good forty minutes, and it's going to be hot as blazes under there, but I will keep you supplied with lemonade to keep cool. You will love the payoff, trust me. Pain is gain, remember? Especially in beauty."

Sally walked to get the pins while Vernadine sat in the white beauty parlor chair, feeling Christmas morning happy. While she watched and studied Sally's combing, parting and pinning techniques, she inquired about make-up styles and how to apply it correctly. "Go to Gayfers Department store, it's downtown, and ask for Rosie. She is a real pro at makeup and she will teach you how to apply it. There is also a great ladies' fashion and shoe department. They usually have fashion shows twice a year. It's a real treat," Sally said enthusiastically.

While Vernadine was getting the pins removed from her hair after spending thirty minutes gasping for breath, and red as a beet from the hair dryer, one of the other stylists applied simple makeup. An alabaster foundation, loose setting powder, red lipstick, light pink cream rouge, eyeliner and mascara. A pair of clip-on earbobs from another customer was placed on Vernadine's earlobes, and a red scarf was found from another station and tied around Vernadine's neck. Every detail fit nicely with her white eyelet dress. Sally finished Vernadine's new hair-do and sprayed her hair.

When Sally turned Vernadine around in her white chair, after the cloud of hairspray cleared the air, Vernadine looked at herself in the mirror and found herself speechless and awestruck. She never dreamed she could look like that. The girl that looked back at her was a stranger. If she had not known it was herself, she would have thought "now, she is pretty", but now she was actually saying it to herself: "You are pretty!" She wanted to cry from happiness, but dared not mess up her fresh make-up, so she held her tears at bay.

Sally just oohed and ahhed over her transformation along with everyone else in the salon. They all agreed they had never seen such a dramatic change in anyone like they were seeing in Vernadine. Sally was a genuine artist, and Vernadine was her subject. For the first time in Vernadine's seventeen years, she felt feminine and beautiful. Two words that had never been used in her personal assessment vocabulary.

After paying for her services and hugging everyone in the beauty parlor goodbye, she walked outside onto the oak covered sidewalk and stopped just outside of the door. She drew in the deepest breath she had ever taken in her life and then slowly exhaled as she stood in a moment of disbelief and exhilaration at how she felt and how she looked. Only twenty-four hours earlier, she had felt broken and beaten down on that dusty dirt road with no idea what she would do. But today, she was changed, rejuvenated, hopeful and determined to move ahead with her life in a new town full of possibilities. She mumbled a prayer of thankfulness under her breath, then lightly placed her hand on her stomach and said to the growing baby in her womb, "It's me and you, little one; Momma will take care of us. Just leave it to me. Somehow, someway, I will make it work." She turned on her heel and walked two doors down to the Oakleigh Realty Company and applied for the receptionist's position. Fortunately for her, the office was quiet and the Broker was in his office. Twenty minutes later, after a brief conversation, she had landed her first job and would begin the next morning at 8 AM. She was off and running.

On a cloud of excitement, her next stop was the ladies' dress shop and the general store. She picked up two new dresses from the clearance rack and a modest pair of heels. She bought face powder, rouge, mascara, eyeliner, lipstick, hairspray and another pack of bobby pins. Out of the fifty dollars that her parents had given her at the bus station, she had forty left. Thankfully, she thought to herself, she now has a job. Loaded down with her new purchases, she stepped back onto the sidewalk and headed back to Aunt Marie's house. She couldn't feel anything except the warm bay breeze blowing on her skin and the beat of her heart as she made her way to the front door of the cottage. "Aunt Marie, I'm home."

"Oh, great! I just baked an apple pie and the coffee is almost ready. Come sit in the dining room with me and you can tell me about your afternoon," Aunt Marie yelled from the kitchen.

"Yes, ma'am, I will be right there. I just need to put a few things in my bedroom."

Vernadine smirked to herself in anticipation of how Aunt Marie would react to her transformation. She smoothed her wind-blown hair, reapplied a little more lipstick, smoothed her dress and took another deep breath. "Well, this is it, Vernadine," she thought to herself. "You have made your plan, and now it's time to tell Aunt Marie about it all. Prepare yourself for backlash and resistance, but stay strong. You can do it!" She almost shouted out loud. She knew she would not want to leave Aunt Marie's house over a disagreement about her plan, but she also knew that she could not bring scandal and chaos into her home. She loved her too much for that. If Aunt Marie could not agree with her plan of keeping her baby and raising her child as a single parent, then she would inquire about the garage apartment for rent that she saw posted in the real estate office. She knew her money would be tight, but she would make it work. One way or the other. She drew in another deep breath to calm her nerves and told herself to stay focused as she made her way into the dining room. It was showtime.

Vernadine's 'Story' and Aunt Marie's 'Uprising'

Mobile, Alabama
June 1944

When Vernadine entered the dining room, Aunt Marie was in mid-sip of her freshly brewed and very hot coffee. As she looked up to behold the 'new' Vernadine, she spewed the coffee in her lap and screamed in a burst of pain. As she quickly grabbed her linen napkin and dabbed her hot lap, she choked on what remaining coffee was in her throat. "Vernadine Turnipseed! Is that really you?" Marie exclaimed.

"Yes, Ma'am, Aunt Marie, it is. What do you think? Are you okay? Should I get some salve for your lap?"

"No, Child, I am fine, but thank you. You made it to Sally's, I see." Aunt Marie said.

"Yes ma'am. After my nap, I took a chance on getting an appointment and, as luck would have it, someone had just canceled. I only had to wait a few minutes, long enough to eat her cheese wafers and tea sandwiches. They are delicious. Her salon is the prettiest place I have ever seen. I felt awkward at first, but the receptionist and Sally were so kind to me. We discussed hairstyles and before I knew it, I was in her chair and then underneath the very hot hair dryer. Another of her stylists applied makeup while Sally was styling and spraying my hair. Sally found the earrings and the scarf, so she gave them to me to complete my look. Well, what do you think?"

"Well, I knew Sally was great at her profession, but your transformation is the absolute best I have ever seen. You look so pretty and so grown. Your mother would not even recognize you, I don't think!"

"Thank you, Aunt Marie. I am glad you are pleased. I feel like a completely different person, and I think I am going to like this new me very much," Vernadine said, as she radiated confidence.

It occurred to Aunt Marie that she had never noticed confidence in Vernadine before. "Here, I have lost my manners. Let me pour your coffee and give you a slice of this warm apple pie. Let's have a party. Your coming out party!" Aunt Marie busied herself and served Vernadine her afternoon treats.

"Aunt Marie, I have to tell you a few things and I would like for you to allow me to finish speaking before you offer your input," Vernadine inhaled. "First of all, I got a job today! You are looking at the new receptionist of the Oakleigh Realty Company! My first job! To prepare for it, I bought two new dresses, a new pair of shoes and some makeup. I start tomorrow morning at 8 AM. At first, I will be answering the phones and taking messages for the broker and agents. I will also be assisting the agents in setting up appointments for showings and calling for feedback to pass along to the sellers of the properties. Mr. Jones, the broker, said there would also be typing and errands to run as well. The pay is not that high, but it is enough to get me on my feet and get started. I am so excited about it I could bust. Momma and Daddy will be shocked, considering my situation with the baby and all, but they will also be proud of me. I know you are wondering about the baby and if I told the broker about it? I did not. I told him I am a war widow, new to town, living with my aunt to get on my feet. I can tell him about the baby in due time." She paused and wiped her mouth with the linen napkin. "Aunt Marie, I am not giving my baby up for adoption. I am going to keep my baby and raise it alone. I can work to provide for the two of us. Spit's Creek is four hours from here, and no one knows anything about the baby back home, and Mobile is far enough away that I can completely start over with a new life and history. The people here will never need to know the truth, and they would believe that my husband was killed in the war and never judge or question my pregnancy or baby. It will work, I promise you. I am sure some people may have heard my name because of the 'queen of basketball' thing, so I am wondering if I should change my last name or just say it's a strange coincidence that I have the same name as this basketball girl? It makes it less complicated to stay with the same name."

Vernadine noticed Aunt Marie sat quietly, and with a gaping mouth, as she explained her plan. She never saw Aunt Marie lick her lips or swallow. Marie sat there frozen, with a fixed and stunned expression. She knew she had offered another huge shock to Aunt Marie and genteel southern ladies are not equipped to handle too many shocks in a short period of time. They often take to bed with a headache or some other ailment after an overload of problems. And, this problem could most definitely bring much scandal to her aunt's irreproachable reputation.

Vernadine continued, "Aunt Marie, I will completely understand if you do not want me to live with you anymore. The last thing I want to do is bring shame on you or my parents. That is why I feel it is best to lie low, keep my head down, and live behind this story that I have created. Your friends do not know me or my parents. No one knows anything about me or my family. This makes it easy to start a new chapter in my life. I do not want my baby growing up in a family without me. I know it is scandalous and improper to be unmarried and pregnant, but this is my real-life situation. I would never forgive myself if I abandoned my child. It is not the baby's fault; it's mine and Slim's," Vernadine said with conviction.

Aunt Marie finally spoke up, "Is there not any chance that you and Slim could get married and live a happy life together and raise your child in a respectable home?"

"No, Ma'am, I do not see that as a possibility. Slim still doesn't know about the baby, and if he did, I feel certain he would ask me to marry him, but it would be for the wrong reasons. What kind of marriage would that be? A marriage in name only, that's what. I want to live loved by my husband, not tolerated and unhappy. I know it's a difficult situation and certainly one I did not plan on, but I have to take responsibility for myself and my innocent child. I am determined to work hard and give it my all. I know it will be very difficult being a single mother, and I would be lying if I did not tell you I will need your help, if you are willing, but I do not see any other choice. I can do this, Aunt Marie. If it kills me, I will try my best to be a great mother who provides for myself and my baby." Vernadine reached for her mother's floral handkerchief to wipe her eyes and the sight of it brought forth new tears. Her mother and father. It will devastate them.

Thinking of her parents, she realized she would have to call them very soon and break the same news to them that she just gave to Aunt Marie, but she would wait a while to re-muster strength. She knew that telling her mother she was pregnant was the hardest thing she had ever done, but this might be even harder.

"Aunt Marie, I know I have put too much on you already, but if we can keep this plan and everything I have just told you between you and me for a while, I would be ever so grateful. I need time to get adjusted to my new plan, work for a while in my new job, prepare for the baby the best I know how, and get my bearings. If we could both act as normal as possible when we speak to my parents, that will buy me some time. Oh, I feel terrible asking you to help me with my undercover plan. I know it is not who you are, and that you will despise the secretiveness of it all, but please try to understand as best you can. I will make sure I protect you from the perception my parents may have that you, too, have been deceitful. I certainly don't have all of the particulars worked out. That is why I am asking for time," Vernadine pleaded.

"Vernadine, this is a tough position for a woman of my spiritual convictions and community standing to be placed in. This is scandalous. Why, it could shame me from my church, the Ladies' Auxiliary League, the Master Gardener's Club, and no one would step inside my home anymore for afternoon teas, nor would I receive any invitations for tea at anyone's home. I could lose everything I have worked for all of these years, community standing, that is. I am respected. I am a Christian woman. I am still considered a beauty, even in my aging years. I am delicate and fragile, like a true Southern lady is supposed to be. I have never had one blemish on my reputation. This is so distressing." Aunt Marie fell on her sofa, grabbed her fan on the side table and fanned with one hand while she dabbed unseen perspiration from her upper lip with her handkerchief, all the while staring at the portrait of her deceased husband above the beautiful wood carved mantel on her fireplace.

They both sat there with no words between them for what seemed like an eternity. Vernadine felt like she could just die, right there on the spot. She was panicking on the inside, fearing that Aunt Marie would just completely tell her 'No way', when Aunt Marie sat up against the back of the couch and dabbed her lip and brow again. She put her fan back on the side table, took a deep breath, and sighed.

"I will get you a cool glass of lemonade, Aunt Marie. You look like you could use it. I will be right back." Vernadine rushed to the dining room table. When Vernadine returned from the dining room with the cool refreshment, Aunt Marie stood up and walked over to the window overlooking the sidewalk. The ice clinked in the crystal goblet as she sipped her lemonade, deep in thought.

"Vernadine, everything I just told you about my reputation and beauty and spiritual convictions is all true. Let me ask you, have you read *Gone with the Wind*? It's a wonderful story of the old south. It's long as the dickens, but goodness gracious, it's gripping. I could completely relate to Melanie Wilkes. Margaret Mitchell was certainly thinking of women like me when she wrote that character. Her grace and manners were above reproach. Her loyalty to family and marriage and Christian duty was the cornerstone of her character. I can completely understand her, as you can see. I even wrote a letter to Margaret Mitchell applauding her efforts in such a wonderful Southern story. The main character of the story, as you probably know, is Scarlett O'Hara. What a vixen and a mess of a woman; a woman in complete rebellion of her upbringing. She was too independent and free thinking for that era, and even for today, we would consider her scandalous. But she completely mesmerized me. I could not wait until her next dilemma arose to see how she would handle it."

Vernadine took a seat in the chair beside the fireplace, not knowing where this conversation was going, but she knew she had to listen attentively out of respect.

"I have lived," Aunt Marie continued, "and acted exactly the way my parents taught me to be. I have never stepped out of line as a daughter, a student, a parishioner, a wife, a community servant, and social leader. And you know what? At this very moment, I find all of that very boring and unexciting. I couldn't wait to read more about Scarlett because I admired her spunk and backbone. I admired her willingness to throw herself out there, knowing that she would be shunned and publicly ridiculed. She had a mission, however noble or self-serving it might have been. And, at my age, I am ready for some excitement. It's overdue. Why not take a risk and shake things up around here? The thought of having one more conversation about my azaleas and gardenias with the gardening club I have been a member of since the beginning of time makes me sick. I am tired of the expectations, the social demands, and the rigidity of it all."

Aunt Marie was wildly pacing the floor and waving her handkerchief in the air. Every couple of minutes, she would take a sip of her lemonade for sugar and fuel, and start again. This time, it was Vernadine who sat with a gaping expression. She was shocked, flabbergasted, and amazed that her sweet, noble, beautiful and petite aunt was raving this way. Aunt Marie quickly walked over to the sheer curtained windows and, with strength and renewed passion, flung the windows open. "It's too stuffy in this house. I need air.. moving air. I feel it's time for some changes around here. Not only in this neighborhood, but Mobile, and everywhere. And I am sick of these curtains and brocade pillows. Here, help me tear them down and let's take these and the pillows to the Salvation Army. You know, come to think of it, Scarlett also tore down her curtains too, but for different reasons."

As Vernadine and Aunt Marie ripped down the curtains, light poured into the living room. All at once, the beautiful room looked old and dusty and faded. They looked at each other and laughed. "This is terrible, Vernadine. Everything looks so old and worn out and outdated. This house is a reflection of me. It has looked and felt this way for years, kinda like the way I feel on the inside. But letting the light in reveals truth. Vernadine, you are my light. I feel inspired and excited and jubilant. You, my dear, have brought life back into this dusty and dark house, and the thrill of living and adventure back to me. So, I say all of this to tell you, of course I will help you with your plan. Together, we can be a combination of Melanie Wilkes and Scarlett O'Hara, polite and gracious when we need to be and hot as fire and brimstone when life calls for that. You will stay here and live with me, you and your baby, as long as you want or need to." Aunt Marie grabbed Vernadine and gave her a tight hug.

"Thank you, thank you, thank you, Aunt Marie," was all she could manage to say in between the tears and sobs. For the second time today, she deeply exhaled. She felt completely drained, but at the same time, she had never been more exhilarated. She was a new woman, a soon to be new mother and now a career girl. She was on her way, she just knew it.

"Well, as Scarlet would say, 'After all, tomorrow is another day.' That is a correct statement if I have ever heard one. It's been a very eventful day for you and I know you must be tired. You need to rest up for your first day of work tomorrow. Let me warm us up some of my leftover beef stew and cornbread, and we can have an early dinner and get to bed. Your new life begins tomorrow, Vernadine, and I think you are going to need all the energy you can muster. Why don't you go take a warm bath and get your clothes ready for your first day as an independent career woman. I will call you when the dinner is ready," Aunt Marie said as she walked to the kitchen on a cloud of excitement and hopefulness. She could feel the winds of change blowing around her, and she was alive and aware and wide awake for the first time in years.

The next morning, the streams of sunlight and the melodic chirping of the birds roused Vernadine from her peaceful slumber. She could not recall the last time she had slept so soundly. The feather bed and soft quilts had lulled Vernadine to sleep the minute her head had touched the pillows. The air of excitement from the day before was still hanging around like an old friend. Vernadine jumped out of bed and found her robe. She brushed her long curls and made her way to the kitchen, where Aunt Marie was busy preparing a breakfast of bacon, scrambled eggs, biscuits and gravy. Vernadine's mouth watered as she poured herself a cup of coffee. The smells of breakfast made her a bit homesick. She could see her mother in her own kitchen getting breakfast ready for her father. The thoughts of her parents reminded her she could not delay the news of her "new plan" to her parents for very long, but right now, she had to focus on the day. Today was the first day of her new job and the first day of her independence. After enjoying her breakfast, Vernadine dressed for the day in one of her new dresses, pinned her hair up, applied a small amount of makeup, made the bed and straightened her bedroom. She stepped off of the front porch at 7:50 AM, refreshed, and strolled the few blocks to Oakleigh Realty Company. She arrived promptly at 8 AM.

"Good morning, Mr. Jones," Vernadine said as she put her purse and gloves on her new desk.

"Good morning, Vernadine. You are right on time. I have a few meetings this morning, so I am afraid that you will be on your own. The receptionist before you left us in a pickle, so there is no one to train you. I will try to train you in between meetings, but the primary task is answering the phone and taking messages. I know you are not familiar with any of our properties for sale or for rent, so use this notebook and flip through until you find the address of the property. I alphabetized the addresses. For each address, you will find the price and basic information. Take a message, then call the agent and pass it along. Most of the agents, there are twelve of them, usually come in daily. Each has a box with his or her name on it right here. Place all information for the agents in their boxes. Otherwise, if you have any other questions, save them for me, and I will check on you between meetings. And, oh, in the event anyone calls with a busted pipe or overflowing toilet, look in the notebook and call Mr. Green; he is our maintenance man. He will get right on it," Mr. Jones said as his first appointment entered the office.

"Oh, my," thought Vernadine, "this will be a baptism by fire. I sure hope I don't mess it all up!" Right then, her first phone call rang and jolted her back to reality. "Good morning, Oakleigh Realty Company, Vernadine speaking. May I help you?"

And so it began, her first step towards working out 'her plan' and adulthood. She was smiling as she spoke on the phone to the caller. "This is going to be great fun," she thought to herself.

Vernadine 'The Real Estate Queen'

Mobile
1944-1959

Sheridan Esther Turnipseed was born on December twenty third in 1944. Vernadine and Aunt Marie had clung to the story that Vernadine was a war widow, so when Sheridan made her appearance, a steady stream of well-wishers visited Vernadine and her new baby, bringing gifts, casseroles, and congratulations. All of the support touched Vernadine, Aunt Marie, Fletcher and Irene and they even felt a little guilty that they were living a lie, but the excitement over Sheridan's arrival gave them reason to celebrate and that was all that mattered to them. They had come too far to back down now. So far, their 'secret' had stayed a secret.

Since her first day in 1944 as the receptionist, Vernadine had excelled in her duties at the Oakleigh Realty Company and she had become an invaluable member of the team. She handled phone calls, showing appointments, leaky faucets and overflowing toilets like a pro. She had spent months watching the Realtors and thought to herself that she could do that job too, so by the time 1959 rolled around, Vernadine had worked herself into the premier agent of Mobile County. Through hard work and grit, she had raised her daughter, work her way up to top producer and was the current president of the local real estate association. She was highly respected and her appointment book and bank account were full.

After fifteen years in Mobile, Vernadine would never have imagined her life would have turned out this way. The once heartbroken, scared, and desperate young girl was now a happy and successful businesswoman and the proud mother of her beautiful daughter, Sheridan. Yes, she was very proud of her accomplishments and her life. After years of saving money, Vernadine purchased a weekend home. She chose a white clapboard cottage with blue shutters on S. Mobile Street in Fairhope. The two-bedroom cottage sat next door to the First Presbyterian church, overlooking a park and Mobile Bay. It was a dream and the perfect escape from the crowds and traffic in Mobile. A slower, more intentional pace was always the perfect place to land after a busy week of contract negotiations and life with a busy teenager. Sheridan made friends quickly with the neighborhood youth and the girls spent hours soaking up the sun, splashing in the bay, walking to the drugstore for ice cream and lipstick, and dreaming about their future husbands. Vernadine enjoyed gardening, painting, and lazy afternoons on the front porch with coffee and a good book. She would stare at the water lapping the shore for hours, grateful and amazed at how God had provided for her and her daughter. Her blessings were many and, for that, she was thankful.

Through the years Vernadine had thought about Slim and wondered if his life had turned out as well as hers. Irene had kept Vernadine up to date on her friends from home, and it didn't take too long after her departure from Spit's Creek to learn that Slim and Marigold had married. She hoped they were having a happy life on one hand and, on the other, she could not help but harbor resentment against Slim. She knew now, on that fateful afternoon on the dirt road with Slim, he already knew Marigold was his dream and not her. For some reason, he would not tell her his true feelings.

"Momma, what are you thinking about?" Sheridan asked as she ran onto the porch, breathless.

"Oh, I am sitting here counting my blessings. You know what? You are by far my biggest blessing ever. You have brought so much joy to my life, and I love you deeply. I hope you know how much you are loved," Vernadine said as she stroked Sheridan's cheek and swiped a stray hair from her sweaty face.

"Yes, Ma'am, I know you love me. I was just thinking, as I was walking home, this town is like a fairytale. The beauty here is breathtaking, and I just walk around in amazement that we live here. It's like being on a permanent vacation. Please never sell this home, Momma. I want to always come here, no matter where I end up. Will you promise me that?"

"I promise," Vernadine said as she grabbed Sheridan and pulled her in for a hug. "I promise, dear child of mine."

In fact, Vernadine knew she had no intention of ever leaving Mobile and her small cottage in Fairhope. Aunt Marie had already told her that her home would be Vernadine's when she passed away. Aunt Marie had already set the wheels in motion for Vernadine and Sheridan to become her heirs. Since Aunt Marie was childless, it was exactly what she knew she should do. Vernadine and Sheridan had become just like her own daughter and granddaughter over the last fifteen years and, because of them, the recent years had been rich and full and happier than she had ever expected her later years to be. Vernadine had made a great living for herself and Sheridan, and they wanted for nothing, but at Aunt Marie's passing, Vernadine would be quite wealthy. They were both comforted knowing Vernadine and Sheridan would have no reasons to worry about anything ever again, at least materially. Money doesn't buy happiness and love, but it sure helps. From the day of the awakening in 1944, when Aunt Marie tore her curtains down, she made the decision that she, too, would turn over a new leaf and lease on life. Vernadine's decision to keep her baby and raise her as a single mother and join the workforce inspired Marie to make some of her own changes. She decided she no longer wanted or desired to be the fragile beautiful flower of a woman she had always been. She withdrew her memberships from the Ladies Auxiliary, the Oakleigh Garden Club, and the

Daughters of the American Revolution. To the dismay of her friends, Aunt Marie began trimming her own hedges, cutting her own grass, and painting her picket fence. She traded her floral print dresses and white lace gloves for overalls and leather work gloves. Rumors were also surfacing that a young Roman Catholic Senator from Massachusetts named John Fitzgerald Kennedy may be the next Democratic Presidential nominee, so she began volunteering at the Mobile County Democratic headquarters on Government Street every weekday morning, except Tuesdays when she went to see Sally at Sally's Hair Boutique for her weekly hair appointment. She made telephone calls and stuffed many envelopes in the campaign fundraising effort. In the 'Bible Belt', the thoughts of John Kennedy being the President seemed completely outside the norm and too progressive for the conservative and mostly Protestant folks, so Aunt Marie turned on her charm and passionately pled with her community to donate to his campaign, a campaign that promised "A Time for Greatness" and "We Can Do Better." The current President, Dwight D. Eisenhower, had been a good President. Being a War Hero and older, he fit the mold of what most folks would agree was 'presidential' and fatherly. But change was brewing under the surface all over the country. Folks were sensing the need to shake things up a bit. They wanted progress in industry and thinking. The youth of America and Aunt Marie were ready for a new direction, and John Fitzgerald Kennedy and his beautiful wife, Jacqueline, fit the bill.

In the few months after John Fitzgerald Kennedy became the thirty-fifth President in 1961, Vernadine noticed Aunt Marie was slowing down. She was listless and had no desire to do anything. The Doctor was called and he informed Vernadine that Aunt Marie had advanced heart disease and she would not be with them for much longer. At the same time the news registered about Aunt Marie, Vernadine received news that her father, Fletcher, had suffered a massive stroke and was not expected to survive long. Caught in the middle of the devastation between two loved ones, Vernadine and Sheridan packed their suitcases and headed off for the four-hour drive to Spit's Creek. Vernadine called one of Aunt Marie's friends to stay with her aunt while they were out of town. She also alerted Aunt Marie's pastor and Sunday school teacher to please keep a check on her aunt, with explicit directions to call her if Aunt Marie's condition declined further.

In the previous fifteen years, Vernadine had not once returned to Spit's Creek. The memories were painful. She had managed to keep her life a mystery and a secret from the prying eyes of the community and First Believers Victory Church. Irene and Fletcher had agreed to Vernadine's 'story', and because they could not stop her, they helped protect her in the ways that they could from home. The church family and the community knew that Vernadine had moved away shortly after graduation to help a sick aunt, but her parents provided no other details. They didn't even disclose which city she was living in. When asked, they always found a way out of the conversation. They left the community and church family to speculate. Protecting Vernadine and Sheridan had always been their chief priority.

On the ride to Spit's Creek, Vernadine was quiet as she remembered the last time she made this trip and how her departure seemed now like a different lifetime. Looking at Sheridan, riding quietly beside her, Vernadine was proud. Sheridan was beautiful and smart, and for that, she was very thankful. She was so happy knowing that Sheridan would not face the same ridicule that she had for not being pretty and feminine. It brought her great comfort knowing Sheridan would have opportunities for college and opportunities to marry a nice man from a nice family. Sheridan had been raised by two very strong women. She had grown up in a beautiful home in a lovely neighborhood; she had ballet lessons, etiquette classes and she wore beautiful, stylish clothes. She was involved in her youth group at church and sang in the choir. Vernadine and Aunt Marie spent countless hours and plenty of money ensuring that Sheridan grew up a proper southern young lady. The results were successful. Vernadine's heart was full of love and pride over Sheridan and she congratulated herself for her success and thanked the Lord for His blessings on their lives. As she looked at her dark-haired, blue-eyed, freckled daughter, her heart swelled.

Sheridan broke the silence and asked, "Momma, please tell me why we never go to your hometown? In all of my fifteen years, this will be the very first time I have been to Spit's Creek and the house you were raised in. And the high school gymnasium that is named after you? I know very little about your past. I know nothing about my father. I only have my life in Mobile as my story and your story. I don't have background information to build upon. It's as if we just appeared on this earth with no history and no family before us. When I am asked about my family or I am asked where my father is, I have nothing to say other than telling them about you and Aunt Marie and my grandparents. Momma, I am fifteen, not five. I deserve to know what my history is and why it is the way it is. I should not have to live my life inside a mystery. I know that you have worked very hard in your career, building a life for us and being my mother. You and Aunt Marie have taken great care of me, and I am thankful for everything I have and knowing that I am loved. So, please, will you tell me our history? Your history?," Sheridan said as she intensely stared at her mother as a single tear ran down her cheek.

Vernadine knew one day she would have to tell Sheridan the truth about her father and why their life was in Mobile and not in Spit's Creek, but she never collected the right words in her head. And now, she was sitting next to her daughter, who was almost grown and pleading for information. Vernadine took a deep breath and knew that any more delays in telling Sheridan would not be justified. There were still three hours of the car ride yet to go and that would be plenty of time to tell Sheridan her story and their history. And so, with another breath and a quick prayer, she spoke.

As Vernadine was finishing her story to Sheridan, they crossed the Buford County line. Sheridan listened with great interest for three hours to her mother's explanation of events. Through many tears and some laughter, Vernadine filled in the gaps for Sheridan and told her about her father, Slim Perkins, and why he was not involved in her life. How could he be? He didn't even know she existed. Vernadine explained to

Sheridan that she and her parents agreed it was best for him not to know in the beginning, that time would settle it all.

In the last fifteen years since Vernadine's disappearance, rumors ran rampant, as one would expect. Some said Vernadine became a German spy and was killed years ago in Berlin and her parents were so ashamed of her that they erased her from their memories and lives. Others speculated Vernadine became a well-known basketball coach for a college out West and she was living with another woman. Such topics were not discussed in large groups, but that was the favorite rumor in the ladies' group at First Believers Victory Church. "Poor Fletcher and Irene," they would say, as they shook their heads and popped their chewing gum. "Imagine the disgrace. They tried so hard to raise Vernadine the right way, but sometimes children just don't take to their raisin'. That sin nature we are born with just takes over sometimes no matter what." They also agreed they always felt something was a little 'off' with Vernadine. A woman that looks more like a man is a recipe for disaster. The ladies would nod in agreement. "We will pray for their broken hearts and for Vernadine's salvation." This always made the ladies feel better about themselves and their own salvation. What would the town's folk think when they saw Vernadine and Sheridan tomorrow?

The 'Queen of Basketball' Returns Home

Spit's Creek
July 1959

It was dusk when Vernadine and Sheridan rolled into Spit's Creek in her brand new black convertible Lincoln Continental. She always felt so Presidential and important in that car. After all, she had worked very hard for it. It amazed Vernadine at how nice and practically unchanged her hometown looked. Memories began flooding her mind, and as they did, she would point and tell Sheridan stories about the 'Clip and Curl' and the hairspray lacquer 'glamour glue' that would hold a hairstyle completely unchanged until the next hair washing. Passing Haegdorn's department store reminded her of how awkward and large she was in high school, and if she bought anything to wear from the store, she had to shop in the ladies' department. She remembered how embarrassed she felt and how out of style she always was compared to her peers. This memory, of course, fondly reminded her of the white eyelet dress with the red bow and angled collar her mother had sewn especially for her graduation because she couldn't find anything to her liking in the store.

They passed the Second Baptist Church and the First Methodist Church and it amazed her at how large both churches had become. She told Sheridan that the bake sales from her basketball games had helped contribute to the growth. Thinking about that brought feelings of pride about her contribution to the Lord's work in Spit's Creek, even though she knew it was a sin to be prideful.

In the next block, the street parking was full. "Oh, look, Sheridan, it's Mrs. Ruth's café and people are still lining up for her 'Catfish Friday's'! Her catfish dinners are legendary. Before every home basketball, everyone ate at Mrs. Ruth's. She had to begin serving supper at 3 PM just to accommodate the crowds. There were even write-ups in newspapers as far as Birmingham about her café. She did really well during the basketball seasons of 1943 and 1944. I like to think I helped her with that, being the 'queen of basketball' and all, and attracting droves of people to town to see the girl basketball player." They both laughed.

"Momma, you are famous, and I didn't realize just how much so until now! Just think, I have had you as a momma for fifteen years, and I did not know the extent of your legacy in Buford County and sports history in Alabama. And now, you are still carrying on that tradition as the 'queen of real estate' for Mobile County! You know what, momma? You are amazing!" Sheridan said, as she beamed from ear to ear.

What the two of them did not notice during their chatter was everyone on the sidewalks and street had stopped dead in their tracks. Everyone was staring at them; gawking at this beautiful car riding down the streets of Spit's Creek with the mysterious strangers as passengers. Someone yelled "It's the President! It has to be!"

Another one yelled, "No, it's not stupid. Do you see any flags on the front of the car? Do you see secret service men surrounding the car with motorcycles?" Even though it wasn't the President, they continued to stare. They just knew it was someone important.

"Are you hungry, Sheridan? I am feeling peckish myself. This four-hour car ride has left me famished," Vernadine said as she rubbed her stomach.

"You mean stop at Mrs. Ruth's?" Sheridan asked.

"Sure, why not! These folks won't recognize me and I am fine with that because I am too tired to walk down memory lane. We are free to eat anywhere we choose and this is the only café in downtown open for supper. If we don't stop now, we will eat fried egg sandwiches at Momma's. Fried catfish with the fixin's sounds better than a fried egg sandwich," Vernadine said, and Sheridan agreed.

Vernadine made a fast U-turn and parked on the next block. She let the top of the convertible up, dusted her nose with powder, and put on a fresh coat of lipstick. She removed the scarf from her hair and brushed lightly on the top to smooth it out. She made a quick check of her teeth to make sure there were not any peanuts remaining from the RC Cola and peanuts she had eaten a couple of hours ago.

Sheridan smoothed her hair as they stepped out of the car and hand pressed the pleats on her skirt. She grabbed her purse and off they went. Sheridan whispered to her mother, "it's show time, Momma." and they both chuckled.

Vernadine knew it was true. The 'basketball queen', who had disappeared fifteen years before, without a trace, was making her re-entry into the community and on a 'Catfish Friday' no less. Her timing could not have been better.

When Vernadine and Sheridan stepped onto the sidewalk to enter the café, the crowd silently parted, like they were royalty, and let them through. The hostess seated them and took their drink order. "Your waitress will be right with you, Ma'am." The hostess tipped her head, and turned around.

Vernadine and Sheridan looked around at the noisy café and noticed most of the folks were staring, pointing, and talking about them. Most figured she was a rich socialite from Birmingham or Atlanta, heading to the beach for the weekend. Some speculated she was the Governor's wife, Mary Joe Patterson, and that possibly she was? Who else but politicians and rich people drive Lincoln Continental's? At that moment, a young girl approached their table and asked for Vernadine's autograph. "Could you please autograph this napkin for my mother? Her name is Rose; and could you please put your title underneath your autograph too? Momma wants it for her scrapbook. Thank you, Mrs. Governor." Vernadine chuckled as politely as she could and explained to the young girl that she was not Mary Joe Patterson. "Well then, who are you? Everyone is dying to know!" the young girl pleaded.

"Oh, Honey, my name is Vernadine Turnipseed, and this is my daughter, Sheridan."

Vernadine thought, "so much for the quiet re-entry to town."

At the moment Vernadine was talking to the young girl, the bell on the front door rang and two new diners walked in. The smile and joviality Vernadine felt immediately dissipated as she sat there looking straight at Slim Perkins and his wife, Marigold. By this point, the young girl had returned to her table, told her mother the identity of the mystery woman, and now the buzz in the café was deafening. Everyone was shocked!

"What? There is no way that is Vernadine Turnipseed," was the consensus among the diners.

"That woman over there is beautiful. Vernadine was not a beauty at all. In fact, she was quite masculine and unattractive for a girl. She must be an imposter!" said another diner.

"I heard Vernadine was killed in Germany for being a spy in the war. I also heard she was living in California with another woman, or something like that! It's all so mysterious." said the waitress.

Because of the raucous conversations in the dining room, Mrs. Ruth separated herself from the deep fryers and set out to find out what was going on. As she stepped into the dining room, she noticed groups of people huddled around tables, chattering with excitement and pointing and staring at the woman and teenager sitting at a table. Mrs. Ruth walked over to the large group huddled up beside the window tables, excused herself, and said, "What in the blazes is going on out here? What is the problem? Are we at war again and I don't know about it? Has someone died? Somebody please tell me!" she screamed.

Vernadine leaned across the table and said to Sheridan, "I think we need to leave. This is a scene, and we caused it. Had I known anything like this would have happened, I would have settled for a fried egg sandwich. This is embarrassing, everyone staring and talking about us and wanting autographs. I am just a girl who grew up in this town, living a somewhat normal life, and wanting to eat fried catfish for supper, NOT to be THE fish in a bowl. Let's go!"

"Momma, are you kidding me?" Sheridan laughed. "This is way too exciting! This is the craziest thing that has ever happened to me. No way do I want to leave. I want to see how this scene plays out! Please, Momma, let's stay. I want to see everyone's reaction when they realize it is really you. If I didn't know better, by the way they are acting, they had a completely different narrative of what became of Vernadine Turnipseed, the local hero. I mean, since you left without a trace fifteen years ago, your fame and legend from Alabama basketball obviously shifted over the years into some great tale and mystery. Don't you want to know what they have said and thought, and to see their reactions yourself?"

Vernadine listened to the plea of her daughter, and she had to admit to herself that it piqued her curiosity. She was suddenly fearful that the 'story' the community had concocted would be too much to handle; but because she had taught herself over the last few years to have a backbone and nerves of steel, she would pull from her reserves and withstand the battle fire. "Ok, let's stay. I am quite curious, yet fearful at the same time. But, whatever this turns out to be about, seeing it firsthand is exactly what needs to happen." Vernadine took a sip of her iced tea and noticed her hand had a slight tremble. She took a deep breath and sat up straight. Sheridan was beaming from ear to ear with excitement and anticipation.

Slim was panic stricken when he realized what all of the commotion was about on the street and the café. One of his old basketball buddies ran over to his table and told him Vernadine was back in town and sitting right across the café from him. He looked at the woman sitting at the table and thought to himself, "There is no way this woman is Vernadine! She is refined, proper, and distinguished. She is well dressed in expensive clothes and she is beautiful!"

The surprise of seeing Vernadine sent shockwaves through the café and in no time, the whole county knew Vernadine was home. For fifteen years, the rumors had run rampant. Slim figured the lack of information about Vernadine added fuel to the rumor fire and to the mystery of the disappearance of the 'basketball queen'. Vernadine had become a legend again for different reasons, a real-life small town mystery with a Southern flare that had taken on a life of its own, and now here she was in flesh and blood, waiting to order her catfish dinner, and wanting to eat in peace without everyone staring at her. With all of the emotional flurry in Slim's mind, his mouth went dry and his knees went weak. He plopped himself back on his booth seat and took a very long gulp of his sweet tea, then wiped the top of his lips with his shirtsleeve. Marigold immediately attended to him, looking concerned and asked, "Are you okay, Honey? You look like you have just seen a ghost. Your face is white as a sheet and you are breathing heavy." Slim was so lost in his own shock that he heard nothing Marigold had said to him. She shook his arm, and that seemed to knock him back to reality.

Vernadine watched the entire scene between Slim and Marigold play out with great interest and a smirk on her ruby red lips. She knew Slim wished he could crawl out of this busy restaurant without anyone noticing him, but that would be impossible. She also knew his mind was racing, replaying the last conversation they had on the dirt road near Vernadine's house that fateful afternoon. But, instead of crawling out of the restaurant, he rose from his seat, collected himself, adjusted his shirt and smoothed his hair, murmuring something to Marigold, then began the walk towards Vernadine across the restaurant. The restaurant noise quickly faded from Vernadine's consciousness and all at once the only two things she heard were silence and her breathing. Controlled panic set in as she looked at Sheridan, who she knew would finally come face to face with her father, the father that she knew existed, but of which she knew very little of.

Before Vernadine had time to rehearse or plan anything to say, Slim was standing at the edge of her table wearing a half-smile on his sweaty face. "Vernadine Turnipseed, is that really you?" Slim asked.

"Hello, Slim, it's been a long time," Vernadine said.

Sheridan sat straight up in her chair. Her eyes bulged and her breathing sped up. Somehow, she knew she was finally looking at her father. She dared not speak until spoken to, so she just stared and listened.

"You have changed. I mean, you look really nice," Slim blushed as he commented, afraid of sounding petty or childish.

"Thank you. I would have to agree with you. Growing up has had definite advantages for me," she commented.

"Where have you been all these years? I did not know what became of you shortly after graduation and the last time we talked," Slim said.

"Well, I have been in Mobile for a little over fifteen years. I moved there to help take care of my Aunt Marie, fell in love with the town and its beauty and people, so I just stayed. I have been selling real estate now for fourteen years and have really enjoyed it. Moving there was the best thing I could have done. We are happy there and my business has been successful. Oh my goodness, where are my manners? This is my daughter, Sheridan. Sheridan, this is Mr. Perkins," Vernadine said boldly.

The moment Slim focused on Sheridan, he felt strange. He knew something looked familiar about her, but he couldn't place his finger on it. "So pleased to meet you, Sheridan. How old are you?" He asked.

"I am fifteen, Mr. Perkins. I am in the tenth grade and I attend an all-girls high school." He thought to himself, 'she is so pretty' as she spoke.

"So," Vernadine said, "What has become of your life these last fifteen years? Is that your wife over there? I believe her name is Marigold?"

Slim tried his hardest to act proud and confident, but he now knew that she must have known for a long time that he had lied to her that fateful afternoon about needing to figure out his future.

Before Slim spoke, Vernadine was looking at Marigold and laughing to herself. The irony was too much to bear. She felt that at any moment she would burst into gut-wrenching, doubled-over, coughing laughter, a real undignified hysterical fit. She also knew if she did, she would blow the perception of her new persona. So, she pinched her leg, braced it firmly on the Sheridan's seat, and pushed hard. She coughed into her napkin and sipped her iced tea repeatedly to keep herself from bursting out into uncontrolled laughter. The fact of the matter was Marigold Lily Wright Perkins had become quite obese and unattractive over the years. She bore no resemblance to the beautiful and innocent version Slim married. The beauty of Marigold was fleeting, temporary, skin deep and had hit rock bottom. Vernadine figured, by the way Slim was stalling, it embarrassed him at how Marigold had changed. His dream of Marigold's eternal beauty had not exactly played out the way he had thought it would. And now, standing there looking at Vernadine and her composed and refined beauty, he was doubly embarrassed. Marigold had been a good and faithful wife, and for that, he was thankful. But he also discovered after they were married that she possessed no goals and aspirations for her life outside of matrimony and child rearing and helping her father at the church. She had no interest in travel or business or adventure or nature or anything. The glow and newness wore off of their marriage after the first few years, but he loved her and she loved him, and somehow they made it through. They had three children in a short time and his oldest daughter, or so he thought, was thirteen.

"Uh, um, yes, that is my wife Marigold. I don't believe you two met before you left town." Slim gulped and kicked the foot of the booth they were sitting in, feeling stupid for the last half of his remark.

"No, we did not have the opportunity to meet. She arrived in town at almost the exact moment I left town, if you recall? She sure made an impression on many folks quickly. I understand you married her after a very short courtship. But, I have heard through the years about her beauty and service in the Methodist church. I am sure she is a nice person. Just curious though, is she ill by chance? Maybe a low producing thyroid or underactive metabolism? I don't mean to be rude, but she may need a doctor. A friend of mine in Mobile was skinny one minute and blown up like a blimp the next, and she had a lot of issues. Unfortunately, she never could get healed and died from a heart attack a few years ago. You know fat and bloating puts a lot of undue stress on your heart. Fat helps with wrinkles, though. I mean, when your skin is stretched out, it hides a lot of damage and age on the surface. But, I am sure y'all already know this. From where I am sitting, I can just see my dear departed friend as plain as day, right before she died; and it's just like she rose from the grave right here at Mrs. Ruth's café! Oh, my! It is so strange! I know I must sound vulgar, and I certainly don't mean to be, but it is our Christian duty to help our fellow man or woman and spare heartache as much as possible. Just do me the favor, and tell her what I said. I am sure she will appreciate it. It may just save her life. It would be sad if anything terrible happened to her." Vernadine smiled through concerned eyes and black mascara.

Sheridan sat silent through the entire conversation, and after her mother told Slim to tell Marigold what she had just said about dying from obesity, she excused herself from the table from sheer hilarity. She made her way to the bathroom, closed the door and from out of the walls a cackle and a boom-boom-boom beating sound vibrated in the dining room. Sheridan was inside the bathroom, beating on the bathroom stall while laughing uncontrollably. She could not believe her mother had just said the mean things she did and with such a straight and concerned face to boot. Vernadine tried her hardest to divert Slim's attention from the obvious, loud noise and high-pitched laughter coming from the bathroom. Vernadine knew she had just set a terrible example for her daughter to follow, but right then she just didn't care how bad of a mother she was, given the circumstances. Vernadine had waited fifteen years to throw pain and meanness back in Slim and Marigold's faces, the two people who made this sweet life together in their marriage and family. This was the life that was supposed to have been hers with Slim, not Marigold's. The fact that she had to run away from Spit's Creek, her parents, and everything she knew and loved, because of her pregnancy, could have been prevented if Slim had asked her to marry him instead of Marigold.

After she collected herself from running down bad-memory lane, she realized Slim was still standing there frozen. He was completely stunned at the events of the evening and this last bit of friendly advice from Vernadine about his soon-to-be-dead Marigold was just too much. Vernadine said, "Slim, it's been so nice to see you and Marigold and all of the folks in the café. We have to get going soon to Momma's. You know Daddy is sick. But one last thing before Sheridan rejoins us, the beautiful young lady you met tonight is your daughter. She knows very little to nothing about you. I have not told her many of the details surrounding our brief relationship in our senior year of high school. I have not even confirmed with her tonight that you are her father. I believe she instinctively knows by my observations of her facial expressions. She is a very bright and beautiful young lady, and she has been the greatest joy of my life. I did not tell you about her because I did not want you to marry me for the wrong reasons, however, by the looks of things, I think you can see for yourself that I am not the same girl I was then, and it's obvious Marigold isn't either. That's all water under the bridge. We have lived a glorious life, Sheridan and I, and I have many things to be thankful for. I cannot even envision what my life would have looked like had I stayed in Spit's Creek. Looking at everything I see here tonight through the lens of a thirty-two-year-old woman who has experienced life in a grander, more refined city, I know now that I made the right choice. I am not sure what questions Sheridan is going to ask or if she wants to see you again. I just don't know what she will want to do? I will not try to stop her from seeing you because she deserves to know more about you and her history. She has been robbed of that and left to wonder about her father for years. I did everything to protect her from hurt. I have made many mistakes along the way as her mother, but I could never be accused of not protecting her heart and doing my best to offer her love and security and some of the finer things in life that I never knew existed until I left here."

As wrapped up in the one sided conversation as they were, they had not noticed that the loud noise from the bathroom had quieted, and as Vernadine said her last word, Sheridan seemed to appear on cue. Vernadine grabbed her hand quickly and they shot out of the door before Slim had time to say anything.

Sheridan yelled, "nice to meet you, Mr. Perkins," As her mother drug her out of the café. They left Slim standing beside the booth with his mouth hanging open and his shoulders slumped. There were no words forming in his mind. He was completely dumbstruck and now the 'disappearance' of Vernadine made complete sense to him. Knowing that he had broken her heart because he chose Marigold over her was difficult enough, but now knowing she was pregnant with his baby and she did not tell him, and that was the reason she left town unbetrothed, was a hard pill to swallow. The heartbreak and fear Vernadine must have felt had to have been too much to bear. Staying in Spit's Creek as a celebrity, knowing the whole county loved her; to only disappoint everyone with an unplanned and out-of-wedlock pregnancy would have been too much humiliation and shame for her and her parents. The questions started rising in his mind as he stood frozen in the same spot. 'Why didn't she tell me?' 'Why did she walk away carrying the secret and fear all alone?' 'I would have married her, and we would have probably had a decent life together. I have a daughter I do not even know!' He watched as Vernadine and Sheridan disappeared in a cloud of dust in her black convertible Lincoln. Slim turned around, headed straight for the door; not looking or speaking to anyone, and walked straight to his truck; leaving Marigold sitting in the café alone.

Home at Last

Spit's Creek, July 1960

Vernadine and Sheridan were happy to arrive home after a long day of traveling and after the dramatic episode at the café, they were exhausted.

When Vernadine walked into her childhood home, the smells and sights soothed her troubled and anxious heart. The day's events had left her rattled and landing in her childhood home was like a salve to her heart. Even though Sheridan had never visited her Grandparent's home, somehow everything seemed familiar to her. Vernadine had described her childhood home in precise detail, and Sheridan felt immediately welcomed and comforted. After the day's events and revelations, she also needed comfort.

Vernadine hugged her mother tightly. All of the emotions she had suppressed for many years came flooding over her, and there was nothing she could do to stop them. She clung to her mother for a long time, while her mother soothed her with words of love through her own tears. There was so much to talk about. She had missed the loving touch and sound guidance from her mother, and talking over the phone was not the same as being in her presence. Irene sensed that there were other things troubling Vernadine besides her concern for her father, but they would have time to talk about it later. Right now, Vernadine needed to see her father.

Irene let Vernadine go and said, "Your father is in his bedroom. He will not know you are there, the doctor has said, so brace yourself for that. The stroke was severe and the doctor isn't holding out much hope for a recovery. In fact, he said he is at risk for another and more severe stroke. I just want you to be prepared. The man in the bed is not your father, at least mentally, but somehow I believe he hears every word spoken to him and he will know it's you. Sheridan and I will go to the kitchen for some hot cocoa if you need us. Otherwise, take all the time you want. We will be just fine."

Vernadine gathered herself and walked down the hallway to her father's bedroom. She prayed as she walked, asking the Lord for strength to bear what she was about to see.

The bedroom was dimly lit, with only one lamp burning on the dresser. A fan was blowing to circulate the air, and the curtains were gently swaying. The quietness of the room was deafening, and her father appeared very small to her. Not at all the man she knew and fondly remembered in her mind. Fletcher had always carried a quiet strength in his large frame and he was intimidating to those who didn't know him, but to Vernadine, he was gentle and kind and strong and he was her protector.

She sat down in the wooden chair beside the bed and touched her father's hand. His hand was wrinkled and bruised and cold. She rested her head on the side of the bed and began weeping. The tears wouldn't stop.

"Daddy," she said through muffled sobs, "It's me, Vernadine. I am home, Daddy, and Sheridan is with me. We are here to take care of you and help Momma. I am so sorry, Daddy, it is so hard to see you like this, knowing there is nothing I can do to help you. Can you hear me, Daddy? Squeeze my hand if you can hear me, please."

There was no movement. Vernadine tried squeezing his hand again to see if he might move, but he didn't. So, she just kept talking and talking, and praying in between, for her Father. She wanted to believe he could hear her, so she just talked. She caught him up on the latest news from Mobile and her real estate career. She talked about Sheridan and how good she was doing in school and stories about her friends. She talked about anything that came to mind.

"Oh Daddy, I have missed you so much. I am sorry I have been away from you and that we haven't seen each other very much these last years. I know it's my fault we were separated. You were only trying to protect me from harm. Please forgive me for disappointing you and Momma. You raised me to make better choices than I did and for that, I am sorry. Thank you for loving me despite my poor decisions and for loving Sheridan how you have. She has been my greatest joy, and I am sad that you and momma didn't get to spend more time with her. She is quite an amazing young lady, and I am so proud of her. Daddy, can you hear me? Daddy, you would love my black Lincoln convertible. When you are better, I will take you for a ride in it and you can drive it."

Vernadine knew she could talk all night to her father. There was so much to tell him. But after her taxing day, she resigned herself to go to bed. Tomorrow she would tell him the story from the café, and seeing Slim and Marigold, and how Sheridan knows Slim is her father. "Good night, Daddy. I will see you first thing in the morning. You don't worry about anything, ok? I love you, Daddy."

She straightened the covers and kissed him lightly on the head and walked out of the bedroom, leaving the door cracked. She walked into the kitchen to find her mother was washing the mugs from the hot cocoa and Irene explained Sheridan had already retired to bed. Vernadine kissed her mother on the cheek, told her good night, and walked to her bedroom. She closed the door and fell onto the bed and cried herself to sleep.

The next morning, the smell of fried bacon and ham in the cast-iron skillet gently woke Vernadine from her slumber. She opened her eyes and looked around at her childhood bedroom for the first time in years. She could not remember how many mornings she awoke to her mother cooking breakfast in the kitchen and the smells filling the house with yummy fragrance. Along with the ham and bacon, she smelled freshly brewed coffee, and she was sure she caught a whiff of her mother's special cinnamon coffee cake with a streusel and nut topping. Upon that thought, she decided she would get up for the day. She brushed her hair and teeth and put on her robe and slippers and made her way to the kitchen.

"Good morning, Momma. Boy, it sure smells good in here! Did I smell your cinnamon coffee cake, or was I dreaming?" Vernadine said as she made her way beside her mother to kiss her on the cheek.

"Now, you don't think that I could have you home and not fix your favorite coffee cake, did you? I just took it out of the oven." She lifted the linen cloth off of the top of it and showed it to Vernadine. They both smiled at each other, happy, deep down inside to share this moment they had not shared in years, but had always remembered fondly.

"So, tell me, how did you sleep in your old bed?" Irene asked.

"I slept like a baby. I had all but forgotten about the lavender and yellow striped wallpaper with the little white flowers scattered about and the matching curtains and bedspread. I think I blocked out all of the details of home so the separation would not seem so personal and real. I built a wall around my old memories just so I could force myself to focus and concentrate on what was ahead of me. It wasn't easy, but I did it. Thankfully, because of Aunt Marie and her love and warmth and comfortable home, I was still surrounded by family and some familiarity. She has been a blessing in so many ways for Sheridan and I. She has loved us like we were her own, and we have never felt out of place or like an inconvenience to her. I know in her heart, after being alone for some time, that the added noise and excitement was good for her, and I am sure that has given her a reason to live longer. I am worried about her though, her doctor says she has a bad heart condition. She has been a rock. By looking at her, you would never know how strong and determined she really is. In fact, the day we tore the curtains down in her parlor, well, she just broke loose. She got involved in local, state and national politics, she quit hosting or going to tea parties. She said that was a waste of her time, she had more important things to do. She stopped entering her roses and azaleas in the annual garden club contest, too. And, did you know she even had a boyfriend who was a Republican who drank whiskey, smoked cigars in her parlor and told off-color jokes? Why, I even saw her smoking and drinking one afternoon in her parlor! She had the radio turned up as loud as it would go with the latest Frank Sinatra hit. I made sure she didn't see me, even though by this point in her life, she did not care what people thought about her. Yes, she is a real enigma, and she roars with laughter as she repeats the gossip she has heard about herself from one of her well-meaning friends. 'Poppy cock,' she would say. 'I don't give a dang what people are saying. Life doesn't last forever.'

And with that, she would lay her head back and really bust a gut. I know her behavior was shocking to her proper set of genteel friends, but something in her broke out, and she never looked back! It was a sight to behold. I saw many times in our years together how she gave me strength when I needed it, and in return, I did the same for her. I think she considered me a 'modern woman' and that's what she wanted to be with the years she had left. In my mind, she succeeded."

"Really? Well, your father and I didn't know about those behaviors in Marie!" Irene said. "And, I guess by the way you're describing her transformation and state of mind, she wouldn't have cared what we thought anyway! Well, it doesn't matter now. We always knew you would be safe and cared for in her home, and I see where your and Sheridan's being there have added years and excitement to her life. I am happy about that for all of you. We are so thankful for all she has done for you and Sheridan. Yes, I can see where she would have seen you as a 'modern woman' and how that inspired her for change. I sure hope she is okay." Irene wiped the corner of her mouth for crumbs and took a sip of her coffee.

Vernadine was on her second slice of the cinnamon coffee cake and had enjoyed the moments listening to her mother speak. The fear and sadness and anxiety from the day before had completely disappeared, and just like that, in the presence and warmth of her mother, she was a little girl again. She flashed back to the days of her childhood when problems left themselves at the front door. The days when feelings of inferiority and humiliation could be left at school, and nothing outside of her safe home, with her parents as her protectors, could touch her. Thinking on the days when she felt 'less than' sitting beside girls with outward beauty and talent and attention from the boys in school, she knew she could go home and crawl into her safety net. Some things never change. She always had the love of her parents.

It was at this very moment she realized the events from yesterday, coupled with her past, had forced her to forge a life for herself she had not planned for in her youth. The hurt and sadness had propelled her direction and path. The inner strength she had to summon from deep within caused her to create a new life and identity for herself. She finally realized, sitting at the table with her mother, she had won her own race, the race to outrun herself and all of her insecurities. She had run the race with determination and diligence, all in the name of self-preservation, only to discover that in everything, she finally loved herself. Her true self. A woman of inward and outward beauty, a woman of talent and business sense, a woman of taste and learned refinement, and a woman who had raised a beautiful daughter.

All at once, upon the realization she was capable and smart and funny and beautiful and a good mother, her biggest burdens and fears released their powers over her once and for all. She knew there was not one thing she had to prove or defend about herself to anyone anymore. She was finally free. Free from the demons of self-pity and fear. Free from the demons of regret. Free from the demons of outward beauty or intellect. The last piece of the puzzle in self-acceptance was talking to Slim yesterday and realizing that she had made a life she was proud of and she had the love of her daughter. She felt proud and full and satisfied for the first time in her life.

With a sip of coffee, deep in these thoughts, she resolved and resigned within herself she would love herself completely. And because of that, she could finally tell her mother what had happened the day before, without shame or embarrassment or any fear of judging from her mother. She had broken the promise of the secret made between the two of them by telling Slim the truth about Sheridan; but she also knew eventually the truth would have to be told and now was the time. She would face this situation the way she had faced the last fifteen years. Full steam ahead.

"Momma," Vernadine said, "I am going to wake Sheridan and ask her to come to the kitchen. It's time we continue our talk from yesterday's car ride and the scene at Mrs. Ruth's last night. There are some things you need to hear, too. It's time to clear the air. All of it."

Dealing with the News

Spit's Creek
July 1960

It was nearly dawn when Slim realized what time it was. Had it not been for the looming summer thunderstorm approaching, he may have sat there even longer, deep in thought. Every human emotion struck Slim while sitting beside the creek bank, and he was relieved that the band of teenagers who frequented the swimming hole had not shown up last night. The only visitors were the lightning bugs, frogs, crickets and mosquitos, and for that, he was thankful.

Slim knew there was absolutely nothing he could do to turn back the hands of time; to tell Vernadine he loved her and wanted to marry her that sad afternoon, or to change the outcome. No, that opportunity was long gone. Now, he was left with the pure facts of a situation that, until hours ago, did not know existed. He had a daughter of fifteen years old who was a stranger to him. A beautiful piece of him that had been living in Mobile and he had absolutely no idea. He could not believe he missed the clues or prompts from Vernadine about the baby. Or were there any? He tried his best to replay every date, ball game, church service, or walk on the dirt roads of Buford County and the conversations and dreams they discussed; but no matter how hard he tried to remember, nothing would come to mind.

And then there was Marigold. What would he say to her and their children, his parents and friends? He knew he would lose the respect of the ones he holds dear. He was certain Marigold would not understand. On their wedding day, they pledged loyalty, honesty, purity and longevity to each other. No, he was not pure, and he had lied about it to Marigold. He knew telling her the news would devastate her. How would she be able to trust him again? He had been a faithful and loving husband all of their years of marriage and had never been tempted to stray; but telling her this news would give her reason to worry and wonder and doubt and question everything and anything he had said or done these last fourteen years. Hopefully she would believe that his not knowing about his daughter would excuse some of the pain. How could the not knowing about something qualify as a lie? He knew in his heart that Marigold would be completely crushed at the news, and he also knew that his heart was broken, too.

He stood up from the damp creek side, dusted off his pants, and walked to his truck. Before cranking the truck, he muttered a prayer from his broken and sad heart. "Lord, I don't even know where to begin. I am devastated over the news of Sheridan. I am afraid that I am about to break Marigold's heart and cause great pain for my family. Lord, please forgive me for my sin of being an absent father to my daughter, who is beautiful, by the way. She has had to grow up thinking that her father did not want or love her. I know she has likely felt lonely, rejected, and unlovable by the key man in her life. I pray, Lord, that you have guarded her heart from any of those bad feelings. I would have been a part of her life had I known about her. Please forgive my anger towards Vernadine. I know she was only doing what she felt was the best thing to do. I know she knew I did not love her enough to marry her and she felt her hands were tied. I know she was afraid and embarrassed, but dang it, she kept all of this from me and I am so angry. I would have figured something out. I feel so guilty and ashamed. Please help me, Lord, as I return home and face my wife with this news. I need your help now, probably more than ever. I know I cannot change what has happened, but I ask you to go before me and soothe the hearts of my loved ones. I pray You give me the right words to say and the right way to say them. Thank you, Lord, Amen."

The minute Slim finished his prayer and opened his eyes, it startled him to see someone standing there. "Slim, are you okay?" Sheriff Frank 'Bull' Smith yelled from outside the truck window. "Marigold called the station hours ago in a panic. She said you walked out of Mrs. Ruth's café last night and you looked like you were in a trance of some sort and you were white as a sheet. She said you said nothing to her or anyone before you walked outside and drove off in your truck to parts unknown. Are you sick? Should I drive you to the County hospital?"

Slim stared ahead, not looking at the Sheriff, and said, "No Bull, I am not sick and I don't need to go to the hospital. In fact, I was just about to head towards home. I must have lost track of time. I am sorry you had to spend your time looking for me, but I am fine. I just needed some time to think about some things alone."

"Can I help you with anything? Or lend an ear to my old pal? You know I am a good listener and I will swear on my badge and oath to keep our conversation private and confidential. Slim, we have known each other all of our lives and this sort of behavior is not like you. Does this have anything to do with the re-appearance of Vernadine today at the café?"

Bull waited for Slim's response. He could just see the wheels turning in Slim's head as he was trying to figure out what to say to Bull.

"No, it's nothing about Vernadine, even though, like everyone else, it shocked me to see her again after fifteen years and no word from her all of this time. Did you hear she has a daughter? She's beautiful, her name is Sheridan. And, did you hear how different Vernadine looks and acts and that she is driving that fancy Lincoln convertible around town, kicking up dust everywhere she goes? You wouldn't even recognize her. It's amazing, the transformation. She is a big-city girl now, with all the drippings of success and money and refinement. By the look on everyone's faces at the café, they were all shocked, too. Just wait until you see her. You will not believe it. She said she is here because her father, Mr. Fletcher, is very sick and her mother needs help. I heard he had a massive stroke or something serious like that? Anyway, what a crazy idea asking you if you have heard! Of course you have. I forgot, for a minute, where we live, there are no secrets in this town." Slim reached across the cab seat and grabbed his keys and put them in the ignition, ready to turn the switch.

"So," Bull said, "You are sure you are okay? You still didn't give me a clue on what in the devil is wrong with you? But if you don't want to talk about it now, I am here anytime you get ready. I am very curious to see Vernadine and her daughter. I can't wait to see what all the fuss is about. Goodbye, Slim," Bull walked to his patrol car, pulled away from the creek bank, and disappeared into the storm. Slim cranked his truck, mumbled another quick prayer, and turned his truck towards home. He knew he was going to need all the spiritual help he could get to face the storm approaching his home.

When Slim pulled into his driveway he noticed a light shining through the living room window. He knew Marigold was sitting on the couch waiting for him. Slim opened the squeaky screened door and fumbled with his keys. Upon opening the door, through tears and a smile, Marigold welcomed him home and explained her fears and anxiety over the last few hours. She grabbed him and clung to him tightly. She looked over his body and face for apparent signs of injury. When she reconciled herself to his well-being, she said, exasperated, "Where have you been? I have been worried sick for hours. I finally called the Sheriff's office for help. You have never done this before! Are you okay?"

In a quiet and resigned voice, Slim said, "yes, Bull found me beside the creek bank and told me you had called frantically looking for me. You have been so worried about me, and I am sorry. I am okay. I just needed some space and time to myself to think. I know in all of our years together, I have never walked out on you or left you stranded. I am sorry for that, and I hope you will forgive me. You and our family are everything to me, and I would never want to hurt any of you. I know none of this makes any sense to you. My behavior, I mean. It's been a long and fretful night. Maybe it's best if I just go to bed and we can talk after I get some rest and clear my mind?"

Slim took off his shoes and socks, and Marigold said, "No sir, this is not something that can wait. You owe me an explanation of what is going on with you! I will make some coffee and breakfast. I am sure you are hungry. Remember, you left the restaurant before eating? Not that you may remember, because you looked demon possessed as you walked out on me." Marigold turned and walked to the kitchen without leaving Slim time to respond. He knew she meant business, and there was no way of getting out of this. He quickly thought of a few excuses he could throw out to her that she might just believe and settle her down for a while; but none of them sounded real or believable, so he settled down in his recliner to wait for his coffee and breakfast and Marigold. What he really wanted was sleep and more quiet. Talking to Bull was straining enough, but this conversation with Marigold would completely drain him.

After a few minutes, Marigold returned with the coffee and breakfast and waited for him to eat a couple of bites. In between sips of coffee and a bite of food, she said, "Well, what is happening with you?"

Slim wiped his mouth with his napkin and took a deep breath. "It was crazy seeing Vernadine last night, wasn't it? You didn't meet her before she left town, but she was really different back then. I mean physically different and really, everything different from what you saw last night. You have heard me tell you the stories about the 'queen of basketball' and our championships in 1943 and 1944, and when we graduated high school the gymnasium was re-named for her, and the beginning of that summer when you came to town and I met you at church? "Yes, I remember all of that." Marigold said. "Well, we had been boyfriend and girlfriend for over a year by the time we graduated. We thought we were in love. We planned and dreamed and talked about what young people in love talk about. She was a great girl. Few people recognized that about her, but I knew. She was not typical in any stretch of the imagination. Maybe that's what fascinated me about her, initially. But the more time I spent with her, the better I got to know her. I realized underneath her gruff exterior was a tender and loving heart. She was the one who invited me to church with her, and that's where I met Jesus. Right there at the First Believers Victory Church, sitting in a pew next to Vernadine and her parents. So, the Sunday I went with some friends to First Methodist, the day we met, was the last day I saw or talked to Vernadine. I knew that morning, sitting in church, looking at you, that I could not fully give my heart to Vernadine. I knew I would try any means possible to catch your eye and heart. I also knew because I was feeling this way about another girl, one that I didn't even know, that it would be wrong to marry Vernadine. So, that same afternoon after the picnic on the grounds, I called her house asking to see her. When I arrived and saw her in her best dress, with makeup on and her hair styled, I knew I was in trouble. I knew I would break her heart that afternoon. We took a walk down the dirt road in front of her house and I made up lame excuses and lies why we could not marry. I didn't tell her it was because of you, or the potential of you, or that I didn't love her enough to marry her. No, I just lied and told her I needed time to figure out my future because I didn't know what I was going to do with my life. The conversation was one sided. She didn't say a word. But as she stood up and walked away, she was crying. I felt like the worst person on earth. She did not deserve my cowardly behavior, but I was seventeen and stupid and wrong. After that day, she just disappeared. She has been gone for fifteen years without a trace. Then, you and I began dating and got married, and well, you know what happened. I have never regretted marrying you. You need to know this is not about that. I did not see Vernadine today and feel like I had made a mistake in the path I chose or the wonderful life we have had together. Nothing at all about me and you." Slim took another sip of his coffee and cleared his throat.

"Well," Marigold asked, "then what is this about?"

"When Vernadine and I were dating, we were normal teenagers. One evening, we sought a place to be alone during a break between games at the 1944 Championship tournament in Tuscaloosa. One thing led to another and, well, you know what I am trying to say? I swear it only happened one time, because after that, I started going to church with her and her parents and we decided it was best to not place ourselves in tempting situations, and we didn't. We wanted to remain as pure as we could after compromising purity, if that's possible. So all these years have passed and not one word from or about her, other than the ridiculous rumors that circulated around town. Seeing her today was not what I expected at all, and then when we talked, she told me a story."

Marigold was on the edge of the couch, waiting for more words. "I asked her where she has been for all of these years? She told me after talking on the dirt road, she left town. She moved to Mobile and has been living with her aunt all of this time working as a real estate agent. She has been successful, as you could see, by her car and clothes and refinement. Did you notice the young lady with her? She introduced me to her fifteen-year-old daughter, Sheridan."

The lights went on in Marigold's mind, and her eyes opened wide. She braced herself for the news she feared was coming. 'Fifteen years', she thought to herself. By doing quick math in her head, she knew what he was about to tell her.

"Marigold, Vernadine, disappeared because she was pregnant. Pregnant with my child. I swear I had no idea about any of it. I feel terrible for the pain I caused Vernadine and Sheridan. She has grown up without a father. Without me. And I have left Vernadine to carry the load alone." Marigold stood up from the couch and began pacing the floor. Wiping her face and eyes with her handkerchief. Slim knew he had deeply wounded her and that nothing he said could take away the shock and the pain. He sat there, staring as Marigold remained silent, while streams of tears rolled down her cheeks.

Marigold turned around and faced Slim. "You mean to tell me that you have lived with me for years, and you never let me know this happened between you and Vernadine? You took vows with me, pledging loyalty, honesty, purity and faithfulness, 'til death do us part' in front of God and witnesses. When we sat together with my father in pre-marital counseling, did it not occur to you to be completely honest with me about all of your past? Why didn't you tell me, Slim? Did you think I would walk out? That I would look at you differently or tell you goodbye? Is it the same cowardice in you that made you lie to me like you lied to Vernadine? Did you have so little faith in me and our love that you felt it was best to start our life together with a lie? Let's just get it all out right now! What else have you lied about? Why should I believe you now, even if you swore on the Bible? Is this your only lie to me?"

Marigold turned and headed out of the living room and said, "On second thought, maybe it is best to talk later! Much later. I will say things to you now that will be hurtful." And with that, she was gone. Slim heard the bedroom door close and lock. He turned out the light beside his chair and fought demons in his mind, unsure of what would happen next.

A few hours later, Slim was awakened by rustling in the kitchen and the laughter of his children. He rose from his chair and stretched his back. Every part of his body hurt, but the overwhelming sadness in his heart from the conversation with Marigold was a more painful hurt. He wished there was a pill for the pain he felt, but he knew there wasn't. He knew he would have to sort everything out with prayer and conversation with Marigold. When Marigold heard Slim enter the kitchen, she didn't turn around to greet him with her usual cheerful and happy demeanor. Instead, she stood steadfastly at the stove. Slim walked to the coffeepot and poured him a cup of warm courage and energy.

"Hello, Marigold. How did you rest?" He knew that was a dumb question, so he walked over to her and gently touched Marigold's shoulders and slowly turned her around to face him. He noticed her eyes were swollen, and she was quietly weeping. He pulled her to him and hugged her. She nestled her face into Slim's chest and continued to cry.

"Marigold, my love, I am so sorry for not telling you about me and Vernadine. I did not know my mistake in not telling you would cause this much pain. Yes, I was afraid of losing you. I was afraid that you would find me unworthy of your love. I wanted to tell you, but I was too afraid of the outcome, because I loved you more than anything else in the world. I was in disbelief that you, this beautiful girl, would want to marry me. So, I decided not to tell you. Losing you would have devastated me. The life that we have built together is beautiful, and I wouldn't want to do anything to harm or destroy it! I was not trying to be deceitful, but yes, I was a coward. After time passed, I didn't think about what Vernadine and I did anymore, and I figured that my lie would be hidden forever. But now, I see I am not free from my lie and that I have hurt you. Can you please try to understand? You know me, Marigold. I know it's hard to believe me right now, but please try to find it in your heart to forgive me." Slim wiped his eyes then stepped away from Marigold, waiting to see if she would say anything.

Through the tears in her eyes, Slim could see her facial expression soften. He could see the love through her tears and he smiled, feeling relieved. "Slim, I have not slept one wink. I have cried and prayed and cried and prayed more, trying to find peace in my heart over this news, not only of Vernadine and what y'all did, but also about your daughter, Sheridan. This has been the worst situation we have ever faced together. I know we are blessed more than we know because marriage has difficulties and arguments and discord, but somehow, we have escaped trying times. We have lived in harmony and trust and love. For that, I am very thankful. We have a beautiful family together, and God has been so good to us. Now, in light of the situation, it's even clearer to me how blessed we are. I know you are a good man. I know you are trustworthy and honest and live by your convictions. You have taken care of me and our children without complaint and you have loved us deeply. You show your love to us all constantly and we are a happy family. I know there is nothing we can do to change the circumstances we are in. It's all in the past, but what we have to face is the future. You have a daughter who does not know her father, a daughter who has a part of her past as one big question mark, and that makes me sad for her and for you. I have enough love in my heart and enough forgiveness in my heart to accept the facts as they are. Our family just grew by one overnight, and we will figure out how to bring Sheridan into our family in a way that is comfortable for her. She ultimately has to decide to be a part of our family, so we can't force the issue. We can offer her acceptance and love, and leave it to her to decide. Sheridan has absolutely nothing to do with how she came into this world, and she is not the one at fault. She deserves to know her father and you deserve to know your daughter. I think you should call Vernadine and ask to meet Sheridan somewhere private, but only if Vernadine agrees. Tell her about our conversation. Ask Vernadine if she would talk to Sheridan about properly meeting you, so she can get the full story from both of you about her unknown past." Marigold wiped her eyes again and sat down at the table.

"Marigold, you are a genuine gift among women. I have had all sorts of bad scenarios playing in my head about how this would go today, but you have exceeded my hopes and brought me even more joy and peace. Thank you for loving me the way you do and for your understanding, even though it's hard to do. I will call Vernadine this morning and see what she will agree to. Thank you, my beautiful and loving wife. I will keep you involved in each step and no more secrets, Ok?" Slim pulled her close and kissed her sweetly on the head, then sat back in his chair, rejoicing at his gift from God and the miracle of love, mercy, grace and forgiveness. 'Hopefully,' he thought, Vernadine would be agreeable to their plan.

Sheridan Learns the Truth

"Sheridan, dear, are you awake?" Vernadine knocked and spoke through the door.

"Yes, Ma'am, I am," Sheridan said softly.

"Please come to the kitchen after you dress? Your Grandmother and I would like to talk to you while you eat your breakfast. Your Granny made my favorite cinnamon nut coffee cake and I can't wait for you to try it," Vernadine smiled as she spoke.

"Yes ma'am, I will be right there. I am starving!" Sheridan said, with more strength in her voice.

Vernadine walked towards the kitchen and stopped by her father's bedroom to check on him, and upon opening the door she could see he had not moved since last night. With her shoulders slumped, she walked over and took his hand and stroked it gently, and began speaking softly to him. "Good morning, Daddy. I hope you are doing better today. I know you can't talk to me and I understand, but I pray God is healing you on the inside, this very minute, and you will be your old self soon. It's a beautiful sunny July morning with a gentle breeze blowing. Momma's wind chimes are swaying and singing on the back porch, and the fresh laundry is flapping in the wind. Here, let me open the window so you can feel the morning breeze and hear the chimes."

Vernadine opened the window and stared at the beauty of her old home place. So many memories flooded her mind of the loving and peaceful home of her childhood. She looked at the clothesline where her mother had hung the wash this morning like she has all these years, and it was at that same clothes line where they hatched their 'plan' for Mobile and her leaving town. After a few more minutes of reflection, she turned around and said, "I will check on you later, Daddy, I love you," she said as she closed the door and walked down the hall to the kitchen where Sheridan was happily chatting away with her grandmother and already asking for a second slice of the coffee cake.

"Good morning, my beautiful one. I hope you rested well. I slept like a baby. I can't remember when I have slept so well! So, I see you like the coffee cake?" Vernadine kissed Sheridan on the cheek and tousled her hair, and poured another cup of coffee before sitting down.

"Oh momma, you are right about the coffee cake, it's delicious! You know I have always loved Aunt Marie's blueberry coffee cake, but Granny's cinnamon cake is making my choice a hard one to make!" Sheridan said with a mouthful of cake.

"Yes, I love Aunt Marie's blueberry coffee cake too! It's amazing how certain foods and smells can wrap you in the softest and most loving blanket." Just as if on cue, the telephone rang and Vernadine heard the loving, yet weakened voice of Aunt Marie. "Oh, hello, Aunt Marie! We were just talking about you. How are you feeling?" Vernadine asked as she sat down with a smile on her face.

"Oh, I am fine. Just tired most of the time, but I am still kicking. I called to check on Fletcher. How is he?" Aunt Marie asked in labored breaths.

"Well, he is not doing well, but we are hoping for a recovery however long that will take. Sheridan and I will be here for a while to help Momma take care of him. He has a great doctor, and we are trying our best to follow his directions. I will call you every couple of days to check on you and keep you updated on Daddy. Do you need anything? Your Pastor and members of your church know you are alone, and I hope they are checking on you like they said they would? I am not sure how long we will be here, but I am only a phone call away. Remember, I left my phone number in the kitchen beside the telephone in case anyone needs to contact me. We love you, Aunt Marie."

"I love you too, Child. I will be perfectly fine and I have regular visitors from the church, so I feel attended to. I will talk to you in a day or so." And with that, Aunt Marie hung up the phone.

Vernadine sat back down at the table, grabbed Sheridan's hand and said, "Momma, Sheridan knows who her father is. I told her everything yesterday afternoon on the car ride here. It was time to tell her what happened and why. Then, after seeing Slim at the café last night, I could tell from Sheridan's facial expression, even before Slim said one word, she knew he was her father. I told Slim Sheridan is his daughter. I did not leave him any time to speak or ask questions. We bolted out of there as fast as we could, leaving him standing in the middle of the café dumbfounded and white as a sheet. Sheridan knows why we decided it was best for me to move away and what part you and daddy played in the plan. I confirmed Slim's identity to Sheridan once we started the drive home from the café."

Irene began softly weeping tears of relief. Relief Sheridan finally had all the answers to the questions that had loomed and haunted her entire life. Relief the mystery was solved and hopefully she could begin to move forward in her heart with peace and hope. Sheridan touched the top of her grandmother's hand and softly said, "Granny, it's all okay. I understand now why everything happened the way it did. I am not upset at any of you for making the decision you thought was best for Momma and me. In fact, I see bravery, love, commitment and sacrifice in what the three of you did. And, Aunt Marie. She took a risk, too. All for me and Momma. I still have questions, but I am at peace with what I have learned. Thank you for loving us." Sheridan hugged her mother and grandmother tightly as the telephone ringing jolted them back to present.

"Hello, Turnipseed residence." "Hello, Mrs. Turnipseed, this is Slim Perkins. I am sorry to hear about Mr. Turnipseed. Is he doing okay?"

"Hello, Slim, thank you. No, he does not seem to be improving from the stroke, but we are keeping a check on him, and the Doctor comes over every day," Irene replied.

"Well, I am sorry. I know this has to be a difficult time for all of you." There was a pause and Irene knew why…. "Mrs. Turnipseed, may I speak to Vernadine?" Slim asked.

Irene held the receiver in her hand and covered it to muffle her voice.

"Slim wants to speak to you!" Irene whispered loudly. "Do you want to talk to him?"

Vernadine was completely drained. The events over the last two days had taken a toll on her mental strength, but she knew she had to take the call and hear what Slim had to say to her. She owed him that much. "Yes, Momma, I will take the call. I will talk to him in the living room. Just hang this phone up when you hear me answer the other one, please." Vernadine pulled herself up from the table and looked at Sheridan on her way out.

"Hello Slim," Vernadine said. There were no 'how are you's' or 'isn't this a pleasant morning'. There was no need for niceties or formalities now.

"Vernadine, I need to talk to you about Sheridan. I need to know why you didn't tell me you were pregnant! Why didn't you let me know? I can't get over the shock of learning I have a daughter that I knew nothing about. You lied to me, or covered up the truth. I have been robbed of knowing my daughter. Oh, I have thought about the 'why's' and 'what for's' all night, sitting beside the riverbank, and I can understand why you were scared and didn't know what to do, but me not knowing is heartbreaking and pure meanness on your part. I want you to know I have told Marigold everything. Of course, she was upset initially, but more at my not telling her you and I had an intimate relationship than over the news about Sheridan." Slim took a deep breath and continued. "I stayed up all night going through our past, wondering why I didn't know about the pregnancy and how could I have missed something so big and important. For all of these years, did it ever occur to you to tell me about our daughter? The Vernadine I remember was kind and sweet and honest; not cunning and secretive. Your silence has deceived not only me and Sheridan, but others too. Marigold told me this morning she accepts Sheridan and will welcome her into our family if Sheridan wants to get to know us, her other family. We want her to know she is welcome at any time, for as long as she wants. Vernadine, I would like to meet Sheridan properly and sit down and talk to her. I want to know who she is and she deserves to know who her father is. "Would you agree to arrange a time and place to meet today or tomorrow?" Slim asked, waiting for Vernadine to speak.

"Yes, I will talk to her and ask her. I told her I would not make her do anything she didn't feel comfortable with in regards to meeting you or trying to build a relationship with you. So, I say all of this to let you know, it's up to her. I will tell her what you have said and I will ask her what she wants to do. I will call you after I talk to her. As far as not telling you about my pregnancy, I wanted to, but after the last talk we had on the dirt road, and your cool demeanor towards me, I couldn't tell you. I must have misunderstood our relationship. We had talked and planned and dreamed of a future together, so naturally I expected you to propose marriage to me that afternoon, to tell me you had everything planned out. I wanted to marry you, live our lives together, and raise our child. Do you really think I wanted to leave Spit's Creek, you, my family, and everything I had ever known? No! Is the short answer. Do you think I could remain here not married and pregnant? I left here scared to death, moved to a city alone, with nothing but a suitcase and fifty dollars to my name. You are angry? Don't talk to me about your anger. I was devastated. I have waited years for the opportunity to tell you how angry and hurt I was. Imagine, if you can, how you would have felt if you were in my shoes? Imagine, if you can, how you might have done something different if you were me? Thankfully I had a place to go. A safe and loving home away from the gossip, shame, and shunning that I and my family would have suffered had I remained in town and all because of a few minutes in the back of a school bus with a boy. The shame and embarrassment would have crushed me and my family. And Sheridan, growing up a laughingstock. A bastard child with a respected and well known mother. No, Slim. If I had told you about the baby, most likely you would have asked me to marry you under obligation and not from a real desire to be my husband. Oh, we may have had a tolerable life together, but who wants just tolerable in a marriage? Not me. I had to leave, Slim. I could not see any other pleasant option. I left without you knowing because that was just how it had to be. When I heard the news about your marriage to Marigold I was crushed. Salt poured into an open wound is an excruciating pain. Because you married so soon after my departure, I knew I had made the right decision to leave. You did not love me enough to marry me and you could not bring yourself to tell me. I understand your anger and resentment, but I felt I had no choice but to go alone and leave you here. I don't really care how you feel now or how you felt then. The decision to leave was the best decision, under the circumstances." Vernadine said.

"As difficult as this is to wrap my mind around, I understand, or I am trying to, really I am. I will wait for your call. Thank you, Vernadine." Slim said as he hung up the phone.

Vernadine returned to the kitchen to two expectant faces.

"Well, what did he say?" Irene asked.

"Slim wants to meet Sheridan and talk to her. He would like to get to know her and he wants Sheridan to know him. Slim is upset, as I would expect, but he said he is trying to understand why I left without telling him about the pregnancy. I was able to get some things off of my chest, and right or wrong, I have waited years to tell him my side of the story. I let him know I didn't care if he was upset or not. Facts are facts. I told Slim I would talk to you, Sheridan, and see what you want to do. I told him it was completely up to you to see him or not. I will not force you to do anything you don't want to. I told him I would call him back after talking to you with your answer," Vernadine sighed as she spoke.

The three of them sat at the table in silence. They stared at each other, at the walls, at the cake, at the vinyl tablecloth with small strawberries on it, just waiting to see what Sheridan would say. No one moved, except for Irene as she circled her wrinkled hands around and around. Finally after a few minutes, Sheridan inhaled and Vernadine and Irene sat straight up in their chairs in anticipation.

"Momma, thank you, for finally telling me the truth about Mr. Perkins. I am relieved to finally know the identity of my father. I have had to stand by and watch my friends hug their fathers, talk about their fathers, and have their fathers take them to daddy-daughter dances at school. I have been sad many times about not having a father. I have cried myself to sleep so many nights that I have lost count. Oh, please don't get me wrong, I love you so much, Momma. You are the best momma a girl could have. You have been my everything, and you have always let me know I am your everything too, but it's not the same. I have imagined and witnessed how a father's love and attention to his daughter is different from a mother's love and attention. I have felt empty and lonely for a father's love." Sheridan wiped her eyes with her grandmother's handkerchief and lay her head down on the table.

Vernadine sat quietly while Sheridan spoke. She knew everything Sheridan said was true because she knew the love of a father that her daughter didn't. Her heart broke as she listened to her daughter. Vernadine raised Sheridan's head and said, "Sheridan, Honey, it's okay what you are telling me. I completely understand and in no way am I upset or are my feelings hurt. I hurt for you," Vernadine reassured Sheridan as she waited for her to continue.

"Thank you, Momma. I know it's hard to hear what I am saying, just like it's hard for me to tell you, but it is the truth," Sheridan sniffled.

"I know, Sheridan, it's ok. I love you dearly and I will be completely fine with whatever decision you make about talking to your father." Vernadine touched Sheridan's hand. "What would you like to do?"

Irene blew her nose and wiped her eyes. She had been here before, at this table, making life-changing decisions with Vernadine, and now she sits with Sheridan at her important crossroad. Her heart ached for both of them, so she remained as quiet as she could and offered love and support. She smiled lovingly at Sheridan as she waited for her to answer.

"I want to talk to Mr. Perkins, Momma. Can you please ask him if he can talk this afternoon, here in the front living room, around 3 o'clock?," Sheridan said.

"Yes, that sounds just fine. I will call him now." Vernadine rose from the table, grabbed the telephone book, found Slim's number, and dialed the phone.

The telephone rang and a woman answered the phone. "Hello, is this Marigold? This is Vernadine Turnipseed. Is Slim available?"

"Hello, Vernadine. Yes, this is Marigold. Slim is available, just one minute," Marigold said politely.

"Hello, Vernadine," Slim said.

"Hello, Slim. I spoke with Sheridan and she has agreed to see you. She wants to know if you can come over to our house at 3 o'clock this afternoon? You two can talk privately in the living room," Vernadine said.

"Yes, that will be just fine. I will be there. Do you happen to know Sheridan's favorite flower? I would like to bring her a bouquet," Slim said.

"Well, let's see. I know she loves tulips and daisies, but since its summer, you will not be able to find tulips, so daisies will be just fine. Her favorite color is green, just in case you add a bow. We will see you at 3 o'clock. Thank you, Slim, Goodbye."

Vernadine hung up the phone and realized her head was swimming and her stomach was in a knot. All of the excitement from the morning had taken its toll on all three of them. Vernadine turned around to face Sheridan and said, "He will be here at 3 PM to talk to you. I told him you two would have your privacy, so don't worry about me or feel you cannot be the completely beautiful, smart and funny young lady you truly are. Your father is a very nice man. Talking to him over the last two days has reminded me of that. You will be in safe hands. I want you to talk about anything you are curious about. Hold nothing back, because I know he is curious to know everything about you, too. Now, if y'all will excuse me, I think I will lie down for a while. My head is hurting," Vernadine hugged her daughter and her mother, and turned to walk to her bedroom.

Once she closed the door, she drew the curtains for darkness and lay on her bed and cried tears of relief, and joy, and sadness all at once. Vernadine knew a burden had been lifted from her heart and mind; a burden she had carried for years. She was happy the air was clear and the truth exposed. She was relieved for the opportunity to finally tell Slim what happened and why. She was happy her daughter could now know she has a father who loves her and wants be involved in her life. As her mind raced and prayers of gratitude rolled out of her heart to the Lord, she drifted into a peaceful sleep.

The Long Awaited Reunion

Spit's Creek
July 1960

Sheridan rose from the breakfast table on a cloud of excitement and nervousness, with lots of questions in her mind. "What if my father doesn't like me? Will he think I am pretty? Will he think I am smart? Is he proud of the person I am becoming? Is he upset I've been gone for so long? Is he wondering why I didn't try to find him?!" Sheridan mused.

Before leaving the kitchen, Sheridan thanked her grandmother for a wonderful breakfast and for her support and love. She expressed her gratitude for helping her mother keep her secret. To spare her the embarrassment and shame in the face of the community. She knew it had not been easy for her grandparents remaining in Spit's Creek with the questions, rumors and stares from neighbors and friends. She hugged her grandmother and told her she loved her.

Irene had been holding back tears and nerves all morning, but with Sheridan's kind words, she fell apart and said "Oh, my dear child, your grandfather and I didn't know what to do to protect Vernadine, so we did the first thing we could think of and called your Aunt Marie for help. We didn't want to send her, alone and scared, to a home for unmarried and pregnant girls."

What Irene didn't tell Sheridan about 'the plan' was her mother was supposed to give her up for adoption after her birth. Irene knew this part of the plan would crush Sheridan if she knew and it was best to leave that crucial and hurtful detail out. Irene came out of reflection and continued.

"But when your mother walked into the house that Sunday afternoon after going for a walk with your father, we knew something had gone wrong and that our 'plan' would have to accelerate. When your momma got on that bus, I thought I would die from heartbreak. I thought, 'there goes my only child, to a city she doesn't know, pregnant with my grandchild, alone and scared.' It was a frightening time. We made it through, day by day and year by year. If you could have seen the transformation your momma made after leaving here, you wouldn't believe it! I know, I will get some old photo albums out and show you pictures of your momma from her younger years after supper! Ok?" Irene said with excitement.

Sheridan was overwhelmed with all the activity from the last two days, but it surprised her at how optimistic and jubilant she felt. She was looking forward to listening to her father tell her about his life. She couldn't wait to see the pictures of her mother, to learn more about her past; and she hoped, starting today, there would be no more mysteries and questions about her family. She felt the missing pieces of her heart falling into place, and that made her very happy.

It was 1 PM before the morning's excitement quieted down. Sheridan wanted to look her best when her father arrived, so she gathered her bathing items and drew a full tub of very warm water for a long relaxing bath. She pinned her hair up, poured her favorite bubble bath and watched in delight as the bubbles formed. She tip-toed into the warm water and relished happy thoughts until the water chilled.

After her rejuvenating bath, she looked through her dresses and decided on a lavender one with a small white bow on the hip. She brushed her hair and teased the top. She rubbed a light coating of rose colored lip gloss on her lips and finished her look with white sandals and a pearl necklace. She looked at herself and felt pleased. Surely her father would agree?

At 3 PM on the dot, the doorbell rang and Vernadine answered the door to a smiling and fidgety Slim.

"Hello, Slim. Thank you for coming. Sheridan is ready and she will be with you in a minute. You can have a seat in the living room. I have some lemonade and oatmeal cookies, and I will bring it in for you two in a moment," Vernadine smiled as she departed the room.

Slim felt excited and nervous. He couldn't wait to sit with his daughter and learn about her, but he did not know what Sheridan had been told about him over the years or if she had wrong impressions he would have to overcome. So, he sat down, took a long breath, stared at the bouquet of daisies, and mumbled a quick prayer.

"Lord, thank you for today. This is a special day for me. Lord, please help me say the right things to Sheridan so she will know I love her and that I am not a bad guy. Amen."

As Slim was finishing his prayer, he heard footsteps walking towards the living room. He braced himself.

"Hello, Mr. Perkins," Sheridan said shyly.

"Hello, Sheridan. Thank you for agreeing to see me. I have to admit I am nervous, so please forgive my jitters. Oh! These are for you. I hope you like them. Your mother said tulips and daisies are your favorite flowers." Slim's hands trembled as he handed her the bouquet.

"I love daisies! Thank you for coming. I am nervous, too, so we will both fumble our words, but it's ok." She put the flowers on the table and sat down.

Vernadine arrived with the lemonade and cookies and placed them on the coffee table and closed the door on her way out to give them the privacy she promised. Vernadine mumbled a prayer as she returned to the kitchen to sit at the table with her mother.

"You are lovely, Sheridan. I noticed our strong resemblance yesterday at the café. My thirteen-year-old daughter looks like me, too. I can't wait for you to meet my other daughters. I mean, only if you want to. My wife's name is Marigold. I am sorry about your grandfather. He has always been nice. So, tell me about you!" Slim reached for the lemonade and poured two glasses and offered one to Sheridan.

"Well, I attend an all-girl high school, I play softball, and am involved in my church and youth group. I have delightful friends, and I love living in Mobile. The oak trees, with the draping Spanish moss, lining the streets, are a sight to behold. It's very different from here, or at least the city is. Momma and I live in Aunt Marie's house. It's a cottage in a beautiful neighborhood. Momma's real estate office is just a few blocks away, along with other shops and a grocery store. My school is close by, so I walk to school with two or three of my classmates every morning and afternoon. Oh, and my birthday is on December twenty-third. I am a Christmas baby," she beamed at the thought. "We are staying here the rest of the summer so momma can help Granny with Grandpa. Hopefully I can meet new friends while I am here," Sheridan took a minute to catch her breath. "Does your church have a youth group? I think I would like to go so I can meet some new friends," Sheridan said.

"Oh yes, we have a large youth group at First Methodist church. You can go with us in the morning if you would like. We can pick you up at 8:45 AM and go to Sunday school and church service. You are welcome to bring a change of clothes and come over to our house for lunch so you can get to know your half-sisters and Marigold. Marigold is a wonderful cook and her Sunday lunches are always a large spread. How does that sound to you?" Slim asked.

"That sounds like fun! Let me see if momma has other plans for us." She jumped up and ran out of the living room.

Slim knew getting to know each other would take longer than the lemonade and cookies would allow, and he felt comfortable knowing that in time, they could build a bond between them. Sheridan came back into the room. "Momma said that would be fine for me to go with y'all tomorrow. I will look forward to it."

Slim had a lot to say to Sheridan. He wanted her to hear his side of the story about his relationship with Vernadine and why everything happened the way it did. "Sheridan, I want you to know, if your mother had told me she was pregnant I would not have let her walk away that afternoon on the dirt road. I knew I was very fond of your mother, and we had discussed marriage a few times, but I got nervous and began having second thoughts; I didn't want to rush into anything, being so young and all. But, had I known about you, I would have taken your momma to the preacher that afternoon and we would have married and provided a family for you. There are things I still need to explain to your mother about what was going on with me that day, and the days leading up to our walk, because she deserves to hear the truth. I knew your mother was a great gal. She is talented and funny, misunderstood and special. I knew she loved me enough to marry me, and she would have made a great wife. But in the middle of my confusion I met Marigold at church the morning of the afternoon walk with your mother. After seeing Marigold that morning, and the attraction I felt towards her, I knew it would be wrong to commit to your mother when I felt excitement over another girl. I knew I had upset your mother when she walked away from me crying. But now I know all the details about the pregnancy and about you, and I feel terrible. Your mother didn't deserve to be hurt and cast aside. I swear I am so disappointed in myself. I saw none of the clues about her condition. She gave me no hints about a pregnancy. As you can figure out, because I was distracted by Marigold I couldn't marry your mother. But I loved your mother enough to marry her if I had known about you. I know my words and sentiments must seem jumbled and confusing to you, and I sound like a complete jerk. I understand if you feel anger towards me; you deserve to. I hurt your mother. Your mother has loved you, taken care of you, and molded you into this smart and loving young woman. I am not proud of myself, but I am proud of Vernadine and of you. Your mother has soared and grown into a beautiful woman in her own right. She has taken life by the horns, in spite of her circumstances, and has made a life so much grander than anything she could have had by staying here in Spit's Creek. I am very proud of everything your mother has accomplished. She was always bigger than this town, even though she didn't know it, but she was and still is. I hope you can try and understand what I am saying. With all of my heart, I pray you can muster the strength and desire to forgive me for not being a part of your life for these fifteen years. I hope we can move forward and try to get to know each other and love each other as fathers and daughters do. I know our relationship is scarred, but can you find it in your heart to get to know me and my family?" Slim paused, took a deep breath and relaxed his furrowed brow, waiting anxiously for Sheridan to respond.

Sheridan knew Slim was waiting on her to speak, but her thoughts ran like a wildfire in her head, not one of them in a coherent sentence. Her head was spinning out of control thinking about her mother on the dirt road, feeling alone and rejected and scared and most of all, heartbroken. She knew her mother would not have been the sort to fool around with boys inappropriately, so because she was pregnant with Slim's baby, she knew her mother had to have strong emotional ties to him; that she had loved him enough to compromise her purity with him. That she wanted to marry him. She thought of her mother's vulnerability and her young heart with dreams and plans for the future with Slim and how they were crushed that afternoon. The betrayal her mother must have felt was painful to think about. She couldn't wrap her mind around the details her father just told her. She knew she needed time to think. There were questions for him, but they would have to wait. So, she sat up straight, inhaled and said, "Mr. Perkins, thank you for seeing me this afternoon, I appreciate it. But the truth of the matter is I need time to think about everything you have said. I have questions, but I just don't know what they are right now. I am going to take some time to myself and think. Thank you for the invitation for tomorrow's church and lunch visit, but I need to stay home instead. I hope you understand. Like you, I, too, have a lot to consider and process. I am feeling a headache coming on, so if you don't mind, I will excuse myself." She quietly walked out of the room, leaving Slim on the couch. She passed her mother, but neither of them spoke. She retreated to her bedroom and closed the door.

Vernadine had been eavesdropping on Sheridan and Slim from the hallway, and she heard every word that was spoken. She was thankful for the handkerchief she grabbed at the last minute, because she had needed it to muffle her tears and gasps from Slim's confessions and recollections from that fateful day that changed everyone's life. She knew Slim was sitting in the living room, so she wiped her face, tucked her handkerchief in her pants pocket, and rounded the corner to a devastated and tearful Slim. Upon seeing Vernadine, he quickly wiped his eyes and cleared his throat. "Hello, Vernadine. Thank you for allowing me to come over today." Slim walked to the front door, opened it, tipped his hat, and walked off the porch to his truck. Vernadine was speechless. Like Sheridan, she was just now hearing the truth from Slim. She was heartbroken all over again. Her wounds had not healed after all.

Interruptions of the Heart

Spit's Creek
July 1960

The night of rest, after an emotional and raw afternoon, did not come easily. Vernadine, Sheridan and Irene were all searching for solutions to cover the scars from the past. At 3 AM, a loud noise coming from Fletcher's bedroom shook the house. At once, all three of burst through the door to see what had happened.

The crash had come from the bed falling to the ground. Fletcher had been wrestling with his bed covers, and all the commotion caused the bed to collapse onto the floor. Fletcher was lying on the floor, tangled in bed sheets, completely still. Vernadine rushed to his side, shook him, checked his pulse and felt nothing. There was no breath, no pulse, and no Fletcher. As Vernadine laid her head on her father's chest, Irene knew her love was gone forever. Irene wailed uncontrollably and Sheridan rushed to her side, knelt beside her, and stroked her hair and back. Vernadine lay there, leaning on her father, crying heaving tears, all the while still trying to rouse her father. It was over. The pain and sickness in Fletcher's physical body was now a new body in the presence of Jesus. The only comfort to Vernadine, Irene, and Sheridan now was in knowing that truth, and knowing Fletcher was healed and happy now. It also comforted them knowing one day they would see him again in heaven. But as comforted as they were in the thoughts of that, they were human. The grief was overwhelming. Their husband, father and grandfather was no longer with them in the physical body. How were they going to carry on without his love and guidance? Irene and Fletcher had been married thirty-five years and they were each other's world. 'He died too young', were the thoughts in each of their minds. In the wailing tears, Vernadine left the bedroom to call the family doctor. Within fifteen minutes he was there and pronounced Fletcher dead.

So many thoughts were racing through Vernadine's mind. She would have to take care of her mother through this process; she would have to plan the funeral; she would somehow have to deal with the loss of her father on top of the current pain she was dealing with. She reflected on a saying 'time heals all wounds', but after today, she knew that was not completely true. Maybe the person who came up with that saying didn't suffer true loss and heartbreak? Maybe it was someone's weak attempt at trying to make someone feel better in the face of loss or devastation? But, what she knew right then was whoever came up with that saying was full of crap! She hated that person right now, because if it were true, she would not feel the way she felt from finally hearing Slim's account of their past and the opening of old wounds, and now the death of her father added more pain. 'Time doesn't heal some old wounds', she thought to herself.

Sheridan gently touched her mother on the shoulder, stroked her hair and said "Momma, the doctor is waiting for the coroner to arrive and take Grandpa's body to the funeral home, but your preacher has arrived and is sitting with Granny in the kitchen. I am so sorry, Momma. I wish there was something I could do or say to make you feel better. At least we know Grandpa is in a better place now. Momma, I know you are devastated, and you will be for a long time, but you probably should speak to the preacher and doctor. Grandma does not know what to do, and she keeps asking for you. Here, wipe your eyes with this handkerchief, and I will brush your hair and get a cool cloth for your face. I am thankful we were here to see Grandpa during his last few days and we could talk to him and thank him for all he has done for us through the years. I believe he heard us, Momma. He heard your words and felt your love. He knew his daughter and granddaughter had come home. I am sure that gave him peace and comfort to know Granny was not alone, that we were here to take care of her. He was proud of you Momma. We are all proud of you. You are the rock of this family now, and Grandpa knew he would be passing the mantle to you. It's yours now, Momma. You have to lead and direct. I know you are hurting and you don't know how you will ever adjust to not having your father here on earth. Knowing you cannot call him on the telephone or visit him in person and hear his laugh and gentle way of speaking anymore is hard to come to grips with. I know it's hard to believe this, but I do know how you feel. Being without a father all of my life has left a void in my heart, the void you are now feeling. The sadness seems to take your breath away, but you will move forward. With a lot of prayer and the love of your family, we will get through this. I know your tears are a continuation of your tears from a few hours ago. I knew you were listening in the hallway to the conversation between me and Mr. Perkins. I knew that, like me, you were hearing his side of the story for the first time. I heard you crying, Momma. I couldn't respond to Mr. Perkins because I was angry and hurt he had done this to you; that he walked away from such a wonderful person for someone else who caught his teenage boy eyes. He didn't see your true worth, Momma. Oh, he knew you were a kind and tender person, but that wasn't enough for him. He made up excuses to separate himself from you so he could move on to greener pastures. To Marigold. I know this isn't the time to talk about all of this. I just wanted you to know I know how you feel about your father, and I can understand your hurt from Mr. Perkins. But, right now, please know that I love you and we will get through this together, just like we always have. Now, let me get the brush and a cool wash cloth. You really need to go to the kitchen and start making preparations for Grandpa's funeral." Sheridan hugged her mother once more, stood up, and walked to the bathroom. There was business to attend to.

Vernadine could not help but cry another short river of tears when Sheridan left the bedroom. She thought to herself in amazement how her daughter had to be the best person she had ever known. She was so proud of her. Her maturity and clear headed thinking at fifteen was far beyond her years. Hearing her daughter tell her she understood the void in her heart over the loss of her father was heartbreaking. Knowing her daughter had carried this great sadness in her heart all of her life made her heart break, but to witness her strength was beautiful to see. Vernadine knew any more tears would have to be shed later. For now, she would listen to the guidance of her daughter and wipe her face and brush her hair. She had to face the situation and take the lead. It was time. So with a broken heart and a tear worn face, she knelt back down beside her father, kissed him on the cheek and said, "I will miss you more than words can express, Daddy. I love you so much, and I don't know what I am going to do without you. But I will take care of mother for the rest of her life. You can count on me, Daddy. My life will never be the same without you. My heart will break every single day. I am going now to take care of Momma and talk to the preacher and doctor about plans for the next step. I know you don't want a fancy coffin or elaborate funeral, so we won't do that. I will make sure we sing your favorite hymns, especially 'It Is Well with My Soul' and 'Amazing Grace'. It will be a nice funeral. You will be missed by your family, but I am so thankful to God that he picked you to be my earthly father. You have done exactly what you were instructed to do by the good Lord, and I know right now you are receiving your crown in the presence of Jesus for being a faithful follower of our Lord. I love you, Daddy. Thank you for loving me through everything." And with that, more tears needed wiping away. Vernadine made her way towards the kitchen with a heavy, but determined heart to take care of her father's burial and to comfort her grieving mother. She would get back to her own grieving heart later.

At the Crossroad

By the time the coroner, the preacher, and the ambulance left with Fletcher's body, it was 6 AM. The doctor had given Irene some medication to help her sleep and rest. She had been asleep for an hour. Vernadine knew rest would come soon enough, so she waited while the paramedics prepared to load her father's body into the ambulance. Standing there watching as her father was rolled out on a stretcher, covered in a white sheet, was almost too much to bear. She stared at the white sheet, just waiting for movement underneath, to see signs of breathing. She wanted to pull the sheet off to see her father smiling at her, wondering what all the excitement was and asking why he was covered up. She would grab him and hug him the tightest she ever had, and with tears of joy she would welcome her father back to life and gladly tell the paramedics that their work was done here, that it was a false alarm. But, no movement was to be seen. Standing at the rear of the ambulance, she watched the doors close.

Even though it was August in South Alabama, she had a chill that would not go away. Sheridan brought her a sweater from her grandmother's closet. She put it on, wrapped it around her chest and gripped the front of it, holding on for dear life. At 6:15 AM, the preacher's wife and two other ladies from the church pulled into the driveway. "Vernadine, we are so sorry for your loss. We have brought some food to leave with you and we figured while we were here, we would cook a hot breakfast. I will put the coffee on and it should be ready in a few minutes," said the Preacher's wife. The three ladies hugged Vernadine and proceeded inside. Vernadine was too tired and mentally shot to utter any words, so she just smiled slightly and nodded her head.

By this time, the ambulance was almost out of sight. She stood on her tip toes to see clear to the end of the road, knowing this was the last time her father would take this journey, down this road, ever again. When Vernadine walked inside, the aroma of the coffee stirred her senses. She noticed the phone was ringing, but one of the church ladies answered. She walked to the desk, grabbed a piece of paper and a pen and scribbled a note that read, 'Thank you for stopping by to pay your respects. We are not receiving guests. Please do not knock on the door or ring the doorbell. We are resting. Thank you.'. She signed it, Respectfully, Vernadine D. Turnipseed. She took a piece of tape from the dispenser, walked to the front door, opened it, and taped the note on the glass of the door. She walked into the kitchen to pour a cup of coffee and sat down at the table. The aroma of bacon was filling the air, and the comforting smells were like an old soft blanket to her. In between sips of coffee, she rested her head on the table and did not speak or make small talk. The telephone rang again. This was going to be a disturbance, she knew it. She hated not to respond to the folks in the community that were offering help or condolences, but after that phone conversation ended, Vernadine walked over to the receiver, took it off the hook, and laid it on the table. "Ladies," Vernadine said, "thank you for your kindness this morning and for bringing us food and cooking this delicious breakfast, but after you have completed the cooking, we would appreciate some quiet time. I don't mean to sound harsh, it's just we have been awake almost the entire night and we are very tired. I plan on trying to take a long nap after I eat." The ladies all expressed their understanding and told her they would be leaving after the dishes were washed and put away. Vernadine found it difficult to summon an appetite, but she managed to enjoy one of the warm buttermilk biscuits with orange marmalade and extra butter. It went nicely with the strong coffee. After eating a small bite, she realized how tired she was, both mentally and physically, so she put the breakfast food in the oven and left a note on the kitchen table for her mother and Sheridan. She figured they would be famished when they woke up. Vernadine tip toed into her mother's bedroom and quietly opened the sleeping pill bottle the doctor left and she took two with her to her bedroom. She didn't want to risk tossing and turning, so she swallowed the pills and chased them down with a glass of water from her bedside table. She changed into her pajamas, turned on the box fan for air and noise, turned her covers down, and crawled into the soft cotton sheets. She was asleep the minute her head hit the pillow.

It was dusk when the movement around the house woke her. She could hear her mother and Sheridan talking, and she knew she needed to get out of bed if she wanted to sleep throughout the night. She put on her bathrobe and brushed her hair and pinned it away from her pale and tired face. She felt beaten and bruised, but she made her way to the kitchen to join her family. She was pleased to see that her mother appeared rested and Sheridan was a busy-bee taking care of her grandmother. "Good evening, ladies. I hope you both got some rest. I was asleep the minute my head hit the pillow. Oh, good, you found the food in the oven. I am starving now. Another buttermilk biscuit with bacon and eggs sounds great to me. Momma, are you holding up? I know you don't want to talk about daddy's funeral, but we are going to have to. I told the preacher we would have a plan to him by tomorrow morning. So, after we eat, we can figure things out," Vernadine said while buttering her biscuit. After cleaning the kitchen, the three of them moved to the living room for comfort and discussed Fletcher's funeral. It didn't take too long to plan, as Fletcher had been specific about not wanting an elaborate funeral. After their discussion, they agreed they were all ready to retire for a night of sleep.

The next morning, Vernadine removed the sign from the front door and put the phone back on the hook. She figured their moment of quiet had lasted long enough, and any longer would insult the women who wanted to bring their casseroles and ham and other fine southern delicacies to their house. She called the preacher and gave him their requests for the service. She then called the funeral home and made an appointment to look at the coffins for later in the morning and followed up on the status of the grave digging. She told her mother the night before she would take care of all the arrangements and for her to continue to rest and grieve. Irene was thankful for Vernadine's efforts in more ways than she could express.

On the second morning after Fletcher's death, the women rose from slumber, ate a breakfast of cake and pie with strong coffee, dressed in their best Sunday dresses and loaded into Vernadine's Lincoln to make their way to the First Believers Victory Church for the funeral service and burial of their beloved Fletcher. As expected, the church was full with people paying their last respects to Fletcher. Seeing the people gathered humbled them all, and their handkerchiefs were already damp by the time the service started. Fletcher had requested the choir sing his two favorite hymns. The piano and organ accompanied the angelic voices in stirring and heartfelt song. The preacher delivered a beautiful and precise description of the man Fletcher was in this life and how missed he would be. Vernadine couldn't help but wonder why there were so many people at her father's funeral? Oh, she knew there were plenty of folks in Spit's Creek and Inner Banks that were his friends, or fellow church members, or fellow farmers, but THIS amount of people here? That made little sense to her. She recalled conversations over the years with both of her parents, especially ones right after she 'disappeared'. She remembers her mother telling her over months after she left, she found it odd and sad that her bible study class and sewing club members whispered whenever she would walk in the room, or they would 'forget' to invite her over for coffee and cookies with the rest of the group, but Irene knew what was happening to her was none other than an old fashioned shunning. She had been a faithful and active member of her church for more years than she could count; and her friends in the church were women she had known most of her life. That still did not stop the women from rabid gossip and innuendos over what had happened to Vernadine. When she began hearing the gossip about Vernadine being a German spy, and then later, rumors of her living in California with another woman basketball coach, she was crushed and insulted and betrayed. But, being the consummate southern lady, she brushed it off with a lot of prayer and forgiveness. Over time, the rumors stopped, except for the occasional inquiry about Vernadine's whereabouts. What kept the questions going was the fact that Vernadine never came home. At all.

So, here she sat, in the middle of a community gathering for her father's funeral and found herself harboring anger at some of the people sitting there. She knew in her heart her father's funeral had turned out to be a 'Vernadine side show', like a grotesque carnival act, and this made her blood boil. On the very day she is saying her final farewell to her beloved father, and feeling the sadness and loss of him, she finds herself ready to explode in her church pew as she looks around the church to see most folks staring at her and not at her father's casket or the preacher delivering the final words of goodbye for the man she loved.

Vernadine made the decision, while planning her father's funeral she would not deliver a eulogy. She knew she could not hold herself together without crying and embarrassing the family. But now, sitting here in the church of her youth, upset and angry, a eulogy she could deliver with no tears wrote itself in her mind like a flash. She stood up, right after the preacher said 'Amen' from the closing prayer and said, "Preacher, I have decided I would like to say a few words, after all, this morning to these fine folks who have taken time out of their busy schedules to honor the passing of my father, Fletcher. I would like to thank them properly. I won't be long-winded. I will get straight to the point." Vernadine turned to squeeze out of the pew, but Irene quickly threw her leg up and pushed hard on the pew in front of her to stop Vernadine from moving. Vernadine looked at her mother with a look of irritation, gritted her teeth through ruby red lips and mouthed, "It's okay, Momma, please let me by." And with a look of determination from Vernadine, Irene lowered her leg. Vernadine shifted by, Irene grabbed Sheridan's hand and squeezed it hard, praying to the Holy Ghost to diffuse the bomb she feared was about to go off. Vernadine's intentions were not pleasant and she knew it. As she walked out of the pew, the look she gave her mother told her everything she needed to know.

As Vernadine walked toward her father's casket covered with an old family quilt and family photos, she paused and thought to herself, "Are you sure this is what you want to do today? This is your daddy's funeral. You know there will be other times you can tell people what you think of them, this is your last minute to change your message. You could say, with a smile, thanks to everyone for coming and that you all will appreciate their prayers during this time of mourning." She stopped at her Father's casket, placed her hand on the tattered quilt, closed her eyes and mumbled a quick message to her Father and one to the Lord. "Daddy, please forgive me for what I am about to do. I know this is inappropriate, and you would be so mad at me if you were here, but you can't see these people the way I can. Do you know why people are here? It's to see me. They have been talking about me since I returned home and their curiosity is at an all-time high. There are people here for you, of course, and you would know those few folks that stood beside you and momma during my disappearance and you would be touched. But, the majority of people here, I suspect, have not darkened these or any church doors in ages, nor did they offer friendship to you. I am angry because of that. You know I run rough shod and my mouth has rarely been my friend, so I am sorry daddy, but I can't let this moment pass without saying a few choice words. I know you will understand, the way you always have." And with that, Vernadine stepped onto the platform and positioned herself behind the pulpit. She grabbed the sides of the pulpit and hung on for dear life, she didn't know exactly what she was going to say. She looked down at her mother and Sheridan to see looks of sheer panic. Her mother grabbed her paper fan with a picture of Jesus and a lamb on one side and an advertisement for the funeral home on the other, fanning away like her life depended on it while also dabbing her upper lip with her handkerchief. Sheridan's eyes looked like they would pop out of her head. She gave herself one more opportunity to back off from exploding venom on the crowd, but quickly shook that feeling away. There was no turning back now.

"Good morning," Vernadine said. "Let me begin by saying thank you for coming today; we all appreciate it. For those of you who don't know me, I am Vernadine Turnipseed, Fletcher's daughter. But I suspect you know that already. Oh, I know I don't look like the same Vernadine, the Basketball Queen. Life and its experiences have been good to me, and I have been blessed in many ways." The crowd was stirring a bit, but she continued. "What I must have misunderstood over these last fifteen years, while I was away, was just how large my parents' social circle had become. Why, I had no idea the social barriers had changed and now peanut farmers and bank presidents and hog farmers and lawyers sit together as equals and have barbeques and Sunday lunches together, or play bridge and drink too much scotch when the Preacher and his wife are not at the party. Somewhere along the way, my mother forgot to fill me in on just how many new friends they had made over the years. I mean, why else would you be here at my father's funeral if you didn't feel a personal loss and sadness over a departed friend and fellow brother in Christ? You know, on the way up here, I paused at my father's casket and asked him to forgive me for my shortcomings. You know why? Because as I sat here this morning, watching you walk in and seat yourselves, at first I was touched. I felt happy for my father. That his life had touched so many people in these communities of Spit's Creek and Inner Banks. But as I asked my mother who is such-and-such and who is so-and-so, she kept saying, "Oh, my stars, I can't believe they are here," or "what in the blazes is he doing here, he never said two words to your daddy and me." And, when I was looking around during the service, I noticed most of you were looking at me and my daughter and not the preacher. This means one thing... y'all are here for the Vernadine Turnipseed carnival show. Plain and simple. Well folks, here I am! Take a good, long look. I am sickened by almost each and every one of you. So, while I have your undivided attention, let me clear a few things up in the nasty rumor mill. When I left Spit's Creek, I didn't leave here because I had been recruited as a German Spy. I didn't leave here to move to California to live with a woman basketball coach either. I understand how both of these rumors could grow and take a life of its own, because this is a small town, and y'all are bored and small minded, and that's just what you do. I know I wasn't the most feminine of teenage girls. I mean, I played basketball on the boys' team, after all. But with these rumors, not one of them was true, and the pain and shunning you provided my parents over the years was hurtful to them and the finest example of why Christians are often called hypocrites. Some of the meanest and most spiteful people I know sit in church on Sunday morning's, all dressed up, powdered up, smiling, singing their hymns and offering loud 'Amen's' during the preacher's sermon. Shame on you! Now, please don't think I am looking at myself as someone who is perfect and sinless and without fault. No, I am just quite the opposite. I have to pray a lot for forgiveness and direction in my life. When I left Spit's Creek I moved to Mobile. I have built a successful real estate career and I live a fine life there. I didn't leave alone when I was seventeen years old. No… along with carrying my suitcase and purse, I was carrying my precious daughter, Sheridan," Vernadine turned and smiled at Sheridan. The gasp in the church was audible. Then the murmuring began.

Since Vernadine began her 'talk' not one person had moved or stirred. Even the fanning had stopped. But with the news of the 'basketball queen' leaving town to hide a pregnancy, that did it, they could not hold it in any longer. Vernadine stood at the pulpit and just watched the circus. She looked over at her mother and noticed that her fanning had not slowed, but had gotten faster, and she noticed that the 'glamour glue' hairspray wasn't holding her mother's hair-do. Her hair had fallen and was stuck to her head, drenched in sweat. Sheridan sat deer-eyed as she looked around the sanctuary at the crowd, licking her lips in rapid succession due to a dry mouth. "Folks, please quiet down. I am almost finished. Sheridan, Honey, will you please stand up?" Vernadine asked. Sheridan looked petrified, but like everyone else in the church, she was completely under the spell of her mother's words and knew she must obey. "Thank you, dear. Church, meet my daughter, Sheridan. She and I made that bus trip to Mobile together. Isn't she beautiful? You can sit now, Honey. Thank you. She has a father, of course, and yes, I was a sinner who succumbed to lust and temptations of sex as a young, unmarried teenage girl. So, as you sit in the middle of your sanctimonious judgment, I know for a fact there are people in the congregation this morning that were sneaking out and doing the very same thing I did, you just didn't get caught. And because you didn't get caught, your reputation remained spotless. But, you know who you are. So simmer down with all of your nasty facial expressions. Jesus told us it is not our place to judge, but His. So, as I close, I hope this has cleared up any confusion about me and answered questions you have had regarding my 'disappearance', as I have heard it called. So, Preacher, will you come and lead us in a closing prayer and may we examine our own hearts, deeply and honestly, and leave here reminded that in God's eyes we are equal and that sin, no matter what form, is still a sin. Thank you for your attention. Now we will dismiss after the prayer, and everyone who wants is welcome to attend the graveside service for my father. Remember, that's why we're here today after all."

The preacher walked to the podium, wiping sweat from his brow as he moved closer. Vernadine made her way back to her seat in the pew beside her mother. She sat and noticed that her mother would not look at her. She didn't let it bother her because she understood why her mother would be shaken and upset. The Preacher began his prayer. "Dear Lord, I ask You search our hearts this morning. If there is any trace of judgment or malice or hatred, please remove it. Please forgive us for not loving each other the way You told us to. Forgive us for shunning our fellow man. Please forgive us for gossip. Thank you, that through Your life on earth, You modeled true love of humanity. Holy Spirit, please keep us mindful that our thoughts, words, and deeds affect those around us. Thank you for sending Your Son, Jesus, as we celebrate Fletcher's homecoming, Lord. We know he is with You today and we will see him again in the sweet by-an-by. In Jesus' name I pray. Amen."

The crowd departed in complete silence, knowing they had just been scolded and reminded that their actions and words had damaged and hurt each other. A handful of people gathered in front of the church, waiting for Vernadine, Irene and Sheridan. They walked together to the oak tree shaded cemetery behind the church. The preacher said another few words and another prayer. Fletcher's casket was lowered into the ground and the three of his girls each grabbed a handful of dirt and threw it on his casket. Life would not be the same without him. They stood there, huddled together, hugging and crying. The few, loyal friends of Fletcher and Irene walked back to the church to give them privacy. After they hugged and cried and dried their tears, they made their way to the fellowship hall and ate a lunch of fried chicken and fresh garden vegetables, Fletcher's favorite meal.

New Directions

Spit's Creek
August 1960

After the funeral service and lunch at church, everyone was exhausted. The raw emotions from the loss of Fletcher, the funeral planning, and the unexpected turn of events at the funeral service left them speechless on the drive home.

Arriving home, they walked in the door, took off their hats, gloves, and purses then retreated to their own bedrooms for rest and reflection. Vernadine knew she had to return to Mobile soon. She had business and clients waiting and Aunt Marie was very ill. She promised her father she would take care of her mother, but she didn't know how she was going to do it. The thought of her mother agreeing to move to Mobile seemed unlikely and the thoughts of her moving back to Spit's Creek was inconsiderable. The only thing she knew right now was she was bone tired and didn't have the physical or emotional strength to tackle that mountain this minute, so she laid her head on her pillow and took a nap.

Vernadine made a pot of coffee when she woke up at 5PM. Sheridan and her mother greeted her deep in conversation. Vernadine did not inquire and went on about her business of coffee making.

"Momma, Granny and I have been talking about the future, our futures. We have an idea we want to discuss with you. Please hear us out before you make any comments."

"This sounds serious," Vernadine said, with her back towards them. "Okay, I am intrigued. Give me just a second to get the coffeepot on and my full attention is yours."

Sheridan and Irene grabbed each other's hand and sat in silence waiting on Vernadine to join them at the table.

"Mother, would you like a cup of coffee?" Vernadine asked.

"That sounds great, yes, thank you," Irene said.

After pouring the two cups of coffee, adding sugar and fresh cream, Vernadine placed the steaming mugs on the table and said, "Well, I am all ears."

"Momma, like I said, Granny and I have been talking about our futures. I have asked Granny if she felt she could sell her home and move to Mobile to live with us. I told her we have a bedroom for her. I explained to her there are many ladies in our church who are widows and she would fit right in. She would have plenty to do there taking care of us, spending time with new friends, volunteering somewhere if she wants to, and she could even resurrect Aunt Marie's rose gardens and beautiful yard and return it to its former splendor. Wouldn't that be great?" Vernadine agreed that would be great. It amazed her Sheridan was thinking the way she was.

"But, the more we talked about it, Granny's excitement turned to sadness. I told her I know this is a major decision, but something had to be agreed upon, because we don't want her to stay here alone while we live four hours away. Now, I know this is your place to make these decisions, Momma, but it just came up as we were sitting here this afternoon. I know you have to make decisions you think are best for everyone, so please forgive me if I am stepping out of line. And, there's more…" Sheridan took a sip of her sweet tea and the ice clinking in the glass was the only sound in the room.

Vernadine sat there, drinking her coffee, trying to stay open minded, because even though she knew her decision would be the course taken, she had still not wrapped her mind around the logistics of it all. She felt relief for the help.

"Momma, Granny does not want to move away from her home and Spit's Creek," Sheridan said.

Vernadine looked at her mother and said, "Mother, is this true? How can I take care of you from Mobile?"

"Yes, Vernadine, it's true. I cannot imagine moving away from the home your father and I have lived in for our entire thirty-five years together. It's hard enough losing him, but walking away from the home, the memories, the farm land, our church and friends is too much to bear. I know you want me to come with y'all to Mobile, and I appreciate your love and care, but I will be fine here. People here will help look out for me." Irene wiped her eyes with her handkerchief and took a sip of her coffee.

"I promised to take care of you for the rest of your life. Leaving you here is doing the exact opposite of what I promised," Vernadine pleaded. "Surely you can understand that?"

"Momma," Sheridan interrupted. "We want you to hear about our plan. I want to stay here with Granny and live in Spit's Creek. I will make new friends, get involved in church, and take care of Granny. I want to Momma. I know this sounds far-fetched to you and that leaves you and Aunt Marie in Mobile, but I will be just fine."

"Don't you realize it is just a matter of time before everyone in town knows that Slim Perkins is your father? Are you prepared to be the illegitimate child of a man who already has a family? What if you are treated like an outsider? You are, after all. You know no one here. What if life doesn't work out the way you are thinking? This is real life, Sheridan, not a fairy tale. You saw how those people flocked to your grandfather's funeral, not for him, but to gawk at you and me! Do you really think this town will open their arms to a stranger, much less Vernadine's out-of-wedlock child? This is a small southern town, Sheridan. In Mobile, you are shielded. Our lives are private, as they should be. You have friends there and a fine school and a church already. What in the blazes are you thinking? I had never thought about leaving Spit's Creek after high school because I had plans of marrying and staying here, but once I got to Mobile, I felt like a bird. I felt free. I felt creative and in charge of my future. I felt hope. I saw for the first time that the world was bigger than my imagination. Why would you want to move in a backwards motion? And, aside from all of that, you and I are a team. You are my child and we have never been apart. I don't want to live without you." Vernadine stood up and looked in her purse for aspirin tablets. The situation was getting worse. Now she was up against her mother and her daughter. How would she combat both of them? She knew the final say was hers to make, but she did not want her decision to split what little family she had left. So, she decided at that moment to breathe deep, take the aspirin tablets, drink water, and reserve her judgment and growing despair.

"So," Vernadine said, exasperated, "Just how would this play out? I just can't see this working. I would be across the state, leaving my aging mother and fifteen year old daughter alone. It is now my responsibility to take care of you two!"

Irene cleared her throat and said, "Vernadine, I know this is so overwhelming. The last week has been a train wreck, and now we are adding more stress to you and your decision making with our suggestion, but I cannot imagine my life anywhere else but here in Spit's Creek. I am sorry, dear, but it's the truth and I know I would not be happy in Mobile starting a new life again at my age. I also don't want to leave your father. I am sure I sound feeble and small minded to you, but in the bottom of my heart, I know I would be miserable and sad, and that would cause stress and unhappiness in your home. It would devastate me to know I am bringing chaos into your home. You might even resent me for being there. The strain on the relationship the three of us have would be too much. I cannot go with you. I will be just fine, I promise. Sheridan's idea of staying here with me is purely her idea. I would love to have her here, of course, but again, I do not want to be the source of frustration to you or hurt the relationship that you and Sheridan have. Why don't we all take a breather and revisit this conversation later after we have all had time to think. But, Sheridan, this is a major decision for you to be making. If I were your mother, I would be very hesitant to agree to leave you here without me. So, it's probably a good idea that the two of you talk seriously about this." Irene wiped her nose, picked up her coffee cup and took it to the sink for washing. "I am going to the garden. There are peas and okra to pick. I will see y'all later." Irene put on her apron, grabbed her gardening hat, and walked out through the squeaky back screened door.

Vernadine and Sheridan remained at the table, looking at each other and saying nothing. The news of the afternoon was surprising, and neither of them knew what to say or do or think. Vernadine arose from the table, washed her coffee cup and told Sheridan she was going to take a walk and she would see her later.

Vernadine headed down the dirt driveway with no particular destination in mind. The dirt was soft on her bare feet as the afternoon sun baked her skin. She was lost in memories of childhood and young adulthood as she remembered the creek, shaded by oak trees, that flowed year 'round further down the road. She rounded the curve and found the path to the creek. She walked down the path and heard the trickle of the flowing water. When the creek came into sight, she smiled. There was a small beach area beside the shallow water, and a sandbar a few yards into the middle. She walked to the side and cooled her hot feet. The water was refreshing, so she moved deeper into it. She submersed herself into the water and sighed. As a child and teenager, she would spend hours here splashing in the cool water with neighboring children and swinging off the rope swing into the deeper side of the creek. She could see it clearly in her mind, like it was yesterday, but many years had passed since those innocent summer days. Today she had a problem to solve. A big problem and she didn't want to make a hasty decision. Floating in the cool creek water, she closed her eyes and began talking to God.

"Dear Lord, it seems all I do is bring my problems to You, instead of talking to You in the in between times, and I am sorry; but this current dilemma is heavy. I don't know what to do and I am afraid. The thought of leaving my mother and daughter here without me is scary. On the other hand, I understand my mother's feelings, and I am sure I would feel the same way she does. This is her home. This is her life of memories and relationships with her friends and church family. I can't imagine starting my life over at her age. I know she is resilient and could adapt, but I would always know deep down in my heart she was putting on a front for me so I would not feel guilty. That is selfish on my part to think what she feels doesn't matter. But, my life is in Mobile. I have worked too hard to give that up, and besides, I would be miserable living here again. I do not understand why Sheridan would ever consider moving here and living with her grandmother in this dirt road, country and judgmental town! She has her whole life ahead of her, and her opportunities are greater in Mobile. What is the appeal for her to even consider this?" Floating on her back, she opened her eyes and noticed a butterfly resting and fluttering on her stomach. She marveled at the distinct and vibrant colors of the butterfly and tried to remain still so the butterfly would not fly away. She remembered learning in science class that most butterflies only live one to two weeks in adulthood. She thought to herself how sad it is something so fragile and beautiful, something that gives pleasure to the beholder, could have such a temporary life. She imagined how wonderful it would be to sit and watch thousands of butterflies flying around her. Do their wings make a sound? Do they buzz and hum in a melodic choir together? Would they rest on her and create a colorful coat? She paused when she thought about the butterfly's transformation from a caterpillar to a butterfly. Her life had been exactly the same as a butterfly's. She had transformed into this beautiful, hopeful, smart, clever woman in her own right. She reflected that even though her parents could have stopped her from leaving town when she was a pregnant teen, they didn't. They wanted to protect her, shield her, encourage and love her from afar. They knew they had no other choice, so in order to keep her from further heartbreak, they had to let her go. They had to let her try her own wings, so that is what they did. Now, as a parent herself, she finally understood the difficult transition from parent to counselor and friend. She knew Sheridan was only fifteen, and younger than she was when she left home, but Sheridan was a different girl than she was in so many ways. She knew Sheridan was level headed, cautious and very mature for her age. She knew she wouldn't have to worry that her mother wouldn't be taken care of, and her mother was capable of taking care of her daughter. Obviously, there were things going on in Sheridan's mind she didn't understand, but whatever it was, maybe she should trust her daughter and her instincts and wishes? Sheridan had been a bundle of questions since they arrived a few weeks earlier in Spit's Creek. Vernadine knew she had revealed little information to Sheridan about her younger years and no information about her father until recently. She could understand why Sheridan would want to know and understand for herself where her life had begun and what kind of life her mother and father had in Spits' Creek. One thing she knew for sure was she would not be leaving Sheridan in Spit's Creek if Slim did not agree to keep quiet and swear to secrecy about the fact he is her father. Slim and his family would have to keep quiet on the issue. She would not leave Sheridan there to be disgraced, made fun of, or ostracized by the community. The mystery of who Sheridan's father is would have to continue for a very long time, if not forever.

The butterfly flew off and Vernadine remembered she was praying. "See, Lord, I get so distracted in my thoughts, I forget to continue our conversations. Did you send me the butterfly to remind me of my life and the changes I have gone through? Is Sheridan a butterfly too? I think maybe we both are. I know I have explored a new and wonderful life, so I should not keep Sheridan from exploring hers. Lord, will You please protect her? Please keep them both safe. I know we can make this work, and I know You will reveal all You are doing in this new season in due time. I am going to trust You, Lord. Thank You for Your love and bounty. Please protect my sad heart too, as I leave these two precious people here without me. I know everything will be ok. Amen."

With the close of her prayer, Vernadine noticed the sun was setting, so she decided to walk home. Her walk home was lighter and gayer than the walk to the creek. She felt free to tell her family she would agree to their plan and that would leave only if Slim and his family agreed to complete silence. If they agreed, she would register Sheridan for her junior year at Buford County High School, buy her a used car for her soon to be sixteenth birthday, open a bank account at Farmer's Bank and Trust and buy her new school clothes and supplies. Yes, there was much to do. And with these thoughts, she ran the entire way home.

The Butterfly

When Vernadine arrived home from her swim, prayers and jog, Sheridan was sitting on the front porch with two other girls in the swing.

"Hello, Momma, what has happened to you? You are wet and out of breath! Are you okay?" Sheridan asked as she walked towards her mother, leaving the swing in motion.

"Oh, yes," Vernadine said, breathless and excited. "I went for a walk, then took a dip in the creek and ran home. There is a lot for us to do in the next few days, and we need to get busy. I have made some decisions about our futures. While at the creek, enjoying the cool water, I had a great conversation with the Lord and a butterfly, so now I know what we need to do about our plans."

"A butterfly? How did you have a conversation with a butterfly?" Sheridan asked.

"Well, it wasn't a verbal conversation, but the butterfly reminded me of a few very important realities of life. They are so beautiful and delicate and uniquely made, just like each of us. Their life begins surrounded by a cocoon, where they develop and grow and mature. Then one day, when the time is right, they magically emerge, as this magnificent and exquisite new creature, ready to fly and discover their world. The butterfly reminded me how our lives are not really all that different from theirs. We also eventually have to be released from our cocoon, our place of development and safety, fly into the world and make our own discoveries, and find our place in this world. Unfortunately, the butterfly, in all of its beauty, does not live very long, so when we see one, we need to be reminded of our similarity to the butterfly. We are each wonderfully made, for different purposes, but each has a purpose. The black and white butterfly fluttered on my stomach for a long time and I was sad to see it leave, but I was thankful for the reminder of the cycle of life we each have. Butterflies are truly a breathtaking and inspiring creature," Vernadine smiled as she spoke.

Vernadine had been so engrossed in talking to Sheridan about the black and white butterfly and her afternoon inspiration and encouragement from her prayer, that she had not taken notice of the two young ladies sitting in the swing. "Oh, I am sorry, I got carried away. Who are these pretty young ladies?" Vernadine smiled and wiped the wet hair from her eyes.

"This is Birdy and Celia Snodgrass, Momma. Well, technically, Berdithia Lee and Celia Augusta, but Birdy said to NEVER call her Berdithia. That was her grandmother's name, but she strongly dislikes the name and can't for the life of her figure out why anyone would think Berdithia is a pretty name, so it's Birdy and ONLY Birdy! Celia is fine with her name, so it's okay to call her Celia. They live on the next farm down the road a couple of miles. Granny called their mother this afternoon and invited them over for lemonade and cookies so we could meet each other. Birdy and I are the same age and Celia is one year younger. People always think they are twins because they are so close in age, and they are always together. They tell everyone that they come as a package deal!" Sheridan laughed and they all joined in.

It was true, Sheridan was finally happy enough to laugh. She was excited to meet new friends in Spit's Creek, and Birdy and Celia were fun and happy and loved to laugh. Sheridan definitely needed laughter and new friendships in her life. After the past few weeks dealing with her grandfather's illness, meeting her own father, and then experiencing the death of her grandfather had taken its toll on her. And then, there was also the memory of her mother's 'speech' at the funeral service she would never forget and feared that no one else would either. Now she was happy and anxiously waiting to see what her mother had decided about their future plans.

"It is so nice to meet y'all, Birdy and Celia! Sheridan has been anxious to make new friends here in Spit's Creek the whole month we have been here, but as you know, we have been busy dealing with family matters. But now, we are finding ourselves adapting to our new normal and ready to see what life brings next. You girls enjoy your visit. Please excuse me, I need to dry off and change clothes and help momma with supper. Y'all are welcome to stay and eat if you would like. We always have plenty! We have a few board games if that interests y'all after supper." Vernadine smiled and walked into the house.

Irene brought the lemonade and warm sugar cookies to the front porch and set them on the white wicker table that was set with white linen napkins, glass punch cups, and small glass plates for the occasion. She said there was no reason at all why all of her fineries shouldn't be used on more frequent occasions. Meeting new friends is always a celebration, so Sheridan took her place as the hostess and offered the delights to her two new friends. The weather was still very warm and the cool lemonade hit the spot. "I have heard about my momma's hometown for years and I have always wanted to know more about the place she grew up. I think it would be fun to go to the same school and church as she did growing up. I think it would give me an understanding of her I would not get otherwise," Sheridan said.

"You do know that our gymnasium at school is the 'Vernadine D. Turnipseed Gymnasium', don't you? Your mother is a local hero and a mystery all rolled into one. Since your momma left, the basketball team has not won another State championship. She is a legend. I mean, the thought of a girl on an all boy basketball team is a gas! Then to lead the team in not one, but two State championships is a double gas! And that was in 1943 and 1944, long before any 'women's rights!' Your mother is a trail blazer, a true patriot of womanhood. Girls are just as good, if not better than boys! Just think how lucky you have been, to be the daughter of a woman like that! You must have stories to tell?" Birdy said as she edged to the end of her chair.

"Birdy is right," Celia chimed in. "Your momma is a legend in this town. We have looked in the yearbooks at her class pictures and basketball team pictures. They keep all of the past yearbooks in the library, and when we are supposed to be working on book reports, we grab the yearbooks and look at your momma. Just think, Birdy, we are sitting here with her daughter and have just finally met her in real life! Boy, your momma has really changed. She looks nothing like she did in high school. She is really beautiful now. Oh, I don't mean to be rude, but if I didn't know better, I would not believe it is really her!"

"I know," Sheridan said as she wiped a cookie crumb from her mouth with her napkin. "My Granny has been showing me pictures in the photo albums off and on since we arrived. I have to agree with you, and I take no offense. She sure has changed over the years, for the better. Granny said that when Momma arrived in Mobile fifteen years ago, she was young and inexperienced and a small-town girl with simple taste and ways. Granny said when they finally saw Momma for the first time after leaving home, that they could not believe the transformation that my momma had made. In fact, it is like the 'butterfly' story momma told us a few minutes ago. That's exactly how Granny described momma. She said Momma had blossomed and bloomed in ways she did not think was possible for one plain-looking girl. Granny and my Grandfather were so proud of Momma. By the time they made it to Mobile to see her, not only had she changed physically, but she had also gotten a job in a real estate office as a receptionist, and she was also studying to take her real estate exam to become an agent. She passed the exam, began working hard to build her business and continued to refine herself. Now, she is the 'queen of real estate' in Mobile County. I am so proud of her. She has taken life by the horns and hasn't let anything stop her from accomplishing her goals and dreams. She has earned quite the reputation as a competent businesswoman and is highly respected by our community. She has always encouraged me to go after whatever it is I set my mind to. Yes, I am very lucky and very thankful she is my mother."

As the girls reflected on their conversation about Vernadine, the telephone rang. "Momma, can you get the phone? I have a towel on my wet hair," Vernadine yelled down the hallway. Vernadine bathed in a warm bath, washed her hair, and was about to apply a small amount of makeup when her mother called her to the phone.

"Vernadine! Hurry up, the Mayor of Mobile is on the phone for you," Irene said flustered.

"Oh, Momma, catch your breath. It's okay. I am not in any trouble," Vernadine smiled then hugged her mother.

"Hello, this is Vernadine."

"Vernadine, this is Brooks Lawson. I hope I am not disturbing you. I am sorry to hear about your father's passing," Brooks said.

"Hello, Brooks. Thank you. How did you get this number?" Vernadine asked.

"Well, I have to admit I called your office and I simply asked the secretary if she knew how you could be reached and she gave me this number, but asked me to keep it private. Please don't be upset with her. I think she gave it to me only because of my position in the community," Brooks said.

"So, you are only calling to offer your condolences, or is there a business matter that you need to discuss? I will be back in Mobile in a week or so, just in time for the city council meeting. I know there are some zoning issues on the agenda, and there is still the matter of the proposed destruction of the McMillan plantation home on Springhill Road that is of grave concern to me," Vernadine said matter-of-factly and to the point.

"Yes, that is true, we definitely have quite a bit to discuss and hammer out. No pun intended." He laughed. Vernadine did not laugh or respond.

"Uhm, no, the two reasons for my call are one, to offer my condolences for your father, and two, well, there is a fall kickoff dinner and dance at the country club in a couple of weeks, and I would like to ask you to join me as my date for the occasion?" he said nervously.

Brooks knew Vernadine was a tough gal, to the point, business minded and not at all intrigued by small talk, unless it was leading somewhere lucrative or socially impactful, or real estate related. So, her candor did not surprise him. They had served on various committees throughout the years and had known each other professionally, but that was the extent of their association. He admired her grit and determination and he also found her very attractive.

Brooks Lawson had worked his way through Plains University with a job in the horticulture department maintaining the grounds and the football field. He grew up in Mobile, in a modest, conservative and loving all American family. He was the first of his family to attend college and he excelled in his studies in the business school. After college, he moved home and began work in farm equipment sales. He loved riding the rural roads of Mobile and Baldwin Counties meeting with farmers and learning their ways of livelihood. His business thrived. He won awards year after year for his consistently high sales numbers. When asked what he attributed his constant success to, he always smiled and said the farmers and their families were like his own family. He never tried to sell farmers anything that would not benefit them or anything that they truly couldn't afford. His work ethic and personality were his winning combination, and his heart was genuine. He never met a stranger, and people were drawn to him. It certainly didn't hurt Brooks was handsome, standing six foot two inches tall, with broad shoulders, green eyes, dark hair and an olive complexion. The girls swarmed around him.

Years earlier Brooks met a young lady on one of his sales calls, and it was instant love. After a brief courtship, they married at a small white country church and began their life together. Everything in Brooks' life was moving along with blessing after blessing. One day, his bride of less than a year told him she was expecting their first baby. Brooks was over the moon. During the day, he worked selling farm equipment and in the evenings, he and his bride painted the nursery, put together the baby bed, repaired other minor issues at home, all in anticipation of their new arrival. When the day came, Brooks' wife labored for two days and those two days were long and uncertain. The doctor stayed around the clock, with Brooks' mother and his mother-in-law assisting. Complications arose that could not be stopped and in the early morning hours of the third day of labor, Brooks' wife and child died.

Brooks could not understand why God would take his wife and newborn child. He spent months and months in deep depression and he retreated to his home for days at a time. His work and health suffered and there was nothing anyone could do to ease his pain and heartbreak. Finally, after a year of mourning, Brooks got up one morning, dressed for work, left the house and put his mind in overdrive. For the last few years he worked without looking up. His business was all he had.

In the winter of 1959, a group of farmers, bankers and area business leaders approached him about running for Mayor of Mobile. At first, the thought seemed far-fetched and preposterous, but he slowly warmed up to the idea and decided to put his name in the hat. After a grass-roots campaign strategy, Brooks Lawson won the Mayor's race in a runaway election. He was young, handsome, outgoing and smart. The town's leaders and constituents were happy to have him as their top city leader. This new position and chapter in his life was just what he needed, and after years of sadness, he decided he was ready to find love again and someone to share his life with. But, finding an unmarried woman, in the 1960s in the South and close to his age, would be tough. He was up for the challenge and he asked God to help him. Just as he was finishing his prayer, a vision of Vernadine entered his mind. "Yes," he thought, "she is the one!"

Brooks knew Vernadine had gone home to Spit's Creek to help care for her ailing father. He learned later that her father had passed away and word was no one knew exactly when Vernadine would return to Mobile. Vernadine remained on Brooks' mind, so he did some investigating on how he might reach her by telephone and inquire to her well-being and offer condolences about losing her father. That would be the perfect excuse. He also knew that the dance at the country club was approaching and there was no one else he wanted to ask. He knew her agreeing to go with him would be a longshot since they were not social outside of the City Commission meetings, but he had to try. Brooks could not remember feeling attracted to another woman since he first met his now deceased wife. That's when he hatched his plan. He knew it was a gamble to call her office and ask for her number, but he would try that first. To his surprise, the secretary quickly agreed to share Vernadine's number. He was thankful to the secretary and after writing the number on a notepad he sat and stared at it for a long while. After finally getting up the nerve, he dialed the phone. Her quick and pointed answers did not surprise him because that was her demeanor, but he felt in his heart there was more to Vernadine than business and direct answers. He knew everyone had a story to tell, and a past, because he certainly did, but he was willing to risk the nerves in his stomach and the fear of outright rejection to get to know her.

The phone call went exactly as he imagined, and he silently chuckled to himself as they were talking. The phone conversation ended with Vernadine telling him she would return to Mobile in a week or so and she would let him know her answer to his invitation when she returned home.

They hung the phone up and Brooks sat at his desk smiling, hopeful, and proud of himself for having the nerve to ask her on a date. Vernadine on the other hand, stood in the kitchen staring at the phone for five minutes in disbelief that she had just been asked on a date by a man for the first time in her adult life, and by no less than the eligible, handsome, well-spoken and respected Mayor of Mobile. She grabbed the back of the chair in front of her, pulled it out and plopped down. She was without words. All she could think about was the butterfly that landed on her an hour before, and that maybe another butterfly moment had arrived.

The Turning of the Tide

Spit's Creek and Mobile
September 1960

The last month had been a whirlwind. Before returning to Mobile, Vernadine's first order of business was the very important matter of speaking to Slim and Marigold. If they wouldn't agree to complete silence and discretion regarding Sheridan, She would return to Mobile with Vernadine. Thankfully Slim and Marigold understood the importance of keeping their family secrets away from prying and nosey townspeople. With that important matter settled Vernadine situated Sheridan into her old home. With as much assurance as she could muster, she loaded the Lincoln with suitcases and canned vegetables from her mother's garden. She lowered the top of the convertible and slowly drove down the dirt driveway waving goodbye and honking the horn, until she could no longer see her loved ones. By the time she reached the black top, she was full guns ahead, light in spirit, and ready to return to her home. There was so much work to catch up on and there was the matter of Brooks Lawson's invitation that needed a reply.

With each mile closer, as she drove the four hours to Mobile, she realized she had missed her home. She missed the challenge of her work and having to think quickly on her feet. She reminisced about her father, too, and even though she was still sad over his loss, she knew she had settled her mother and she had kept her promise to take care of her.

Since receiving the phone call from Brooks a week ago, Vernadine had thought of little else. She was still in a mild state of shock that someone as handsome and eligible as Brooks would be interested in her. Over the course of a few days, she decided to accept his invitation and she couldn't wait to get home to telephone him and share the news.

Pulling into her driveway was like a reunion with an old and trusted friend. After a few minutes of fond reminiscing, she unloaded her convertible, raised the top and ran inside to see Aunt Marie. She had so much to tell her. All of the details from the funeral and her impassioned 'eulogy', Sheridan finally meeting her father and the ruckus her presence caused in town, the difficult decision on leaving Sheridan in Spit's Creek, talking to the butterfly at the creek, and Brooks Lawson's telephone call. They settled in the parlor and Vernadine began her stories. One by one. Aunt Marie soaked in every detail and said,

"You didn't really say all of those things at your father's funeral, did you? Vernadine that is the most scandalous thing I have heard in a long time! That is really something for the mind to comprehend and I am sure your mother wanted to crawl underneath the foundation of the church building! Bless her poor heart! And Sheridan! Standing up and being officially introduced to the community! I can imagine no one has ever been to a funeral quite like Fletcher's. I assure you, you just gave that community more ammunition to continue talking about you for many years to come. I will say this, you certainly leave a wake when you arrive and depart from most situations. But as I sit and ponder over the shock the congregation experienced during your speech and rebuke, it was high time you had a chance to say something to those gossiping, mean-spirited people in Spit's Creek who ostracized, rejected and abandoned your parents; and those who have kept your name on their lips for far too long now. I am sure, to add insult to injury, it also shocked them to see what a beautiful and smart woman you have become. Actually, I am thrilled for you. I am also proud of you for settling the score and setting the record straight! They deserved every bit of the bitter taste in their mouths your words left. I hope they felt the judgment from the good Lord, too. He says 'Justice is mine.'"

She was about to tell Aunt Marie about Brooks Lawson and his phone call when the telephone rang. Deep in thought and lost in herself, she almost spilled her whole cup of tea from the sudden ringing. "Hello, this is Vernadine speaking. Yes, operator, I will accept the charges."

"Hey, Momma, it's me and Granny! We were just calling to see if you arrived home safely? How was your trip? Is everything okay at the house?" Sheridan asked.

"Oh, hello, Dear. Yes, I arrived about an hour ago. The trip was just fine, no problems at all. It sure is good to be home, I know that. Everything here is just fine. In fact, I am sitting in the living room with Aunt Marie filling her in on all that happened over the last month. How are you and Mother?

"Everything here is just fine. Momma, today we had P.E. in YOUR gymnasium! It was so neat to see your name on the scoreboard and the entrance outside. I just beamed with pride. In fact, word has spread rather quickly I am attending school here, and folks just flock to me like I am a superstar. All because of you! Hopefully, the excitement will die down soon," Sheridan laughed.

"I am sure it is a zoo around you. I hope you don't feel overwhelmed. Just take it in stride. I have been away for so long now, you would think it wouldn't matter, but I guess not," Vernadine said.

"Momma, have called Mr. Lawson yet to tell him you accept his dance invitation?" Sheridan asked in anticipation.

"Well, that's what I was thinking about when the phone rang. No, I have not called him yet. I am trying to gather my nerve." Vernadine exhaled as Aunt Marie's eyes bulged as she began to pull on Vernadine's blouse.

"What are you talking about?" Aunt Marie said loudly. "What man are you supposed to call? I have not heard one word about a man!"

Vernadine leaned over and whispered, "I was just about to tell you when the phone rang. Hold your horses."

"Momma, call him! You can do this! He is only a human after all, not a king or a god. Just a regular man, who happens to be the Mayor. You deserve some fun, Momma! You deserve attention from a man. It's long overdue, and how nice it is to be getting attention from such a handsome man, too! Please call him right after we hang up! We love you Momma, I have to go. Birdy, Celia and I are going to the creek where you talked to the butterfly! I will talk to you soon and write you a letter every day. Hang on, Granny wants to say a quick hello," Sheridan said as she handed the phone to Irene.

"Hello, Vernadine," Irene said. "Everything here is A-Okay. Sheridan and I will be just fine. You have no reason to worry at all. Sheridan has taken to her new friends and school like a duck to water. She is laughing and jubilant and doing well. Now, like Sheridan said, you call that man when we hang up! You deserve love, Vernadine. You are a grown woman who has lived all of your adult years without someone to love and someone to love you. You take a chance and see what happens with Mr. Lawson! I am rooting for you, we both are! Now, I will say goodbye since we are burning up money on this long-distance phone call. We love you and we will talk to you soon." Irene didn't wait for Vernadine to say goodbye, she just hung up. Vernadine knew her mother was pressing her to make the call to Brooks Lawson.

"Vernadine Dawn Turnipseed," Aunt Marie said sternly, "What man!"

Over the years Aunt Marie had suggested, recommended, pointed out, invited over and pushed eligible bachelors in Vernadine's direction. Vernadine rejected most of the men. She did have a quick lunch or coffee after work with a couple of Aunt Marie's picks throughout the years, but not one of them made her heart skip a beat or piqued her interest. In fact, she found most of them irritating. The men were too pushy, too conventional, overbearing, too meek and mild mannered, sappy, too educated or not educated enough, not ambitious enough or they were overly proud of their accomplishments. They were too short, too fat or too thin, not gifted with a comely face or attractive physique. It seemed there was something always missing. After hit and miss dates with men that never made it to the second date, Vernadine began to wonder if there were any single men left that would ever appeal to her? As the years passed her by, along with her fleeting youth, she turned her focus to hard work and Sheridan and her family. Somewhere along the line she made peace with the idea of never finding a lasting romantic love. The emotions would hit her broad sided at times, and there would be days of bitterness, anger, self-pity and depression, but with the help of her loved ones and prayer, she would bounce back and start all over again in her resolute mind set. Being single was not the worst thing that could happen to anyone, but dealing with the loneliness was a different matter which required extra prayer and extra determination. And now, after all of this time, a handsome, well spoken, strong and capable man appeared into her life out of nowhere. She was dying to tell Aunt Marie what was going on, and Aunt Marie was pressing in hard.

Vernadine drew in a long breath and began her story about Brooks Lawson. Aunt Marie sat transfixed the entire time. When Vernadine ended her story, she and Aunt Marie hugged and cried for a few minutes. "Vernadine, I am so happy for you! Mr. Lawson is the most eligible bachelor in a four county area! I could not have picked anyone better for you than him. Now, you make that call right now, and please try to add a little pep in your voice. You do have a tendency to always be so matter-of-fact and emotionless on the telephone. We don't want him thinking you are doing him a favor by accepting his invitation. He needs to know you are looking forward to the evening with him. You hear? You are looking forward to it, aren't you?"

"Yes, Ma'am, I am looking forward to seeing him and I will try my best to sound chipper and upbeat. But, you can't stay in the living room when I make the call. I am nervous enough, ok?"

"Ok, I will go outside and water the ferns on the front porch and sweep the sidewalk. But here, this will help your nerves." Aunt Marie shuffled to the dining room, poured a glass of brandy, returned to the living room and handed it to Vernadine. "Bottoms up, every bit of it. Trust me it will soothe your nervous mind."

"Yes, Ma'am, thank you," Vernadine smiled and tossed the warm brandy down her throat. She took a deep breath, tapped the line connection, and nervously dialed each number slowly, watching the dial roll around and around. After the last number was dialed, she almost hung up, but she took a deep breath and waited for an answer on the other end.

"Good afternoon, Mayor's office, may I help you?" said the perky receptionist.

"Good afternoon. This is Vernadine Turnipseed, may I speak to Br.." was all she was able to say.

"Oh, hello, Miss Turnipseed, the Mayor is expecting your call. Please hold on one minute while I ring his office."

The nerves in the back of Vernadine's neck pulsed and her temples throbbed. She knew nothing about dating. The short dates, with the wrong men, had taught her nothing. She knew real estate and motherhood and committees and church functions, but not men and dating. 'This will not go well', she thought to herself. She grabbed the telephone and stretched the cord to reach the liquor cabinet. She fumbled opening the cut-glass decanter and quickly poured another swig of brandy and downed it. Vernadine thought, 'Well, Scarlett O'Hara always drank brandy in times of trouble, so I can too.'

"Hello, Vernadine. How are you? I guess you made it safely back to our fair city?" Brooks said.

"Uhm, yes, I arrived this afternoon," She choked from the vapors of the brandy.

"Well, the reason for my call is to give you my answer about the dance. I have decided to accept your invitation. Please give me all of the details," Vernadine exhaled. 'So much for sounding upbeat and cheerful', she thought to herself.

Brooks silently laughed to himself. He sensed Vernadine seemed extremely nervous and anxious, and the clinking of glass from a decanter gave her away. "How wonderful! Thank you for accepting my invitation. The dance is next Saturday night and the dress is formal. The club hosts this dance every year for their members and it has become quite a tradition. I could not go alone to such a grand affair, and I am pleased you will accompany me. I will pick you up at 7PM. There will be dinner and drinks and a band. I hope you like to dance? You will, of course, with your long-standing professional career, know many, if not all, of the people in attendance," Brooks said.

"Well, that sounds just fine. I will be ready at 7 PM next Saturday night. Thank you for asking me. It sounds like fun. I cannot remember when I had an occasion to wear formal attire. I will look forward to it," Vernadine said with confidence added from the brandy.

"Well, since we still have over a week before the dance, would you like to join me for dinner downtown this Friday evening? I can pick you up at 7 PM. This gives us an opportunity to talk and get to know each other before the dance," Brooks asked.

The sounds from the glass decanter top clanked again, and there was a brief silence on the phone. "Oh, yes, that would be fine. I will see you Friday evening. Thank you," Vernadine said.

"Ok, then, it's a date! I will see you in a couple of days. Goodbye Vernadine and thanks again!" Brooks said.

"Goodbye, Brooks, see you Friday." Vernadine said as she hung the phone up.

Brooks didn't let the fact that Vernadine drinking liquor that early in the day dampen his desire of wanting to know her better. He knew she was an upright Christian and morally convicted woman, who ran her business and life with the highest of standards. She was nervous about the dance and dinner date, and that's all there is to it. In fact, he found it rather endearing that a woman with such a tough exterior could have a crack in her armor and expose human emotions. "Yes", he thought to himself, "I think I am going to really enjoy getting to know Vernadine Turnipseed."

New Horizons

Mobile
September 1960

When Vernadine ended her conversation with Brooks Lawson, she realized it was 2 PM and she was tipsy from the four shots of brandy she consumed for bravery while talking to Brooks. She had a decision to make. She could keep sipping her brandy and relish in the thoughts of her upcoming dinner date with Brooks and have an early bedtime, or she could brew a pot of strong coffee, splash her face with water, then make two emergency phone calls. The first call would be to Sally's beauty salon to schedule a last minute hair appointment for Friday morning; and the second call to her favorite ladies' dress shop to ask the owner to pick out a few dresses for her to look at. She knew everything had to be perfect. An opportunity like this doesn't come around every day, or in her case, never.

She thought about it and chose the coffee, brewed extra strong, and the phone calls. This was a call to action. She could get back to the brandy another day, especially if the potential relationship with Brooks didn't pan out. She collected herself and calmed down before she called Sally's. Any hint of intoxication sensed by Sally would become hot news at the beauty salon, and before she knew it, word all over town would be 'Vernadine has a drinking problem, bless her heart, all alone with no man. She drinks for emotional support.' To keep the wolves at bay, she waited one full hour and drank three cups of coffee before calling anyone. She had worked too hard on herself and career to cancel it all out from four shots of brandy in the middle of the day. While waiting the hour to lose the effects of the brandy, Aunt Marie returned inside and went straight to her questions. "Well? How did the call go?"

"Everything is great. I accepted his dance invitation for a week from Saturday and he asked me to join him for dinner this Friday night so we can get to know each other better. I agreed to that as well." Vernadine beamed through every pore of her body. She felt like she walked on clouds and there was not a care in the world that could cause her sadness at this moment. She remembered what excitement from love and romance felt like, and the prospect of both, even though it had been years ago with Slim. Love feels the same at any age, she figured and she was in love with love.

She dialed the beauty salon and tapped her nails on the dining room table. Sally answered the phone. "Hello, Sally, it's Vernadine. I have a favor to ask. I know you are very busy, but I have a very important meeting Friday, and I need my hair rolled and styled before then. Could you possibly work me in?"

"Hello, Vernadine. My, this sounds important! As luck would have it, I just had a cancellation for Friday afternoon at 3 PM. Will that work?" Sally asked.

"That's perfect! I will be there," Vernadine said.

"Ok. I have you down. Will you have to slide your dress over your head, or is it a zipper? Because if it's a slide over, be dressed before you come in," Sally said.

"Well, I am not sure yet, but I will make sure it zips, because I don't want to mess up your handiwork! Thank you so much, Sally, I will see you in two days." Her next call was the ladies' dress shop. "This is Vernadine. Could you possibly pull two or three dresses aside for me to see? I have a special appointment Friday night, and I need a new dress. It's for a dinner. I would prefer a dress that has a side zipper if you can find one."

"Yes, I can think of three dresses that would work for you! Size twelve, right? I will pull them right now. When can you come in? I will be here until 5 PM today," The shop owner said.

"I can be there in less than twenty minutes. Thank you so much!" Vernadine said.

Vernadine raced to the bathroom, brushed her teeth, and rinsed with mouthwash. She washed her face, reapplied powder and her signature red lipstick. She brushed her hair and pinned it up. She put on her favorite silver clip-on earrings, changed her blouse, grabbed her purse and keys, and headed the few blocks to the dress shop. When she arrived, the bell on the door rang, announcing her presence. She was instantly met by the shopkeeper and directed to the dressing room. The shopkeeper had three beautiful dresses for her to choose from. Two of the dresses were pastels and those didn't feel appropriate because they reminded her of spring. The third dress was navy blue, and she loved it. She tried the navy blue dress on and it fit perfectly; it accented her long lines and it was very becoming on her mature figure without being too flirty or revealing. She asked the shopkeeper to package it up for her. While waiting on the dress to be wrapped, Vernadine spotted an orange scarf and orange and white earrings with a beaded bracelet to match. Without really realizing it, she had outfitted herself in the school colors of Plains University, Brooks' alma mater. She felt maybe it was too much, but she didn't mind. She knew she would also need a new lipstick shade with more orange in it than she normally wore, but her skin tone could pull it off. After purchasing the dress and accessories, she stopped by the drugstore for a new lipstick shade and a new pair of hose. She returned home to look at her purchases as she spread them across the bed. She pulled her navy blue heels from the closet and laid them at the foot of the bed. She felt pleased with herself and couldn't remember the last time her stomach was full of butterflies. 'Butterflies, they keep showing up', she thought to herself and smiled.

Because she was in such a great mood, she returned to the living room, turned on her favorite Frank Sinatra album and poured another brandy. "Fly me to the Moon, let me play among the stars, let me see what spring is like on Jupiter and Mars. In other words, hold my hand. In other words, baby, kiss me..." She sang along and swayed around the living room, lost in the words of her favorite Swooner. She felt alive for the first time in years, and all because of the promise of a dinner date and a dance with a handsome, smart, and kind man.

By the time Friday morning arrived, Vernadine thought she would pop from excitement. She resumed her work the day before as a distraction. There was plenty to catch up on from a month's absence, but her heart wasn't in it. She had worked for years and that is all she had done; work and care for Aunt Marie, Sheridan and her parents; so she was ready for a change of pace and routine and in desperate need of excitement and romance.

She walked on clouds into Sally's Beauty Salon at 3 PM and was escorted to the hair washing station. The warm water and massaging of her scalp relaxed her, and she took her first full breath in two days. She realized then she was a nervous wreck. Sally washed, rolled and styled her hair and coated it with enough hairspray to hold for a solid week. This reminded her of Zilly and Dilly's salon back home, and the thought of that made her chuckle. She knew after a few days, her head would itch something fierce, but by then, she could wash it herself and soothe her itching scalp. The date with Brooks would be worth all the pain.

After her hair appointment, she went home and took a nice long bath, taking care not to get her hair damp. She took her time applying her favorite rose scented lotion and body powder. She sat at the vanity table and began her makeup application. The new orange lipstick was just fine, not too brassy or loud, and she dabbed her lips with a tissue. The new navy blue dress fit like a glove and the scarf, earrings, and bracelet looked just as good as she thought they would. She slid on her blue heels, grabbed her compact and lipstick from the vanity, put them in her purse, turned her lamp off, and made her way to the living room. At 6:55 PM the doorbell rang. She gasped and quickly took another look at herself in the foyer mirror. She appreciated Brooks' promptness. Promptness was a religious belief for her. Being late, even by a few minutes, was a cardinal sin, so she already admired that trait in him and felt reconfirmed in her decision to spend the evening with him.

Upon Vernadine's opening the door, Brooks, the talker, politician and salesman, was speechless. He was immediately taken with Vernadine's demure beauty. She looked breathtaking, in his eyes, and he found himself without complete composure or the ability to form a word for the first time in ages. Vernadine noticed Brooks' appreciative lapse and said, "Good evening, Brooks. Thank you for being on time," Vernadine smiled a wide smile.

"Good evening, Vernadine. Thank you for agreeing to have dinner tonight. You look beautiful," Brooks said through blushing cheeks.

"Thank you," Vernadine said nervously. "Would you like to come inside? I would like to introduce you to my Aunt Marie. She really wants to meet the Mayor," Vernadine smiled and stepped aside as Brooks walked into the foyer. Brooks' cologne whiffed through the air and his fresh shave, new haircut, and navy blue suit set her heart and mind ablaze. 'Is this a dream?' She thought to herself. Aunt Marie sat demurely on her settee, propped with floral pillows, offering a big smile as Brooks and Vernadine rounded the corner. "Aunt Marie, I would like to introduce you to Brooks Lawson," Vernadine said as she seated herself in a high-back chair next to Aunt Marie.

"Hello, Ma'am. I am pleased to meet you. Your home is so lovely," Brooks said with a political flair. "I am sure you may feel nervous about Vernadine having dinner with someone she does not know very well, but I assure you, I will take good care of her and mind my manners the entire evening," Brooks said smiling. The three of them laughed.

"Yes, I know you will. You have too much riding on this if your behavior is not completely honorable, Mr. Mayor," Aunt Marie chided and smiled through her thin lips covered in frosted mauve lipstick.

"Yes, Ma'am, you are right about that," Brooks agreed. Brooks looked at Vernadine and realized again, just how beautiful and comely she looked sitting in the chair next to her Aunt. A picture of manners and grace, mixed with grit and nerves of steel. He felt happy and reassured about his decision to get to know Vernadine better, and even though he did not know exactly how everything would play out, he felt a sense of hope, promise, excitement and wonderment at the mystery of it all. Like Vernadine, he also had butterflies in his stomach, but nervousness would not hold him back from taking the journey to see where it would lead. "Vernadine, are you ready to go? I made reservations at Constantine's for 7:30 PM. I hope you like Greek food?" Brooks asked.

"Oh, yes, I do! Constantine's is one of my favorite restaurants," She smiled as her heart skipped another beat. "Aunt Marie, I will see you later. Please don't wait up for me."

"You two have a wonderful time together. It was a pleasure meeting you Mr. Lawson," Aunt Marie said as she waved her hand holding her handkerchief.

Brooks escorted Vernadine to the front door and opened it for her. Vernadine stepped onto the porch, closed and locked the door. Brooks held her elbow as they made their way down the porch stairs towards the car. Vernadine was thankful for the darkness outside, because she could not contain her smile. She was beaming from ear to ear and wanted to enjoy the moment without anyone seeing her. She knew she would die of embarrassment if her feelings of excitement were one sided. But if she had only turned around, she would have seen the exact expression on Brooks' face. For the rest of the evening, neither of them lost their smiles or giddiness, and they both wished the evening would never end.

From their first date, they were inseparable, and devoted all of their free time to being together. They enjoyed dances, dinners, and Sunday church services. They took long walks in the park and strolls through downtown Mobile. They made frequent trips to Vernadine's house in Fairhope overlooking the bay and a few trips to Spit's Creek to check on Irene and Sheridan. The consensus was overwhelming from her family; they immediately liked Brooks and expressed their happiness for both of them. Brooks and Vernadine knew they were in a race to make up for the lost time and years spent alone, never knowing if there would be someone special for them, so they relished their blessings and growing love for each other.

When Vernadine felt secure enough, she told Brooks her story of being 'The basketball queen' and about Slim. Even though she was afraid of losing Brooks, she told him about the moments on the school bus at state playoffs and all of the events leading up to her arrival in Mobile. Brooks was shocked. He wasn't shocked or judgmental about the pregnancy, but somehow, he had not connected the dots together about the 'queen of basketball', and he remembered his fascination with her even back then. He could not believe the Vernadine he knew now could ever fit the mold of an athlete playing on an all-boys' basketball team. He knew he admired and loved her for who she was, and he could feel his chest growing in pride at his good fortune in finding such an interesting woman.

Brooks told Vernadine his stories of working his way through college at Plains University, returning home after college and selling farm equipment. He told her about meeting and marrying his wife and the tragedy of the death of his wife and newborn child. He told her about his year of extreme depression and withdrawal from life and society. He told her of his surprise and shock at being asked to run for Mayor at such a young age and how all of this brought him to meeting her in City Council meetings. Brooks adored Vernadine and after a few short months of dating, he knelt down on one knee, in Vernadine's living room, and asked if she would do him the honor of becoming his wife. Vernadine did not hesitate and accepted his proposal through tears of pure joy. Aunt Marie was right there, excited and tearful herself. She was so happy Vernadine had finally found true love from a good man. She deserved it. Aunt Marie wasted no time in collecting the brandy decanter and three glasses as she thought of the perfect words to toast the love birds. Before the toasting and celebrating began, Vernadine knew her mother and Sheridan would want to share in her good news. She excused herself and made a phone call. It surprised Vernadine to hear they had been expecting her phone call with great anticipation and that Brooks had phoned a few days prior asking both Irene and Sheridan for their blessings of matrimony. The phone call ended with tears of happiness, hope, celebration and best wishes for a new and wonderful future together. The future Vernadine had dreamed about for years now was finally coming true.

Vernadine pinched herself on her good fortune in finding such a loving and handsome man, and she floated on clouds. Finally, at thirty-four years old, she could begin planning a wedding and a life with a truly nice man. Brooks felt the same way about his new life and adventure with Vernadine. A new and happy chapter of life was on the horizon and they couldn't quit smiling about it and thanking the Lord. They knew there was much to do in preparation, and they didn't waste a minute. Sorting through both houses and decisions needing discussion would take some time. They planned the wedding for the end of May, in the front yard of her Fairhope cottage, under the large oak trees, at sunset overlooking Mobile Bay.

Where is Louanna?

Late April 1961
Spit's Creek

With high school graduation only a few weeks away, the town buzzed with excitement as it did every year, and hopes ran high for the future of each of the graduates. Parents walked with their heads held high; confident that their son or daughter would be the next big success in their careers and endeavors. The families prayed their children would have the opportunities that skipped their generation and the generations before them; the chance to move on to bigger and better futures, to carve out a life of comfort and wealth in towns larger than Spit's Creek. The optimism was electric.

With acceptance letters in hand from Plains University for the upcoming fall term, Birdy and Sheridan began making plans for their new journey together. There was so much to do to prepare. Waiting through the long and hot summer in Buford County would be grueling, but this summer promised to be one full of excitement and happiness.

Along with the jubilance and optimism in town, there was also foreboding and fear. No one had seen or heard from Louanna Parsons for two weeks. The law enforcement agencies issued an all-points-bulletin throughout the states of Alabama, Georgia and Florida asking for help. Mr. and Mrs. Parsons were inconsolable and in a constant state of worry and panic. The thoughts of their beautiful little girl in harm's way, or worse, left them devastated. Louanna's father took a leave of absence from the Alabama Mill, and spent his days driving around Buford County searching every field and stream and deserted house and barn. Louanna's mother also took a leave of absence from the hospital, but she never left her house. Marigold Perkins and the ladies of First Methodist Church organized an indefinite schedule for meal delivery to the Parsons' house, hoping to relieve the stress of cooking. A prayer vigil, led by retired Pastor Wright, was held on the steps of the courthouse five days after Louanna was reported missing. The community turned out in mass for a show of support. The vigil concluded with Bull Smith making a public plea asking for help. He announced he and his deputies, along with the city police department, would lead and organize search parties in the efforts to find Louanna. The Parsons and the community were thankful for Sheriff Smith's commitment to uphold the office for which he was elected.

The following Wednesday morning, Birdy and Celia wheeled into Sheridan's driveway in the red VW bug and honked the horn. Sheridan ran out of her house, leapt off of the front porch, and jumped into the backseat. Birdy tore off like a shot, kicking up dust and dirt all the way down the driveway. Irene stood at the screened door shaking her head. "Teenagers," she said aloud as she wiped her damp hands with her apron. She couldn't help but think about Vernadine at that moment and feel sadness. There was not a time she could recall when Vernadine raced out of the door to greet her close friends; friends waiting on an adventure with life ahead of them. She was comforted knowing Vernadine had finally found her one true friend and love in Brooks Lawson, and her days of being lonely were over. Days of promise and fulfillment were ahead.

Before arriving at school, the girls made a quick stop at Mrs. Ruth's café. Barely missing a dog in the road, Birdy buzzed into a parking spot, and the girls raced inside and ran to their favorite corner booth.

"Good morning, Girls. You here for your regulars, or something different today?" Mrs. Ruth asked while wiping the table next to theirs.

"No, Ma'am, we will have our regulars," the three said in unison.

"Coming right up, along with your orange juice," Mrs. Ruth said as she walked away.

"Mrs. Ruth," said Birdy, "I think I will have a cup of coffee instead of orange juice today." Birdy turned around to face Sheridan and Celia with expressions of shock and horror on their faces.

"Birdy!" exclaimed Celia, "Why are you ordering coffee? That's a grown up drink. You are seventeen. No seventeen-year-old drinks coffee! Don't you know coffee stunts your growth? And if you haven't noticed, you are already short enough!"

"Would y'all shut up!" Birdy fired back, "I am just trying it. I saw a movie the other night where Elizabeth Taylor was drinking coffee and she looked so glamorous. She was even smoking, too. I am considering trying a cigarette soon. Who wants to do it with me?"

"You have lost your mind!" Sheridan loudly whispered.

Celia spoke up and said, "Don't you know Momma and Daddy would kill you if they thought for one minute that you were smoking! What would Momma's Sunday school class think if they knew their teacher's daughter was smoking like a no-good hoodlum? And, Daddy at his Lion Club meetings, having to hold his head up, with everyone talking behind his back; whispering he has failed as a father and as the spiritual leader of his family? No, Birdy! Don't do it!" Celia implored.

Right then and there, the challenge and risk was set into motion in Birdy's mind. She decided she would definitely start smoking today. She could always ask one of the guys who hung out in the back parking lot at school for one cigarette. She could be smoking by lunch today. She, too, could be glamorous just like Elizabeth Taylor. At least that's what she hoped for in her mind. "It's time to shake things up a bit," Birdy thought to herself. She felt justified in her new way of thinking. She was ready for new, whatever that was. She was ready to step out a little and try new things. Of the three girls, Birdy was the loose cannon, and even though Sheridan and Celia disapproved of her new plan for coffee and cigarettes, they were not surprised, either. They did fear, however, what Birdy would decide to do next, especially when she was not under the watchful eyes of her parents. All hell could break loose and they all knew it. Sheridan and Celia were already bracing themselves for the impact.

The biscuits and gravy, orange juice, and Birdy's coffee arrived in no time. The conversation between the three girls quieted as they ate; each deep into their thoughts. The murmur in the café centered on Louanna Parsons. There was still no sign of her. Louanna's boyfriend, Tommy Smith, dropped out of school, to the dismay of his parents, within weeks of his graduation. Tommy couldn't bear the gossip, rumors, and finger pointing. Everyone agreed Tommy was the reason for Louanna's disappearance. Who else would it be? The evidence was stacked against him and he was guilty. In Bull's haste to leave the crime scene, along with Tommy's jacket and shoes, he left one tube of pink frosted lipstick, one earring, and a hair pin. All of which were identified by Louanna's parents. The items were bagged and tagged and placed in the evidence vault at the police station. Bull wasn't worried. None of the items recovered could be traced to him. Tommy, on the other hand, was not so lucky. Tommy had been looking for his jacket and tennis shoes for months, to no avail. How did they end up at the river? Formal charges had not been filed, but in the public's eye, Tommy was convicted for crimes against Louanna and law enforcement and Mr. Parsons followed Tommy wherever he went.

His father, Bull, was strangely quiet and absent from offering support and encouragement at home and in the public eye, and Tommy wondered why? He was left to assume his parents thought he was guilty, too. Tommy felt completely isolated and terrified. He knew his life was over before it had time to really begin, and the sadness he felt over that thought was paralyzing. Bull, on the other hand, seemed oddly calm, cool and collected. He stood by, day after day, as the fevered pitch of the town grew with accusations against his own son. Bull's response to the anger and accusations were always the same, "We are working diligently with the Spit's Creek Police Department, following every lead we receive. We are not at liberty to divulge any information in the disappearance of Miss Parsons at this time. We are not prepared to make any arrests, but rest assured, you will know as soon as any new developments arise." There were always questions about his son's presumed guilt, but he remained professional and emotionally stable with his responses. It amazed the townspeople how Bull could continue to serve his county in the midst of his own personal crisis. What the public didn't know was how Bull struggled with the reality of knowing the crimes against Louanna would be pinned on his own son. Bull lacked the moral and spiritual conviction to confess the whole truth, and he was unwilling to suffer the consequences for his crime. Even to save his innocent son. He deliberately left Tommy's belongings on the river bank, knowing he was sacrificing Tommy to protect himself. He would not take the punishment for the crime. Tommy would have to take the fall. Bull flinched at the passing thought but didn't dwell on it for long.

Birdy, Celia and Sheridan arrived to school tardy. Instead of parking in her usual spot in the front parking lot, Birdy drove around to the rear of the school and parked next to a group of guys she knew would help her in her mission of becoming Elizabeth Taylor.

"I am telling Birdy the minute I see her, if she does not pick us up in the front parking lot after school, we will find another ride home. I am not going back to the rear lot. Ever. She knows how we all feel about this! People are already talking about us!" Sheridan hissed.

"I know! I feel the same way as you! I don't understand what she is thinking! Girls like us do not park in the back lot. We have our reputations to protect!" Celia said.

Birdy lingered beside her car and looked around. One guy stood out. A guy she had always thought of as ruggedly handsome.

"Excuse me, hello, I am Birdy Snodgrass. Would you have a cigarette I can bum?" she smiled sweetly as she spoke.

"Sure," said the handsome guy, returning a smile.

"Thanks. Well, I guess I need to go. The bell has already rung and we are tardy. I think I will save this for lunch break. Will you be out here during lunch? I don't know how to smoke. Maybe you could teach me?"

"Sure, I will be out here. See you then," The handsome guy said.

As Birdy made her way to the school doors, she felt giddy and risky. She felt dangerous and alive. Being sneaky with a cigarette and a cute boy was a bigger thrill than she had expected. She couldn't wait until lunch break.

When the final school bell rang for the day, Birdy walked to the back parking lot, started her car, let the convertible top down and drove around to the front of the school to pick up Sheridan and Celia, who Birdy was now calling "the goody-two-shoe twins". Neither Sheridan nor Celia found the new title endearing. They were still mad at Birdy for parking in the back lot and smoking during lunch. On the way home, Birdy zoomed into the quick mart and bought a pack of Pall Mall cigarettes, a lighter and an RC Cola. She jumped back into her car, opened the cigarette pack, lit her second cigarette of the day, and wheeled off towards Sheridan's home.

"Celia, if you tell Momma and Daddy about this I will drop you off in the middle of town every morning on our way to school, and you can walk the rest of the way. See if I care. And, Sheridan, the same goes for you," Birdy said as the smoke billowed from her mouth and caught the wind. Nothing was said the rest of the ride until they hit stopped traffic with police and sheriff cars everywhere.

"What in the world is going on?" the girls said in unison as they craned their necks to get a better view.

"Y'all, isn't that where Tommy Smith lives?" Celia said exasperated.

"Oh, my gosh, it is!" said Birdy.

Tommy walked onto his front porch in handcuffs and two deputies on either side. From what they could see, his upper body was slumped and the deputies were holding him up as they walked towards the patrol car. He looked defeated and broken, and even from a distance everyone could see he was heaving and crying. Tommy's mother followed behind him screaming and grabbing at his shirt. A composed Bull Smith walked up behind her as she collapsed to the ground.

"Oh, no! y'all, they are charging Tommy with Louanna's disappearance!" said Birdy.

"Am I the only one who feels this way, but don't y'all think this whole thing is very mysterious? I don't see where Tommy would ever hurt Louanna. The way he treats her and the way he looks at her. I know she told me during our spring break trip that she didn't like him the way he liked her, but she never mentioned anything about Tommy being possessive or jealous or controlling. He's just a regular jock-type guy who definitely thinks highly of himself, but he does not appear to have a mean streak. I know I am new here, and I may be really off base, but something just doesn't seem right here?" Sheridan said.

"I agree," Celia said. "This whole thing is very strange. You remember, though, we all noticed many changes in Louanna over the past few months. She quickly went from a confident beauty queen, ready to tackle the world, to deflated, depressed and plainly dressed. All of that was so unlike her. I know a lot of the girls have never liked her out of pure meanness and jealousy, but Louanna was really a nice girl. She wasn't a snob or uppity; she just took care of herself, made plans for her future away from here, and couldn't wait to leave. Maybe that's it? Maybe she has run away and is somewhere, right this minute, doing just fine? Maybe the dirt roads and small town living finally got the best of her and she had to get away suddenly?"

"Another thing about all of this that strikes me as odd… have y'all noticed the Sheriff seems so composed all of the time? I mean, the blame has been directed at his son and he acts like none of this bothers him. If I was Tommy's father, I wouldn't be able to hold myself together like he has. I mean, look at his poor momma. She is inconsolable. Her reaction to this tragedy is normal, The Sheriff's is not normal," Sheridan said with an irritated voice. They all just nodded their heads in agreement.

Tommy was ushered into the patrol car, the door was closed, and he laid down on the back seat. The officer turned on the siren and sped away towards the police station, followed by multiple police cars. Bull Smith remained standing resolute in the yard as the whole scene played out. Tommy's mother chased the patrol car until she collapsed in the middle of the street. Birdy cranked the car, shifted the car into drive, and slowly pulled away. She swerved passed Mrs. Smith, who was still lying in the street weeping and wailing and screaming, "Not my boy. Please don't take my boy."

For the rest of the ride home, Birdy, Celia and Sheridan sat quietly. Birdy turned the radio on to fill the silence while the news announcer reported, "Tommy Smith, the son of Sheriff Frank 'Bull' Smith and the boyfriend of Louanna Parsons, has been arrested for suspicion of foul play and harm to Miss Parsons. Neither the police department, Sheriff's department, or Tommy Smith's family were available for comments."

The news spread quickly throughout Buford County about Tommy's arrest, and most people collectively breathed a sigh of relief, knowing the guilty teenage boy was behind bars. The news was bittersweet and even though an arrest was made, an uneasiness and unsettling was felt by everyone. Something about this tragedy just did not seem right to many of the townspeople, and the question that persisted was, 'why would anyone leave a trail of evidence to implicate themselves in a crime?' The insistence from the community to make an arrest took on a life of its own and the law enforcement officers were feeling the pressure for action. Guilty or not guilty, Tommy Smith was the sacrifice to ease the pressure and collective panic.

Tommy wept all night in the solitude of his jail cell. In between sobs, he screamed, "I am innocent. I loved Louanna! I would never do anything to hurt her. Somebody, please believe me!"

The End of the Innocence

Spit's Creek and Mobile
May 1961

The summer of 1961 started off with sweltering heat. The minute the last bell of the school year rang, the three girls ran to the parking lot with reckless abandon, waving and telling friends goodbye. They jumped into the car and sped out of the school parking lot; each taking turns throwing their last term papers out onto the highway.

"Good riddance, Benjamin Franklin," said Birdy...

"Nice meeting you, Martha Washington," said Sheridan.

"I hope we don't meet again for a long time, or ever, Mr. Shakespeare," said Celia.

The girls left a paper trail blowing in the wind. It was summer now.... Birdy turned the radio volume all the way up. Her favorite song, "Runaway" by Del Shannon, was playing, and they all sang along at the top of their lungs. "My little Runaway... run, run, run, run, runaway"....Tonight was graduation for Sheridan and Birdy. Tonight signified the beginning of the rest of their lives, but in the midst of the excitement over graduation and future plans, they couldn't help but think about their beautiful Louanna and the reality that she would not be graduating with her classmates' tonight.

Louanna had been missing for one month, and Tommy Smith's trial was fast tracked to begin in three weeks. The grand jury voted unanimously to try Tommy. Bull Smith worked fast to hire the most aggressive and dogged attorney to defend Tommy at trial. Bull figured he could at least do that for his son, and maybe through luck, the jury would believe Tommy's attorney in pleading reasonable doubt. A hung jury was always a possibility. Tommy was known as a respectable young man and a star athlete; he didn't have a criminal record, even for speeding or drinking by the river. His record and reputation were spotless.

Waiting on the Buford County High School graduates to take their seats for commencement, Vernadine realized it had been seventeen years since she darkened the doors of the gymnasium that bore her name. She couldn't help but remember her days as 'The Queen of Basketball' and winning the championships of 1943 and 1944. The last time she sat in this gymnasium was for her own high school graduation when she wore the white eyelet dress with the red bow. She noticed the gymnasium hadn't changed much over time as she stared at the 'Vernadine D. Turnipseed' scoreboard and her team's pictures with fond memories. She glanced around the gymnasium and noticed Slim and Marigold sitting on the opposite side in silent support for Sheridan.

Vernadine turned to look at Brooks seated beside her and she felt her heart melt. All of the twists and turns of her life, the surviving, the making of a way, on determination alone, seemed all worth it now. She was seated next to the love of her life and surrounded by her small family to celebrate Sheridan's graduation. Vernadine opened her handbag and retrieved the worn handkerchief her mother gave her as she loaded the bus to Mobile and wiped her eyes. Brooks noticed Vernadine's emotions, and without saying a word, he placed his arm around the small of her back and gave a gentle nudge.

The commencement service was jubilant and upbeat. Vernadine sensed the townspeople had forgiven her outburst at her father's funeral, and even though she remained true to the words she had spoken on that sad morning, she felt relieved she was not sitting in the midst of their anger and resentment on such a happy occasion. When the commencement service ended, the parents, teachers, and families sent the graduates off with well wishes for their futures with a reception under the large oak trees.

While the family was together, Vernadine and Brooks shared the progress for their upcoming wedding day and plans were made to depart for Mobile the following morning.

In the excitement of an early departure and loading the luggage, no one paid attention to the newspaper on the front porch. It wasn't until Irene locked the front door, heading for the car, that she grabbed the newspaper and placed it in her over-sized handbag. 'A little something to read and occupy my mind on the four hour car ride,' she thought to herself as she settled into the front seat of Vernadine's Lincoln.

The chatter in the car was non-stop about the wedding. The reception would be on the front lawn after the ceremony, with a main course of shrimp and grits and a champagne fountain. Brooks hired a local jazz trio for lively music and the pastor from the First Baptist Church in Mobile would officiate the wedding.

In a moment of quiet Vernadine said, "I have something I would like to ask the both of you."

Irene and Sheridan said, "Ok", in unison.

"Since Daddy is gone, I don't have anyone to walk me down the aisle. This makes me sad. I know Daddy would be happy for this moment together and so would I. I have been thinking about who I could ask and no one really came to mind, except maybe my broker, who has been a wonderful mentor and friend. I seriously considered asking him, but then the thought popped into my head about the two of you. You two are my heart. I know this is not traditional, but I would really love it if both of you walked beside me down the aisle," Vernadine sniffled as she spoke.

"Oh Momma, that is a wonderful idea! I would love that! And since when have you concerned yourself with traditional ideas, anyway?" Sheridan said as she patted her Mother on the back with a sly smile on her freckled face.

Vernadine glanced at her mother and noticed she was crying and wiping her eyes. "Momma, are you okay? Vernadine asked.

"Oh, don't worry about me. I am fine. Your father missing this exciting time in your life has me teary eyed. I have thought about how your father would be happy for you. He would have liked Brooks. I can hear him saying 'The Lord has His own plan and journey for each of us. It is comforting to know that He is with us in the bitter and the sweet. Our Vernadine has experienced both, but I could not have chosen a better man than Brooks Lawson for our Vernadine.' He knew through these last years you were heartbroken and lonely for a companion. He truly wanted you to find someone worthy of your love. I cannot tell you how many times I overheard his prayers for you as he knelt beside his bed. He would talk to the Lord for thirty minutes each morning after he drank his coffee and ate his breakfast. He would kiss me on the cheek, tell me how much he enjoyed the breakfast, and say 'Well, me and the Lord have got to have our daily conversation. I will see you shortly.' And then he would walk to his bedroom and kneel beside his bed. He never closed the door so I knew what was on his heart. The fervency of his prayers were influenced by what was happening in your life. He pleaded with the Lord to show his favor on you. Your father was a quiet man by nature, but he took his role as your father to heart. He loved you and Sheridan so much, Vernadine. He would be so thankful after many years, his prayers are finally answered, and you have found a wonderful man who truly loves and adores you. Brooks is a fine, strong, loving, Christian man, and that is exactly what your father and I have prayed for. Not to mention, he is also quite handsome, too. I know you are sad your father is not here to walk you down the aisle; he would have never wanted to miss this moment with you. I tell you all of this to say 'yes!' it would honor me to walk beside you down the aisle." Irene said as she wiped her eyes with one hand and grabbed Vernadine's hand with her other.

"Oh Momma, that is beautiful! I can hear Daddy telling me along the way how life is bitter and sweet. I never understood what he meant by that until years later. But, he is so right. I have tasted both, mostly the bitter it seems, but I am so thankful life is bringing me sweetness for the first time in a long time. I have a wonderful family, a successful business, and now the love of a man who has, until now, only lived in my dreams. The biggest miracle of this is that Brooks is real. I keep waiting to wake up from my dream and find it was all in my imagination; but it's not and for that I can't thank the Lord enough for this 'sweetness' He has given me. Thank you for telling me this story about Daddy. You are right. I can hear him saying everything you have said just as if he was sitting beside us," Vernadine said through crying eyes. "I am so thrilled you two will be beside me on my wedding walk, and I know Daddy will be with us in spirit. Having you two with me makes my wedding even more special."

The conversation quieted. Each of them retreating to their own thoughts and silent prayers of thankfulness for all of their good fortune and happiness. Irene adjusted her seat and retrieved her reading glasses and the newspaper from her handbag. In bold letters on the front page LOUANNA PARSONS' BODY FOUND. "Oh my Lord!" shouted Irene, "Louanna's body has been found!"

"Granny! Hand that to me! Let me read it aloud to you both!" Sheridan exclaimed as she grabbed the newspaper and popped the paper twice for reading.

Sheridan drew in a breath and began reading, "The body of Miss Louanna Parsons, of Spit's Creek, Alabama, was discovered yesterday morning by a fisherman in the Chattahoochee River. The fisherman, who requests to remain anonymous, explained he was trolling along the side of the river, approximately five miles south from the popular teenage gathering spot in Spit's Creek, when he noticed something caught in the roots of a tree. He managed to get closer to the tree and discovered a body caught in the roots. The fisherman explained he immediately headed towards his truck and quickly made his way to the Spit's Creek Police Department to speak with the officer in charge. In a matter of less than an hour, the police department, Buford County Sheriff's department and the coroner were on the scene. Law enforcement officers and the Coroner declined any remarks except to say 'the investigation of the death of Louanna Parsons is ongoing.' The article continued with a brief biography of Louanna, noting she would have graduated from BCHS in May. Her father was quoted as saying 'We are inconsolable at the loss of our only child, Louanna. We want to thank all of the law enforcement agencies that have worked together to help bring our Louanna home. We would like to thank the gentleman who discovered her body. We would also like to thank our church and community for taking such good care of us through this tragedy. Please continue to keep Mrs. Parsons and I in your prayers.' The article concluded with funeral arrangements to be announced after the conclusion of the autopsy.

"Oh, my goodness!" cried Sheridan. "Poor, poor Louanna. I know her parents are beside themselves in grief. Even though I have only spent a small amount of time with Louanna, I really liked her. She was so beautiful, and she was very excited about her future. She had big dreams and plans, and now she's dead. I am glad her body was discovered so her parents can give her a proper funeral; but like I have mentioned to Birdy and Celia, there is something very odd going on here. Tommy Smith is a very nice guy, and he loved Louanna even though she didn't feel the same way about him. I cannot see him hurting her in any way." Sheridan said as she stared at Louanna's picture next to the headline. "Momma, Tommy Smith's trial is one week after your wedding. I would like to be there if that's okay you."

"Ok, I understand why you would want to be there, but be prepared to hear and see things that may disturb you more than you think they will. Death by murder is a messy business and I am sad for the Parsons. I can't imagine the pain they are in. Tommy's father and I were in school together. I wonder how he and his wife are handling this?" Vernadine said as the wind tossed the end of her scarf.

"That's just it. Bull Smith has been cool as a cucumber through this whole mess, and I have found his behavior very odd considering his son is the one charged in this crime!" Sheridan said as she rubbed her brow, deep in questions and turmoil.

"Well, the truth always has a way of showing itself, eventually. This whole thing is very tragic. I will mail a card to the Parsons and the Smith's in a day or so offering my prayers and condolences during this sad time," Vernadine said as she turned onto their street. "Ok, we are almost there! There is so much to do before the wedding!"

After the cars were unloaded and everyone put their belongings away, Brooks kissed Vernadine goodbye and left for his home with a promise to see her later.

The following morning, the headline in the Mobile Register read, "Buford County Sheriff's Son Arrested for Murder." The article showed a picture of Louanna, Tommy Smith and Sheriff Bull Smith side by side and noted that jury selection was in progress with a trial date set for early June. After a brief recap of the events leading up to the arrest of Tommy Smith, the article concluded with a comment from Bull Smith. "The community of Spit's Creek is saddened by the death and discovery of Miss Parsons' body. Miss Parsons was a great example of the fine young folks we have in Buford County. The news of her death has hit us all very hard and we are all dealing with the grief. My wife and I are personally affected in this terrible tragedy, as our son, Tommy, sits in jail awaiting his trial. I have hired the best attorney on this side of the Mississippi to defend him, but the evidence and the history of his personal relationship with Miss Parsons stacks the cards against him. We are praying for a miracle and we would appreciate any and all of the support and prayers we can get. We are concerned that we will not see Tommy for a very long time after the conclusion of the trial."

The Bitter and the Sweet

Mobile and Spit's Creek
May-June 1961

Vernadine had not slept a wink. She tossed and turned all night in anticipation and excitement for the sunrise and what this new and glorious day would mean to her. Her journey to this very day had been a long one. Through all of the twists and turns, the heartbreak and sadness, she was finally going to be a bride.

The cottage in Fairhope looked like a fairytale. The front porch was draped with white tulle, white lights, and peach colored flowers. White chairs and tables covered in white cloths were scattered about the yard. The jazz trio played softly as the guests found their seats to wait for the ceremony. The setting, with a backdrop of live oaks and Mobile Bay, was a sight to behold.

"Momma, it's time. We are ready if you are!" Sheridan said through the door. Vernadine opened the door. "Oh, Momma, you look stunning. You are so beautiful! Mr. Lawson is going to just die when he sees how perfect his bride looks!" Sheridan said, as she leaned in for a light hug.

Irene was speechless, and thankful she had remembered to put her handkerchief inside her small handbag. She dabbed her eyes and said, "Vernadine, you are the prettiest bride I have ever seen. If your father could see you, he would be so proud. I knew you would look beautiful today, but you are a vision. Brooks is going to die!" The three of them wiped their eyes and hugged in a circle. "Can we have a prayer before we walk you outside?" Irene said.

"Of course, Momma, that is a wonderful idea," Vernadine said as she closed the door.

They joined hands, stood in a circle, and bowed their heads. Irene began her prayer: "Dear Lord, today is a day we didn't think would ever come, but we are so thankful that this glorious day is finally here. Thank you, Lord, for bringing my daughter such a wonderful man for a husband and companion. I know You know the complete story of all of our lives. The good and the bad, or 'the bitter and the sweet' as Fletcher would say. I know You know through the trials of life we can sometimes wonder if You are really there. But, dear Jesus, we know You see and know everything; and through our pains, sorrows, despair, happiness, and excitement, You are there. Thank you for taking care of my Vernadine and Sheridan. Thank You for Your constant protection and provision. Thank You for the meaning of this day and thank You for allowing me to be here to see this blessed event in the life of my daughter. My prayer is that You will protect and watch over Vernadine and Brooks, and that their life together will be one of pure joy and happiness. Thank You, Lord, for Your timing and Your plan for each of us. Thank You for loving us all. In Jesus' name, Amen." The three dabbed the corners of their eyes and hugged. Irene straightened Vernadine's veil and opened the door to make their way to the front yard. The guests were seated, the music played, and Brooks was standing under the large oak tree, waiting for his bride.

Earlier that morning, before Brooks settled himself under the oak tree, he prayed. "Dear gracious Lord. I am coming to You today with a full heart. The same heart that was broken and sad a few years ago is beating again with pure joy, thankfulness, and amazement at what You have carried me through and for the love of Vernadine Dawn Turnipseed. I am not sure what I did to deserve the love of this woman, who, to me, exemplifies grace, beauty, intelligence, and a loving and giving heart. I want to thank you for my gift. You have given me a renewed purpose in my life. Thank You for the opportunity to grow old with someone. I promise to You I will love and cherish Vernadine until I draw my last breath. Help me be the best husband and companion for her. She deserves it. Thank You, Lord, for life and for your constant care and protection. You know that I sincerely loved my wife and child, and through my bitterness from their deaths, I turned away from You for a long time. I was mad at You for taking them away. But, I know they are both with You. I know they would not want me to live a life of sadness, bitterness, and anger and neither do You. Forgive me, Lord, for my lack of faith and anger. Today is very special to me and one that I never imagined would happen again. You are a loving God. A just God. A righteous God. Thank you seems so small, but from the bottom of my heart, Thank You, Lord, for this day and for this new family."

Vernadine, Sheridan and Irene were waiting for the cue. The music began and the three of them slowly began their walk down the aisle. As she made her way towards Brooks, she dabbed her eyes underneath her veil and noticed Brooks was teary eyed, too. Standing in front of her was her greatest surprise and blessing. She glanced at Sheridan and thought to herself, "well, my second greatest surprise and blessing."

The ceremony was brief and the reception was loud and happy. The guests stayed until the food and champagne ran out. After everyone said their goodbyes, Brooks opened another bottle of champagne, poured two glasses, and raised his glass. "Vernadine Lawson has a nice ring to it! I will promise to love, cherish, respect, and take care of you forever. You are my whole heart and I will strive every day to remind you of that. I will love Sheridan as if she were my own. You looked so beautiful today. You took my breath away. I'm looking forward to our life together. I love you so much." Brooks said as they tapped their glasses.

"Ok, my turn," Vernadine said. "You have made me the happiest woman. In a million years I never thought I would find someone as wonderful as you for my husband. I am so thankful you are mine. Our life together starts right now!" Vernadine said as she leaned in for a kiss.

Brooks and Vernadine made the decision to remain at the Fairhope cottage for their honeymoon. All of the excitement from Sheridan's graduation and wedding preparations left them happy but exhausted.

Evenings on the front porch gazing at the bay, long walks under tree-lined streets, dinners in delicious restaurants were perfectly fine with them. The location didn't matter as long as they were together.

Two days after the wedding, Vernadine received a phone call to hurry home. Aunt Marie was in the hospital and her condition was grave. Vernadine and Brooks jumped in the car and sped back to Mobile. Vernadine rushed inside the hospital and asked to see Aunt Marie. When Vernadine walked in Aunt Marie's hospital room she was saddened to see her once vibrant and full of life Aunt barely conscious. "Aunt Marie, it's Vernadine. I am here. Can you hear me?"

"Yes, child, I can hear you," Aunt Marie said through low and labored speech.

"Oh, Aunt Marie, I love you so much. What am I going to do without you? You have been like a second mother to me. You have loved Sheridan and I like we were your own and I can never say thank you enough. I don't want you to leave us!" Vernadine said through tears.

"Vernadine, you and Sheridan will be just fine. You have Brooks to take care of you now and he will be just what you need. I am so thankful I was at your wedding, and I know now you will be provided for and loved. Out of sheer determination, I hung on long enough to see you finally find love and lasting happiness. Now it's time for me to go. We will see each other again someday. Life on this earth doesn't last forever. Now, don't you worry about me, I will be taken care of in heaven, and I will be there waiting for you when it's your time to come. I am so happy for you and I have cherished these years together. They have brought me so much joy. Please don't be sad. You are still celebrating your marriage, and you deserve a celebration. I will tell your father that you love him when I see him. I love you, Vernadine," Aunt Marie said as she drew her last breath.

Vernadine couldn't move; she was frozen. Losing her father and her aunt in a matter of months was beyond her comprehension. Through all the happiness in her life over the last year, there was also deep pain. The loss of two people who loved her deeply cut her to the core. Even though she was comforted knowing she now had two guardian angels, the loss of their physical presence would never sit right with her. She knew her heart would mourn and grieve the loss of these two souls until her dying day.

Going through Aunt Marie's papers the morning after her death, Vernadine discovered Aunt Marie wanted her to deliver the eulogy at her service. Aunt Marie had handwritten a short note to Vernadine telling her she was the closest person to her and because of that, she was the only one who could do her story and life justice. Aunt Marie asked her to focus on the love they shared, and to ask to God for the strength to say her 'goodbye's' for her. She asked her to remember her church family, her neighbors and her fellow club members, along with anything else she felt appropriate. Vernadine knew she would not make it through this daunting task initially, but she became accustomed to the idea and felt honored from the request of her beloved Aunt. The evening before the funeral, Vernadine sat down at the dining room table and began to collect her thoughts and memories. What could she say without completely falling apart? Unlike speaking at her father's funeral, out of disgust and anger at the congregants, this time she was left without the same bravado that she felt on that sad day. Vernadine closed her eyes and realized she was sitting in the exact same chair she sat in on the day of her arrival in Mobile seventeen years ago. And just like that, memories flooded her mind, and in the course of half an hour she had completed the eulogy.

The funeral was well attended and the altar was covered in flowers. On top of Aunt Marie's coffin sat a picture of Aunt Marie on her wedding day, beautiful and young with a full life ahead of her. Vernadine knew Aunt Marie loved that picture and she had commented on it through the years.

Vernadine walked to the pulpit and said, "Ladies and gentlemen, friends and neighbors, we are gathered today to celebrate the life of a wonderful woman, a woman each of you remember as saintly, charitable, loving, and the perfect picture of Southern womanhood. My Aunt Marie was one of the most beautiful souls I will ever have the honor of knowing. Her love and commitment to her family and close friends was exemplary. She was a woman ahead of her time. She loved her home, her community and her church. She also loved John F. Kennedy and Frank Sinatra." The crowd chuckled. "Aunt Marie opened her home to me what I was seventeen. She took me in and she nurtured and protected me like I was her own daughter. I will never be able to repay her for all she has done for me and my daughter, Sheridan. My heart is very sad at the loss of Aunt Marie and knowing I will not see her again on earth is difficult for my mind and my heart to comprehend. But, what I have of her are my many memories of a life shared together, memories I hold close to my heart like a warm, comforting blanket. Her presence is with me in the home we shared together. All of her stories whisper to me through photographs, the smell of a blueberry cobbler, fresh coffee, and soft feather pillows with white crisp linens. She is here with me. I know she is with her family in heaven that has gone before her and she is as beautiful today as she is in this wedding picture sitting in front of us. I can hear her laughing and asking the Lord if he wouldn't mind the 'great choir of angels' singing her a Sinatra song for old time's sake. Yes, I will miss you so much Aunt Marie. I love you sincerely. Rest well, you beautiful rebel, you, and I will see you again in the sweet bye and bye." Vernadine sniffled as she looked towards heaven and blew a kiss to her Aunt Marie. She stepped away from the pulpit, amazed she had pulled this off without completely breaking down. Her Aunt would have been so proud of her. She knew it.

The Trial

Spits Creek
June 1961

The morning after Aunt Marie's funeral, Sheridan, Irene, Birdy and Celia loaded their cars for a racing drive back to Spit's Creek. Tommy Smith's trial had begun the day before and they were determined to sit front and center in the courtroom and not miss one more detail. Arriving back home, the girls deposited Irene at her house and sped off towards downtown. Cars lined every street, and it was difficult finding a parking place. When the girls ran five blocks to the courthouse, they found it was standing room only. Squeezing through the crowd, they found a spot on the wall to stand in view of Tommy. What they noticed was how weary and beaten down Tommy looked. His face was pale and his eyes were puffy. He looked like he had lost twenty pounds as he stared at his lap or the table, doodling on a notepad to keep himself busy. The man who discovered Louanna's body in the river was finishing up his story. There were no questions asked by either attorney, and he was dismissed. Tommy's attorney, Custis Buck, said, "Your honor, the defense calls the Buford County Medical Examiner, Dr. Richard Graves, to the stand."

After placing his hand on the bible and swearing to tell the truth and nothing but the truth, the medical examiner sat down.

"Dr. Graves," said Custis, "I understand you performed an autopsy on Miss Parsons. Is that correct?"

"That is correct," said Dr. Graves.

"Can you please tell the court what the findings from the autopsy showed? The cause of death and any other pertinent information?" Custis asked.

"Yes, sir, Miss Parsons died from strangulation of the neck. Miss Parsons' body showed severe bruising around her neck and the bottom of her face. She had a broken hyoid bone."

"Dr. Graves, please explain what the hyoid bone is?" asked Custis.

"The hyoid bone is a small U-shaped bone of the neck that is fractured most times in strangulation," Dr. Graves replied.

"Thank you, Dr. Graves. Is there anything else you discovered in the autopsy of Miss Parsons you can share with the court?" Custis asked.

"Yes, sir, during the autopsy, I discovered Miss Parsons was well into her third month of pregnancy." There were gasps and moans in the courtroom. Upon hearing the news of the pregnancy from the Medical Examiner, Tommy Smith let out a loud cry, laid his head on the table and sobbed. After a few minutes of sobs and moans from everyone in the courtroom, the judge tapped his gavel, calling everyone back to order. After a long and quiet pause, Custis asked, "Are you sure, Doctor?"

"Yes, I am sure," replied Dr. Graves.

"Thank You, Doctor. One more question. How often have you seen, in your years as the medical examiner, unmarried pregnant women the victim of homicide?" Custis prodded.

"Well, I don't know the exact number, but I have definitely encountered this situation before. Young unmarried women who are pregnant are definitely vulnerable for homicide in my experience," Dr. Graves replied.

"Would you say in all of your years as a Medical Examiner that you have seen one, maybe two of these similar tragic circumstances?" Custis asked.

"I have seen four or five cases in my tenure as Medical Examiner."

"Why, in your opinion, do you believe young unmarried women are vulnerable victims, as you say, of homicide? Custis asked.

"Objection, your honor," the DA said, "This question is irrelevant and solely based on opinion. We are here to discover the facts, not conjecture or opinion from the witness."

"Overruled," said the Judge.

"Thank you, your honor," Custis said. "Dr. Graves, will you please answer my last question?"

"Thinking back over my cases involving murdered, unmarried and pregnant women, testifying at their trials and learning the story behind their deaths, these women were a threat to the man involved. His life, career, marriage, society standing, etc. If the truth came out about the affair and pregnancy there would be too much to lose. This is a crime of passion. The man figures if he can silence his mistakes, his life can continue on as normal and no one will know his involvement."

"So, in a moment of heated argument or desperation, the man kills the pregnant woman to cover his sins," Custis said.

"Yes, I believe that is what happens," Dr. Graves said

"Thank you, Dr. Graves. The defense has no more questions for this witness."

There was a saying, "Get justice with Custis", that was known statewide. Custis Buck was a known rebel and he held the state record for licensed attorneys in Alabama for nights spent in jail and fines paid for contempt of court. There wasn't a judge in the state that didn't know him, a law enforcement officer that didn't know him, or a criminal that didn't know him. His work load was heavy and his phone rang constantly with folks needing a real go-getter for their attorney. Custis had three former wives, one of those wives being a former beauty queen from Plains University. He had six children, a load of debt, and he liked his whiskey and gambling. Those vices helped contribute to the torment of his existence. Custis grew up in Spit's Creek and he left town after high school to attend Jacksonville State University. He struggled, but graduated from law school in Birmingham, and began his practice in Five Points, downtown Birmingham, in a small third story office overlooking the fountain. Custis and Bull had known each other since childhood. Custis spent a few nights in the Buford County jail off and on, and when locked up, Bull would bring him a plate of Mrs. Ruth's catfish with all the fixin's along with a piece of apple pie and two cups of Red Diamond coffee; one cup black and the other with Irish whiskey. Bull would bring cigars and magazines to make his stay a bit more civilized. These two men were cut from the same cloth. No nonsense, crude and high on themselves. When they arrested Tommy, Bull placed an urgent call to Custis, pleading for his help. Custis agreed and cut Bull a deal on his fee, even though he really needed the money. Bull was appreciative because he knew he needed someone who wouldn't mind playing dirty if it came to it. "Justice Custis" Buck always ran right above the illegal and unethical line of the law, and Bull was just fine with that. It was a point that both of them agreed with. "Justice Custis" had often been called "Perry Mason" because he had never lost a case, but in this case, the odds were stacked against him, and he knew it.

"Your honor, considering the testimony from Dr. Graves regarding the pregnancy of Louanna Parsons, the State asks for an amendment to the original charge of murder to one count of manslaughter and one count of criminally negligent homicide," said the District Attorney.

"Considering the recent evidence, I agree with the additional charges," the judge said as he struck his gavel on the podium.

"Your Honor, the defense objects. Mr. Smith had no knowledge of Miss Parsons' pregnancy," Custis said.

"Mr. Buck, the facts are the facts. Overruled," the judge said.

Tommy Smith could not contain his anguish. He begged Custis to let him speak, but Custis opposed the idea. Tommy argued he was innocent, and he deserved the chance to tell people how much he loved Louanna. He wanted the chance to say he had not seen his jacket and shoes for months. He wanted everyone to know he loved Louanna. He was advised by Custis that there was no way he could escape the charges. The evidence and his personal history with Louanna were indisputable, and because of the news of the pregnancy, his motive for murder was even stronger in the eyes of the court.

After a brief recess, court reconvened.

"Your honor, the State would like to call Sheriff Frank 'Bull' Smith to the stand," the DA said.

"Sheriff Smith, will you please tell the court what transpired on May fifteenth at the riverbank where Tommy Smith's letterman jacket and tennis shoes were found."

"At approximately 2:30 PM we received a call from an anonymous caller asking us to go to the river, the popular hangout spot where the kids gather to swim, because of suspicious articles located in the brush. My deputy and I drove out there, along with the Spit's Creek chief of police. Upon arrival, we walked around the bank and noticed that, oddly, the sand looked like it had been swept by tree branches. There were only two sets of footprints in the sand, which we believed was from the anonymous caller and a friend. The footprints were followed to the brush where we pulled out a letterman jacket and a pair of tennis shoes. When we looked at the letterman jacket, the name 'Tommy' was on the right breast side. Then we looked at the pair of tennis shoes and found the initials 'TS' written in ink on the inside sole of the shoe. I knew then that the jacket and shoes were my son's, Tommy Smith. I couldn't believe it. About fifteen feet from the waters' edge we also found a tube of pink lipstick, one earring, and a hair pin. We photographed all of the articles as they lay on the ground and bagged them. We also took pictures of the sand, the brushy area, and the waters' edge.

"Then what did you do?" asked the DA.

"At this point, Miss Parsons had been missing for quite a few days with no leads. After the discovery at the riverbank and knowing the personal connection between Tommy and Louanna all added up to a very bad scenario. After taping off the scene, we drove back to town, located Tommy and brought him in for questioning for the disappearance of Miss Parsons. My Deputy called Mr. and Mrs. Parsons and asked them to come to the station to identify the tube of lipstick, hair pin, and the earring. The Parsons identified the items as being Louanna's. After many hours of questioning, Tommy was released to house arrest pending charges of kidnapping and foul play towards Miss Parsons," Bull Said.

"Sheriff, at what point did you and the local police department make the decision to arrest Tommy for these alleged crimes?" the DA asked.

"We moved rather quickly. Tommy was arrested two days after his initial questioning," Bull said.

"Sherriff, has your office or the police received any other potential leads since the arrest of Tommy Smith?" asked the DA.

"No, sir, none," Bull said.

"Your honor, the state has no further questions for this witness."

"Mr. Buck, do you have any questions for Sheriff Smith?" asked the judge.

"Yes, your Honor. Sheriff Smith, don't you find it very odd someone would leave their own personal belongings at the alleged scene of a crime? I mean, who would be that careless? I have spoken for many hours to Tommy about this whole thing, and Tommy is not a stupid boy. Tommy has told me over and over again that his letterman jacket and tennis shoes have been missing for quite a while. He did not have possession of these articles, and he did not know where they were. Is it possible that his jacket and tennis shoes were planted at the riverbank by the real perpetrator and used as a set up for Tommy to take the blame? Is it possible that someone else stole Tommy's jacket and tennis shoes from school, or the football field, or from his locker or even from his bedroom?" Custis implored.

"I suppose anything is possible. Tommy has a habit of leaving his belongings strewn about and forgetting where he left them. His mother and I have spent many hours talking to him about the importance of taking care of his belongings. If you were to walk into his bedroom right now, you would think a bomb had exploded. The inside of his truck is the same way. I say all of this to say, yes, I guess someone else could have taken Tommy's jacket and tennis shoes and he not miss their being gone," Bull said.

"Sheriff Smith, did you, your deputies, or the police department question any of Tommy's close friends about the jacket and tennis shoes? And did you ask any of his friends about the true nature of his relationship with Miss Parsons?" asked Custis.

"Yes, sir, we interviewed multiple friends of Tommy and Louanna," Bull Said.

When Custis was questioning Bull, something began gnawing at him about his friend and the facts of the case. He couldn't quite place his finger on it, but after the hours spent with Tommy, he knew in his gut that Tommy was innocent. He knew this because he had defended and won cases for people before who were as guilty as the day is long. There was a dirty, rotting rat somewhere, he just knew it, and he was going to get to the bottom of it, if it was the last noble thing he did while on the face of the earth. The thoughts of this young seventeen-year-old boy, with a life just beginning, having it snatched away from him, made him sick to his stomach. For the first time is his shady legal career, he felt a renewed purpose, passion and appreciation for the law and he promised himself he would change the way he did business going forward. Tommy's case would represent not greed or fame, but truth and justice and vindication for the truly innocent. With these nagging thoughts rolling around in his mind, he continued with vigor asking, "Sheriff Smith, in your years as Tommy's father, have you ever noticed a mean or vicious streak in him?"

"No, sir," Bull replied.

"Yes, I would find that hard to believe myself. I have also known Tommy since he was a little boy, and I have not once noticed meanness or disrespect or any personality traits that would lead me to believe he would just snap and murder someone," said Custis.

"Objection, your honor, Mr. Buck is not on the witness stand and his opinion is irrelevant," the DA said.

"Sustained. Mr. Buck, keep your opinions to yourself," the Judge said.

"Your honor, I am trying to help establish past behaviors of Tommy," Custis replied.

"Mr. Buck, your reputation precedes you. In this court, I will not allow grandstanding or testimony from any of the attorneys of record. Am I clear? I know you are familiar with our county jail, and I will send you back if I have too, and this time you won't get your catfish dinner, Irish whiskey or your cigar," the Judge threatened.

"Yes, your honor," Custis replied.

Bull was squirming in the chair as the conversation became heated and threatening.

"Sheriff Smith, out of all of the friends of Tommy and Louanna you interviewed, thirty to be exact, did any of them mention bad blood or any ongoing dispute between Tommy and Louanna?"

"No, sir," Bull replied.

"Do you ever recall a time when Tommy was upset or mentioned anything negative or spiteful against Miss Parsons?" Custis asked.

"Not to me. I did notice he seemed sad at times, especially beginning late fall or early winter. I overheard his mother ask him one night after dinner what was bothering him and he said Louanna was not available for dates anymore. He suspected she may have another boyfriend, but he never said who he thought it might be. The subject was not talked about again, at least to my knowledge." Bull shifted again in his chair, pulled on his collar and poured a glass of water from the pitcher sitting beside him.

"Sheriff Smith, did you know Louanna Parsons?" Custis asked.

"Yes, sir, I did, but only casually. She came over to our house a few times to see Tommy and we exchanged polite small talk. Other than that, I can't say that I really knew her. She was always respectful and well-mannered each of the times I spoke to her," Bull responded.

"So, your only conversations with Miss Parsons took place at your house?" Custis asked.

"Your honor, Sheriff Smith is not on trial. I see no reason to continue with this line of questioning," said the DA exasperated.

"Mr. Buck, are you going somewhere with this line of questioning? Because the DA is right, Sheriff Smith is not the defendant. Move on," said the Judge.

"Yes, your honor. I have no further questions the Sheriff," Custis said.

When Bull was released from the witness stand, the look of disdain and contempt he shot at his old friend "Justice Custis" was brutal. Bull felt sick and very uncomfortable. He could not understand why Custis would turn on him and put him on the defense like he was the criminal. Something very wrong was playing out here and he felt doom and dread overcome him. He barely made it out of the courtroom before racing to the bathroom to vomit.

After Sheriff Smith departed the courtroom, the Judge tapped his gavel and drew the court to attention and said, "Ladies and gentlemen, the court will reconvene in two days at 9 AM. Tomorrow Miss Parsons will be laid to rest, and the court wants to respect the meaning of this sad day for the family and friends of Miss Parsons," The judge tapped his gavel again and said, "Court dismissed."

Custis collected his paperwork and brief case, and told Tommy to 'have faith' before he was escorted back to his jail cell. Custis walked out of the courtroom and strolled to Mrs. Ruth's café for a dinner of hamburger steak, mashed potatoes with gravy, green beans and a glass of iced sweet tea. Custis was mentally exhausted and looking forward to returning to his motel room to review more documents of depositions and photographs in peace and quiet. He couldn't help but think about the glaring and vicious look Bull Smith gave him as he stepped off of the witness stand. He knew that their year's long friendship may never recover what played out in the courtroom today and that saddened him, but it was as if something else was driving him in his questions towards Bull he could not hold back. Just as Custis turned out the lamp on the bed stand beside him, a memory hit him like a lightning bolt. Months earlier Custis received a phone call from Bull letting him know he had to drive a prisoner to Jefferson County and would be staying overnight. He asked Custis if he was available for dinner the next night. Custis readily agreed and asked Bull to meet him at his office at 5 PM and they would walk across the street to a popular restaurant known for great food and eighty-year-old Scotch. They ended their phone call excited for the opportunity to catch up and visit.

The next afternoon at 5 PM on the dot, Bull walked in to Custis' office and yelled "Hey, Boy, you here?"

"Hey, you crazy man! Are you ready for that Scotch? You look great! I see you had time for a shower and a change of clothes?"

"Yea, I had to get out of that hot uniform and vest! The vest, guns, handcuffs, and belt add about twenty pounds of weight and even more sweat," Bull said.

"Man, what have you been doing for yourself? I haven't seen you this trim and fit since our high school football days! You look great!" Custis commented.

"Well, just watching what I eat and exercising a little. I was getting too big of a spare tire and I hated it. Once the weight came off, I also realized my clothes were the same ones I had been wearing for the last twenty years, so I went shopping. You should try a little exercise yourself, old buddy, it makes you look and feel so much better and it doesn't hurt with the women either, if you know what I mean. Bull lightly punched Custis on the shoulder.

"The last thing I need is a woman! You haven't forgotten that I have three ex-wives? I think I have learned my lesson and run out of luck with women, and I am getting used to the idea of being alone. It's definitely cheaper and easier," Custis laughed. "Have you been stepping out on your wife? Usually men who change their appearance are having an affair," Custis added.

"Well, there is one woman, but you wouldn't know her," Bull smiled.

"Man, you are asking for trouble, believe me on this! Does your wife suspect? I mean, isn't she asking you questions about all of your changes?"

"As a matter of fact, my wife loves the changes and has even jumped on board herself. She's dropped twenty pounds, has a new hairstyle, and new clothes. Our romantic life hasn't been this charged since we were newlyweds. No, I don't believe she suspects a thing. I am more attentive and affectionate with her and she thinks everything is great," Bull smiled.

"So, if things are going great with your wife, why would you feel the need to step out?" Custis inquired.

"Because it wasn't my wife that started this change in me, it was the other woman. She is so beautiful and even before I started improving myself she thought I was sexy and interesting. This woman brought fire back to my belly. My reason for getting up every morning was fresh and renewed, and I started to feel like I was walking on air. My wife is just reaping the benefits. And, before you ask, no, I don't feel guilty about this affair. It won't last long, but the memories will last a lifetime. We aren't getting any younger and the way I see it, this is my last chance to feel young and virile again with someone new," Bull said confidently.

"How do you know that this affair won't last long? Did you have a conversation with the woman and tell her she only has a certain amount of time with you and once the clock counts down, it's automatically over?" Custis queried.

"I know because she won't be in town much longer. She is leaving town at the end of the summer heading off for a new chapter in her life. So, see, that will be the end of it after that. Ok, that's enough about me tell me what is new with you? I see your name in the papers often over some big case you are working on," Bull said.

And, just like that, Custis was hit blindsided as memory played out in his mind. He said out loud to himself, "This can't be! Louanna Parsons *was* leaving town at the end of the summer for college. She was beautiful and looked very mature for her age and any man would agree. I think the woman Bull was having an affair with was Louanna Parsons! I think my friend killed her and her unborn baby... his baby!" Custis fell off the bed and hit his head on the night stand. He lay there, rested his head on the carpeted floor and wept. He knew he was going to have to find the truth, and the truth is often very ugly. He was going to have to prove that his friend murdered this beautiful teenage girl. And worst of all, he knew his friend was sacrificing his very own son for his crimes and sins; and even in the lowest and darkest places in his mind, Custis knew what Bull was doing was the most despicable and disgusting low of lows he had ever seen in his years of practicing law. He knew Tommy's life was hanging in the balance and he was the only one that could save him. For the first time in years Custis picked himself up off the floor and knelt beside his bed and began to pray. Custis knew it would take a miracle to find enough evidence and proof to convince the Judge and the jury that Tommy was innocent and Bull was guilty. Custis also knew a miracle of this size would need supernatural assistance.

On the Run

Louanna's funeral began at 10 AM the following morning. The community turned out in mass to support the Parsons and to grieve the loss of one of their bright stars. First Methodist church was standing room only as the minister performed the service. Mrs. Parsons' cries echoed through the sanctuary the duration of the service as Mr. Parsons physically kept her upright. Losing a beautiful young woman is a hard reality to swallow, and her classmates and her community were not handling it well. The sight of Tommy in the courtroom yesterday when hearing the news of Louanna's pregnancy was heartbreaking. It was obvious to everyone there he had absolutely no idea she was pregnant and his shock and heartbreak were visible. If Tommy was guilty, his reaction might have been completely different, colder and stoic, but because of the genuineness of his emotions, how could the jury not see reasonable doubt? Even though Custis Buck did not know Louanna, he felt compelled to attend her funeral. His sadness from last night's memories and the surety that Tommy was innocent, along with human compassion forced his attendance. Custis noticed Bull and his wife were seated on the pew behind the Parsons. Bull, dressed in his dress uniform, displayed power and support from law enforcement but mostly it was just a show. Until today, the Parsons regularly talked to Bull in a personal regard, but something was different today between them. Mr. and Mrs. Parsons completely ignored Bull. Bull wondered why the sudden coolness, but he figured their grief was too strong, and he was right about that. Custis asked the Judge if Tommy could attend the funeral. Out of surprise, the Judge agreed. He was not sure why he agreed, but he did. Like Custis and Sheridan, and some of the other townsfolk felt, there was something not right about the whole situation. So, with a deputy in tow, a handcuffed Tommy was escorted to the church and seated in the balcony. Custis sat beside him during the service as a show of support. Tommy cried the entire service. Before the service ended, Tommy was escorted back to jail. On his way out of the church, jeers and comments of "killer", "baby killer", and "you will fry in hell for what you have done" were loudly whispered by some of the mourners. Tommy was thankful for the privacy and solitude of his jail cell. When he settled in, he cried for the rest of the day.

After the service, a long line of cars followed the black hearse to the cemetery to lay Louanna and her baby to rest. The Parsons were touched at the outpouring of love from their community. Bull and his wife waited in line to speak to the Parsons' before heading for home. The once warm and kind relationship Bull felt with them was now matter of fact, distant and cold. "Why the sudden coolness?" thought Bull as he and his wife were walking to their car. And once again, the pit of his stomach rumbled and fear tinged his soul.

As Custis was making his way to his car after the graveside service, Mr. and Mrs. Parsons called to him. He turned around. They were both on his heels. "Mr. Custis, we would like to meet with you in private in one hour at our house. Can you meet with us? It's rather an urgent matter," Mr. Parsons said.

"I will be there in an hour."

"Thank you, Mr. Buck," Mr. Parsons said through anxious and teary eyes.

Custis arrived exactly one hour after the graveside service at the home of Louanna Parsons. Mr. Parsons met him on the front porch and quickly escorted him inside. Mrs. Parsons' greeted Custis and offered him a cup of coffee, which Custis gladly accepted.

"So, what is the urgent matter you want to discuss?" asked Custis.

"I know our meeting with you must break some code of ethics or some law, and we apologize if we are placing you in a compromising position. But, we knew you were the only one who could help us. We have proof Tommy did not kill Louanna," Mr. Parsons said.

Custis, in mid-sip, choked and spewed his coffee out onto his lap. "What do you mean you have proof Tommy didn't kill Louanna and her baby?" coughed Custis.

"Yesterday morning I was in Louanna's room picking out a dress and shoes for her burial. I was a total wreck as you can imagine. Picking out burial clothes for your own child is the worst feeling in the world. Louanna was only months away from college and pursuing her dreams. I am not supposed to be saying goodbye to her forever," Mrs. Parsons paused for tears as her husband rubbed her arm. After a moment, she continued, "I had taken two of her favorite dresses and two pair of shoes out of the closet and laid them on the bed trying to decide which outfit Louanna would pick. Louanna always kept her shoes on the floor of the closet in the boxes they came in. She was a very particular girl about her clothes and shoes. Anyway, when I opened one of the shoe boxes to take the shoes out, I found a small key. A diary key. It was not a secret that Louanna kept a diary. We knew about it. In fact, I have bought her many diaries for her birthdays or Christmas. The last diary I bought her was this past Christmas. Because I bought it for her, I knew what it looked like. It was pink with yellow butterflies. I called Mr. Parsons in the bedroom, showed him the key and said, 'We have got to find her diary, help me look.' So we tore her bedroom completely apart and found nothing. Exhausted and panicked, we sat on the edge of the bed thinking more about where she might keep it when I noticed the top drawer of her dresser looked off track and crooked. I knew there was nothing wrong with the drawer to her dresser, so I told Mr. Parsons to open the drawer. When he tried to open the drawer the bottom of the drawer was caught on something. Mr. Parsons pried the drawer out and at the back of the dresser was Louanna's pink diary. We unlocked the diary and began pouring through it. The first entry was December twenty fifth. We stayed up all night reading her diary and looking for the diary she has just completed. We found it in the back of the second dresser drawer and we read that one, too. We also found a box filled with money and a one-way bus ticket to Atlanta on the back corner of her closet shelf," Mrs. Parsons said.

"What did you discover from the diaries?" Custis asked.

"Louanna had been having an affair with Bull Smith since last fall," Mr. Parsons said. "She wrote about everything in detail. The first time they met at the river and all of the rendezvous that took place and where. She even named the motels they would stay at in Birmingham and Montgomery. Her last entry said she was going to tell Bull about the baby, ask him for money, and leave town right after graduation. She talked about being scared and nervous to tell him. She said she is ready for this affair to end and move on with her life. She expressed deep sadness over the unexpected change in her plans and about how she would not get to have the life that she has dreamed about for so long. Louanna had grand plans of travel and culture. Education and romance. Her dreams were lofty, but we encouraged her every step of the way. We encouraged her to dream big, and she did," Mr. Parsons cried.

Custis was speechless. He knew right then God answered his prayer from the night before. This was exactly the proof he needed to exonerate Tommy and point to Bull Smith as Louanna's murderer. Now, he had to read the diaries for himself and introduce the diaries as fresh evidence in the trial. The DA would be angry about this loss, and he would object to the diaries, and try to render them as 'hearsay and forgery', so Custis knew what he would have to do to keep the diaries as evidence and Louanna's voice and pain and fear in the forefront of the jury's mind. All he needed was reasonable doubt.

"Mr. and Mrs. Parsons, I will need to take possession of the two diaries. I will read them both tonight and ask for a continuance and travel to Montgomery and Birmingham to find the clerks at the two motels where Bull and Louanna stayed. I will have subpoenas for both of them to testify at trial as witnesses to the rendezvous. I will also have a handwriting expert look at the writing samples and Louanna's diaries to prove their validity. Thank you for this. I knew Tommy was innocent and I suspected Bull, but you have given me the proof I need. My prayer has been answered and an innocent boy will not go to prison.

Mrs. Parsons handed the diaries to Custis. They exchanged hugs and said their goodbyes. Custis walked to his car and drove straight to his motel room where he spent most of the night reading the diaries. He slept little that night as the details from Louanna's account of the affair played over and over in his mind. He felt deep sadness and anger that his friend, Bull, had embarked on such an affair, at his age, and with a teenage girl on the cusp of a bright future. His last thought before finally drifting off to sleep was of Tommy. He decided that going to see Tommy at 8 AM was the right thing to do. He had to tell him the news before the trial to lift his hope of exoneration, but he also knew Tommy needed to hear about his father's involvement and affair from him first. Tommy would have a lot to process, and he would need help and support.

The following morning, Custis slipped into the motel café for two cups of coffee, two sausage biscuits and two orders of hash browns. He made his way to the jail, checked in with the officer on duty and met Tommy in one of the two interview rooms. Tommy was thankful for the breakfast and hot coffee. After finishing their meal, Custis said, "Tommy, today is going to be a very important day. Louanna's parents have given me evidence, two of her diaries to be exact. The diaries tell a story of Louanna's last year as she describes everything that happened to her. I am telling you this for two important reasons. One, we now have proof you were not Louanna's killer," Custis said as Tommy interrupted him.

"What did she say?" Tommy asked sitting straight as a rail in his chair.

"Louanna had been having an affair with an older man. The affair had been going on since last fall. So, what you thought was correct. She had another interest in someone," Custis grabbed his shirt collar and loosened his tie. This was going to be a long and emotional day. Custis took a sip of his cooling coffee and paused longer. Tommy leaned forward.

"Well. Who was the older man? Is it anyone I know? I knew something was very different with Louanna when she started blowing me off," Tommy said.

"As a matter of fact, you know the man she was having an affair with very well," Custis said. "Tommy, there is no way to sugar coat this news."

"What? Who is it? Tell me!" Tommy implored.

"Tommy, it was your father," Custis said defeated.

Tommy jumped up from his chair, walked to the corner of the room, and began beating his head against the wall amid loud wailing. "Why! Why! Why!" Tommy cried as he sank to the floor. "My own father? How could he? How could he have an affair with my girlfriend? How could he do this to me! He killed her for getting pregnant and then framed me for HIS crime! He was going to let me go to prison for the rest of my life for something that HE did! Where is my father? I want to see him RIGHT NOW," Tommy yelled loudly as he beat his hands on the cement floor. The guards on duty entered the interview room to see what was going on. They picked Tommy up, handcuffed him, and dragged him back to his cell. Tommy screamed the entire way back to his cell, "Why! Why! Why! I hate my father for doing this to me! Tell my father to come her NOW!" The two deputies carried Tommy back to his cell and looked at each other with quizzical expressions. Something big was about to happen they just didn't know what.

"Sheriff, this is Deputy Jones. There is something strange going on down here at the jailhouse with your son and we thought you needed to know."

"What's going on?" Bull asked.

"Well, Tommy's lawyer was just here to see him. He brought him breakfast and they ate together in the interview room. Everything seemed normal until suddenly a loud, screaming and crying voice echoed down the hall. I grabbed Deputy Childers, we ran down the hall and opened the door to find Tommy crying, yelling, and beating his hands on the floor in the corner of the room. We grabbed him and took him back to his cell. Tommy has not acted this violently the whole time he's been locked up."

"Well, what do you think upset Tommy? Did he say anything?" asked Bull.

"Yes, sir, he said a few things." Deputy Jones said.

"Well, what did he say?" asked Bull nervously.

"He kept saying 'why, why, why' and then he said 'I hate my father for doing this to me! Tell my father to come here NOW!'" the Deputy said.

"Is that all he said?"

"Yes, sir, that's all he said to us. I am not sure what he was saying in the interview room or what his attorney said to him that started the whole thing before we went in the room," The Deputy said.

"Take me back to the moment Custis arrived at the jail. What was he carrying?" Bull asked calmly.

"When he checked in at the front desk he had two cups of coffee and a bag of food from the motel café. When he signed in, he had to place everything down on the counter. So, he laid the food down and wrote his name in the log book," The deputy said.

"Is there anything else that you can remember?" Bull asked impatiently.

"Oh, yea, he placed two colorful books on the counter too, that he had been carrying under his arm. I glanced at the book on the top. It was pink with butterflies on it and written in gold letters was the word 'diary'" the Deputy said proudly. "Sheriff, you might want to come down here. I can still hear Tommy yelling and crying from his cell all the way up here at the front."

The phone line went dead.

Bull Smith ran to his patrol car, jumped in, and sped like the devil to the jail. A few minutes later, he arrived at the jail, jumped out of his car without turning off the ignition, and ran inside. He raced passed the front desk and down the hall to Tommy's cell. He unlocked the cell door and went inside where he saw his son in a fit of anguish and rage. Tommy's face was distorted and red and before Bull could get one word out, Tommy rushed over to him and punched him square in the jaw knocking Bull to the floor. Before Bull could get up, Tommy was on top of him beating his head and kicking his ribs. Bull wrestled his way up and pushed Tommy against the wall. "I know what you did, Dad!" Tommy screamed through sobs. "You killed Louanna, and you set me up as her killer. You just wait. After today, you will be a wanted man, and I will be a free man. All of your big talk, arrogance, community standing won't get you out of this. My own father has betrayed me in the most despicable way imaginable. Don't you worry, by sunset or tomorrow morning it will be you in here locked up like the animal that you are! There is no way out, Dad. You will be fried like a piece of country ham in a hot cast-iron skillet when they strap you in to the electric chair and pull the switch. And guess who is going to be sitting on the front row watching you burn from the inside out? Me. I will be there, you can count on that. You murdered Louanna and her baby. What did she say to you? Did she threaten to expose you? Ruin your career? I can see her putting up a fight. She did, didn't she? Those scratches on your face and neck a while back, when you said you got tangled up with a cat. Those were from her, weren't they? This whole time you knew what you did. This whole time you willingly offered me as a sacrifice and you were going to let me rot in prison for years, if not for the rest of my life. You are the most despicable excuse of a man that I have ever known. You are no longer my father. You are out of my life forever, but rest assured I will gladly stick around to watch big, bad, tough, above the law, Bull Smith fall. Fall in the most public way imaginable. Your life is over. Thankfully your childhood friend, Custis, came to my rescue. That's the only thanks you will get from me. Other than that, you are dead to me. Now, get the heck out of here. I don't want to look at your pitiful face any longer. GET OUT, I said!!!"

Bull wiped his bloody face with his handkerchief and stared blankly at Tommy. He turned around, walked out and locked the cell door. Tommy placed his hands on the bars and stared wildly at his father as he made his way down the hallway. Bull walked at first, then began a sprint down the remaining hallway. He shoved open the metal door and it hit the wall. The last thing Tommy heard was Deputy Jones yelling "Sheriff! What is wrong?" as Bull ran passed him. Tommy heard the front door slam shut and the sound of screeching tires on the street as Bull sped away to parts unknown.

Bull raced home, grabbed his overnight bag and threw clothes inside. He grabbed his extra pistol, more bullets, and a large stash of money from the dresser drawer. He changed his clothes and found his truck keys. He knocked his wife down in the hallway as he raced out of the house without saying a word to her. He knew he only had a short amount of time to get a decent head start on law enforcement looking for him. He sped out of town, not yielding to any lights or stop signs. He made it to the highway and headed west. If he could just get to Mexico, he could hide out and never be found. Once inside the Mississippi state line he found a used car dealer in Biloxi; traded his truck for a black Buick sedan, and in the cover of darkness he drove all night, only stopping for gas. By sunrise the next morning, Bull Smith crossed the Mexican border at Brownsville, Texas. Bull stopped at a cantina. He knew he had to keep moving further south and that's what he would do after he finished his beer and his Huevos Rancheros.

With the discovery of Louanna's diaries, and the sudden disappearance of Sheriff Bull Smith, all charges were dropped against Tommy Smith and they released him from his handcuffs and he was again a free man. He shook Custis Buck's hand and then pulled him in for a tight hug. "Mr. Buck, there are not enough words to thank you for what you did for me. You saved my life and I will be eternally grateful. I will never forget you." Tommy said through tears of gratitude and joy and relief. 'Justice Custis' had once again won his fight for his client.

Custis replied, "Tommy, you have changed my life in more ways than I can count, and I will be eternally grateful to you, and you can bet that I will never forget you either." With that, Custis touched Tommy's shoulder to lead him out of the courtroom to a crowd of cheering townspeople gathered on the street. An all-points-bulletin had been released throughout the southeast to be on the lookout for Sheriff Bull Smith.

Custis drove Tommy home and they promised they would keep in touch. Tommy ran in the house, quickly packed a suitcase and hit the road in search of his father. A report had already come in from the used car dealer in Mississippi that Bull purchased the Buick sedan from. The used car dealer reported Bull mentioned something about going to Texas and maybe Mexico for an extended vacation. The authorities were in hot pursuit.

With the conclusion of the trial and order restoring in the community of Spit's Creek, Sheridan, Birdy and Celia were left with the summer ahead of them before college in the fall and Celia's senior year of high school. They walked to the car and commented on the heat and humidity. "I know," Sheridan said, "let's take a swim in the creek where my Momma talked to the butterfly. It's so peaceful there." Birdy cranked her VW and headed out of town with the sun on their faces and the wind in their hair and not a care in the world. Tommy was headed west with a vengeance to find justice.

The End

Note from the Author

Word-of-mouth is crucial for any author to succeed. If you enjoyed *The Bitter and the Sweet*, please leave a review online—anywhere you are able. Even if it's just a sentence or two. It would make all the difference and would be very much appreciated.

Thanks!
Anessa Sewell Kent

We hope you enjoyed reading this title from:

BLACK ROSE
writing™

www.blackrosewriting.com

Subscribe to our mailing list – *The Rosevine* – and receive **FREE** books, daily deals, and stay current with news about upcoming releases and our hottest authors.
Scan the QR code below to sign up.

Already a subscriber? Please accept a sincere thank you for being a fan of Black Rose Writing authors.

View other Black Rose Writing titles at
www.blackrosewriting.com/books and use promo code
PRINT to receive a **20% discount** when purchasing.

CPSIA information can be obtained
at www.ICGtesting.com
Printed in the USA
JSHW022330120423
40256JS00002B/5